LOOT

A BUSTER HIGHTOWER MYSTERY

LOOT

GARY ALEXANDER

FIVE STAR

A part of Gale, Cengage Learning

Detroit • New York • San Francisco • New Haven, Conn • Waterville, Maine • London

GALE
CENGAGE Learning·

LIBRARY OF CONGRESS CATALOGING-IN-PUBLICATION DATA

Alexander, Gary, 1941–
    Loot : a Buster Hightower mystery / Gary Alexander. — First
Edition.
    pages cm
    ISBN-13: 978-1-4328-2717-5 (hardcover)
    ISBN-10: 1-4328-2717-0 (hardcover)
    1. Comedians—Fiction. I. Title.
PS3551.L3554L66 2013
813'.54—dc23   2013014022

First Edition. First Printing: September 2013
Find us on Facebook– https://www.facebook.com/FiveStarCengage
Visit our website– http://www.gale.cengage.com/fivestar/
Contact Five Star™ Publishing at FiveStar@cengage.com

Printed in Mexico
1 2 3 4 5 6 7 17 16 15 14 13

loot: n. stolen money or valuables

—*The New Oxford American Dictionary,* 2001

For Shari

AUTHOR'S NOTE:

Some of the settings in this novel are real, some aren't.

None of the characters are.

The crime was real.

One piece of loot was found years later; a bond in Nevada.

The crime remains unsolved.

Headline in the *Seattle Daily Times:* Tuesday, February 23, 1954

Boxes in 1st Av. Vault Looted

Skilled safecrackers over the weekend broke into and looted the Pioneer Safe Deposit Vaults, 701 First Av. The vaults had withstood the Seattle fire of 1889.

Frank J. Goodman, the owner, discovered the burglary when he opened for business this morning.

The safecrackers, using acetylene torches, cut through a steel wall one and a half inches thick to gain entry to safe-deposit boxes. More than 400 boxes were opened and their contents removed. The vault contained 1800 boxes.

Goodman said it would be days before he knew how much was taken.

The safecrackers left in the vault two acetylene tanks and a foot locker containing two electric drills, concrete bits, goggles, gloves and crowbars.

Detectives termed the burglary a highly professional job.

The company, at street level in pioneer days, now is in the basement. The vault was built in 1884 for a pioneer bank. Goodman has leased the firm since 1949, from Dr. Al Sherman.

The safecrackers apparently picked a rear-door padlock and replaced it to leave no evidence of forced entry, said Victor L. Kramer, chief of detectives.

The safecrackers burned the locks off two steel doors to reach the vault.

Cracks around the firm's front door had been taped, apparently to seal off the noise and odor from the burning.

The safecrackers first attempted to drill a hole in the door of the vault, then moved around to the side, removed some bricks, and drilled through the wall.

CHAPTER 1

Not Long Ago

The lady who came through the door was fiftyish, nice face and body for her age, no makeup, no attempt to hide graying hair. Neutral color slacks and blouses, not baggy, not tight. Not looking for any action, today or any other day.

She was tense, trying to play it cool. After decades as a pawnbroker, Randall Coll believed he could read his potential customers in an instant. Like a book, as they say. Reasons for doing business with him varied, but it was like visiting the dentist. You had to go there, but you sure as hell didn't want to.

He'd bet this was her first visit to a pawnbroker. She was ready to pee her pants. My kind of customer, thought Coll, proprietor of Coll's Jewelry and Loan: (A Family Business), a small shop within walking distance of downtown Seattle.

"May I help you?" Coll asked, hoping he registered as avuncular, but aware that he probably didn't.

"I was wondering about this ring. What it might be worth," she said, taking it out of her purse and giving it to him with a moist hand. "It's old. It's been in the family for generations."

It was old, a marquise solitaire in a heavy platinum setting, a cocktail ring from the Roaring Twenties, high fashion at the speakeasies. When Coll put his loupe to the stone, he was ready to pee *his* pants. It was easily three carats and absolutely flawless, a rock as perfect as he'd ever had in his shop.

Randall Coll turned it between his fingers and shrugged, as if dismissing the diamond as paste. A zircon bought on a TV shopping channel.

"Well?" she asked impatiently.

"You judge diamonds by the Four Cs. Cut, color, clarity and carat weight," Coll lectured. "This stone is a hair over two carats, but there's an inclusion so big you could drive a truck through it."

He offered her his loupe, to see for herself.

She declined with a quick headshake.

Ninety-nine percent of Coll's customers did so, not wanting anything against their faces that had been against his.

"I am not saying it's terrible," he said, sweeping a hand toward his counter case. "Believe me, I've had a lot worse in here. The stone is semi-big, the most important decider. I can offer you nine hundred. Cash."

"Isn't the setting platinum? I mean, it's so heavy. I looked it up online. Platinum is presently going for about seventeen-hundred dollars per ounce. It has a specific gravity of twenty-one-point-four-five, compared to gold's nineteen-point-three, and—"

Randall Coll raised a hand to interrupt. His impulse was to address her as "honey" or "dear" as he tended to do with unaccompanied females in his shop, especially those like her who had done a little homework. Everybody who owned a computer thought they had access to answers for everything. Everyone was an expert.

But this little gal was the type to strongly dislike "honey' or "dear." She was tight-assed and had been to school for more years than he and she knew it. She had "old maid" written all over her. He settled for "ma'am."

Coll shook his head and said in his best false sincerity, "Sorry, ma'am. Not platinum. It's white gold. White gold is gold mixed with nickel, zinc and a little palladium. White gold's not chopped liver, mind you. I wouldn't lie to you and say that it is. I'll go a thousand. Tops."

"I was thinking in the area of two thousand dollars."

In the area of.

Amateur hour, Coll thought. Two-thirds of them did that, arbitrarily doubling his offer. After further dickering, he'd capitulate and pay her twelve-fifty, grimacing as if she'd given him the world's worse screwing.

If they lost face, they'll never return, and he wanted to keep this one on the hook. See what she was all about.

He'd get an easy eight thou from a jewelry wholesaler he knew, cash out of his pocket, peeled from a roll. As desperate as Randall Coll was for money, he'd lose no sleep knowing that the greedy bastard would peddle it uptown to Froufrou Jewelers for fifteen grand minimum.

He sighed theatrically and said, "Ma'am, twelve-fifty and that's stretching it."

She was holding the ring now, looking at it, thinking. Then she let it drop into her purse.

"I guess I'm not prepared to let go of it just yet. I'm sorry for your trouble."

She was as flighty as a jackrabbit. He'd spooked her and she was getting away.

Coll assumed the ring wasn't hot; she wasn't the type. She'd recently fallen into something, maybe an inheritance, but that wouldn't explain her jitters. It had to go beyond that, maybe a money crunch weighing on her.

Her cell phone rang. She flinched, reached into her purse, looked at the little screen, and shut it off hard. A stalker, a bill collector, a boss wondering where she was? She had that look, Coll thought.

"I'm sorry for your trouble," she repeated.

He smiled and said, "Not a problem. Sentimental value. I understand perfectly, ma'am. You're doing the right thing."

As soon as she left, Coll peeked out the door. At the end of the block, she got into a white Toyota Prius.

A tree hugger's kind of car. He wasn't surprised.

Randall Coll jotted down her license number.

Although he had no intention of returning that day, Randall Coll hung his GONE TO LUNCH sign on the door and locked up. Coll did go to lunch, to an outdoor food court around the corner. He bitterly watched yuppies wolf down whatever they pleased while he had yogurt, one of the few foods that his ulcerous stomach tolerated.

Before leaving the shop, Coll had contacted a customer who worked at the state department of motor vehicles. The guy was an occasional drinking acquaintance and he owed Coll big time.

Coll's Jewelry and Loan had bought a sack full of jewelry from him, no questions asked. Later, in his cups, after they'd gone out for drinks, Coll buying and prying, the state employee had told Randall that his wife was cheating on him and the days of their marriage were numbered.

While she was out getting banged by her boyfriend, he'd staged a break-in. A broken window. Drawers flung about in search of swag. Then out the alley. To the front door and in. Calling the cops. Telling them how shaken he was by what happened, how violated. The whole bit.

Since Washington was a community property state, he was merely cutting down the gross assets to be divided, which was only fair, her being a bitch and a slut. Coll cut him off when he started boasting of an insurance double-dip, not wanting nor requiring further details.

Coll gave him the Prius's license number and within seconds got a name: Judith Ann Roswell, and a home address on Seattle's Capitol Hill, only five miles east of his shop.

"At the speed of light. My ass'll be grass if anybody finds out, you know," the DMV guy said, as if Coll should be grateful.

"Have a nice day," Coll said, hanging up on him.

Coll drove south on Interstate Five, debating his next move, if any. He did his best thinking behind the wheel. Still undecided, he got off the freeway at a sprawling suburban mall. Like any mall in the United States of America, it housed chain stores, too-bright lighting, and elevator music. Inside, Randall Coll developed an instant headache.

He neared the first of many cell-phone kiosks. It was staffed by aggressive young men, as they all were. One of the pinheads leaned into his path.

"How are you today, sir? Who's your provider?"

"Where's the nearest pay phone, kid?"

"Nearest what?"

The world was going straight to hell, Coll thought. Alexander Graham Bell must be spinning in his grave.

"A pay phone."

The puzzled kid said, "You don't pay for the first five hundred minutes with our plan, sir. Is that what you mean?"

Coll knew that since cellular phones began multiplying like mice, the pay telephone was a doomed species, a dodo bird in the making, but to this pinhead they'd been extinct before his birth.

He had to find a landline telephone. No way could he make the call he was contemplating on the phone in his pocket, on a phone number traceable to him.

Coll cupped a hand to his ear and mimed inserting coins into a slot. "A. Pay. Tele. Phone."

Blanching at the creepy old guy's glare, the kid said, "Dude. Oh yeah, right. I don't know if they got 'em in here anymore."

A pimply colleague of his said, "Hey, I know what you're talking about, man. Last I saw, there's those phones on the other end of the mall, down by the JCPenney."

As Coll walked off, the second kid fired a parting shot, as if Coll should be grateful. "Hey, you're welcome. And I don't know how long ago that was when I saw the pay phones. Like they may be gone. Hey, wait. Hey, who's your provider?"

It took Randall Coll a while to get to the Penney's. They built these malls a mile long. Because of flat feet, a prostate the size of a glazed donut and growing, and other maladies, he was no speed demon. There were days when Coll couldn't shit and days when he couldn't stop, no happy medium, hemorrhoids searing throughout.

Mall-walker geezers were passing him as if he were a statue, slaloming around people, out of sight in seconds. Most weren't much older than him, but they were taking long strides, jackets and sweaters tied around slim waists, seemingly unfazed by the brutally hard tile floor. They acted as if they were bound and determined to live forever.

Randall Coll despised each and every one of them. He wanted them to fall and fracture a hip. Then die of a blood clot to the brain.

The telephones were there where the pinhead said, stand-up types separated by metal partitions. He remembered when phones lived in actual booths, the ones built of polished wood. Oak, he thought it was. They had seats and doors that shut. He imagined that if any were left, they were relegated to the Smithsonian.

Randall Coll picked up the receiver, white-knuckling it. The only family he was on friendly terms with was a dim-witted nephew named Dicky "Mad Dog" Coll.

In homage to Vincent "Mad Dog" Coll, a homicidal gangster during the Prohibition Era, Dicky had been tagged Mad Dog by the media for his outrageous behavior at his trial. Convicted of murder-two for what the media also tagged the Year's Stupidest Crime, Dicky served eleven years before his release three months ago.

Not only wasn't Dicky insulted by "Mad Dog," he was flattered. He wore the moniker like a medal, for God's sake. Dicky spent time in the prison "libarry" as he called it, studying the life and times of his certifiable namesake, far more time than Randall Coll felt was healthy.

Coll replaced the receiver, then lifted it again. He stared at the steel box that asked fifty cents for a local call; highway robbery.

Randall did a rough tally of his assets, such as they were. A pawnshop full of junk. No savings, no 401(k), no pension. No children speaking to him, let alone willing to care for him in his dotage. On disastrous trips to Vegas, Coll left behind any short-term pawnshop profits and everything else but the fillings in his teeth.

He did own the trailer he'd let Dicky stay in since he'd gotten out. He'd taken it in from a day laborer for a hundred bucks. Coll's Jewelry and Loan: (A Family Business) would take in virtually anything if the price was right.

The trailer was in Kent, a South King County town, ten miles from this mall and twenty miles south of Seattle, in one of the last occupied units in a metallic slum of a trailer park slated for demolition, to be replaced by a self-storage facility.

Randall Coll had even wheedled for Dicky a few bucks a week from the owners as caretaker of the property, to keep an eye on it at night, and to sickle the weeds down. He knew Dicky was as lazy as a slug and wouldn't lift a finger, but that wasn't his problem.

To bring this whack job of a nephew into his scheme was to open Pandora's box, Coll knew. But this was his last and best shot at the gravy train. He needed to research Ms. Judith Ann Roswell before someone else did.

He had nobody else to do the legwork.

Randall Coll fished two quarters out of a pocket.

CHAPTER 2

"Hey, how many baseball fans we got in here?" Buster Hightower asked. "I'm talking hardcore fans."

Half his audience of eighteen in the cocktail lounge of the Westside Bowling Lanes and Casino raised their hands, some hesitantly. They knew that any question from the comic, who was perched precariously on a makeshift platform between the dartboard and cigarette machine, was bound to be booby-trapped.

"That's about the average, huh? I'm a fan. I like to watch grass grow, like how it's growing so well into the month of June, but on account of we live in a condo, there ain't no grass to watch grow in the yard that we don't have, so this is why I watch baseball on the tube instead.

"Toward the end of the games when they change pitchers every two minutes after they wear themselves out throwing four pitches, trust me, the grass doesn't grow at all, whether or not you have any on your patio or not. It's wilted from old age.

"Sports are healthy, good for you, right? But baseball looks kind of unhealthy, you know. All those players and coaches with bulges in their cheeks, there's gotta be a mumps epidemic they can't seem to get rid of no matter how much they spit, spitting out the mumps germs, and they spit all the time. What that does is spread mumps germs yon and hither, which is why they never get over it. You'd think in this day and age of modern medicine you could get a shot for mumps."

Buster paused for laughter, much of it from the ladies, long-sufferers of their menfolk's baseball habit.

"The fashion statement of baseball coaches and managers befuddle me. How come they gotta dress in uniforms like the players and twelve-year-old Little Leaguers?"

Buster paused for laughter, took a swig of beer, and patted his gut.

"Some of those managers, they're my age and also, ahem, not exactly built like Superman. The baseball bosses that're even more geezerly and unpleasantly plump than me, they're really not a pretty sight. Ain't too flattering when you're the size of two shortstops, standing in the dugout for everybody to see, scratching and spitting."

Buster Hightower was tall and chunky and sixty-two years old, a true original in many respects. A stand-up comic since the Watergate days, Buster played at the fringes of his profession, catching-as-catch-can gigs at bachelor parties ("I ain't jumping out of no cake," he'd tell them), rural saloons with chicken wire to protect the performers from flying beer bottles, corporate retreats on low budgets, and NCO clubs. He'd done company picnics, retirement parties, comedy clubs in bad neighborhoods, and dumpy smoke-filled casinos.

The obscure comic was known neither far nor wide for his ranting and raving over politics and other triviality. He was neither mean nor obscene. You want the F-bomb, he'd tell his crowd, go in the can and read what's gouged into the walls. No racism for that boy either.

And if you want him to knock gals because they're gals or you want potty jokes, you'd best mosey on down the street.

Consequently, Buster Hightower severely narrowed his appeal, but he could sleep at night.

"Those signs the managers give the players, where they touch their nose and chin and ears and other places I don't even wanna think about? What if they got an itch they gotta all of a sudden scratch? This is over and above and in addition to their abnormally normal spitting and scratching. Like they missed their shower today and yesterday and last week. Or got tangled up in some poison ivy when they should of been showering.

"The runner on first base, he looks over while the boss is digging at his armpit like crazy for reasons nobody wants to know, so the runner takes off even though the bases are loaded and he's got no place to go. Unless the rules changed just before the game where there's nine outs in an inning and five bases, he's got a problem. It's kind of like trying to force yourself on an elevator that's already got twenty-seven people on it and the door's closing."

In walked Carla Chance, love of Buster's life, with her mystery companion. She blew Buster a kiss and sat at a rear table. Rubenesque Carla, two years older than the comic and an inch shorter at six feet, dressed tightly in primary colors. They were a striking couple.

The guy with her, Buster observed, was half their age and what he thought of as terminally Ivy League.

Slacks and sweater that cost more than Buster's entire lifetime wardrobe.

Handsome as all get out, blond hair just so, dimpled jaw out to there.

Aristocratic came to mind. Silver Spoon City. The guy was definitely a change from her run-of-the-mill policyholders, folks on the same wavelength with Charles Manson and Ted Bundy.

All she'd said to Buster earlier was his name, Tyler Polk (Tip) Taylor III, and that he was named after three consecutive US presidents. They were meeting at her Last Chance Insurance Agency to try to write him an auto policy. No other agency Taylor had approached could.

That left Carla Chance and her LCIA, Carla who could write

anyone in the entire solar system except Buster Hightower.

Buster opened his mouth to continue, but stopped to observe a bizarre event. Phil, the Westside Bowling Lanes and Casino's manager, rolled in a cart with a bottle of champagne in a bucket of ice, surrounded by glasses.

Phil was older than Buster, a bowling alley lifer who entered the profession in his teens as a pinsetter. He had compulsive bowler written all over him. The pot gut, the slumped shoulders, the radioactive bowling-league shirt, and the bored look he copied from the pros on television when they threw a strike and walked back to their seat.

Phil seemed bewildered as he set up Carla's table with the bubbly and glasses, three of them, a temptation to Buster to wrap up immediately and have a sip or four.

They had to have called ahead and asked Phil to run out for it, Buster knew. He'd never ever seen champagne on the premises. Whatever wine the Westside had was screw-top, vintage: last Wednesday.

Phil was having a hell of a time getting off the cork. The wire and foil made it a three-step process, a good argument for sticking to screw-top.

Buster said, "Where was I? Oh yeah, baseball. They call a game quits or stop it before they start it on account of quote-unquote inclement weather. One raindrop lands on the umpire's face mask and suddenly the game ain't clement. Answer me a question. When have you ever heard a nice day having clement weather? Me neither and I'm calling off this bit on baseball because I just spotted a cloud outside.

"You watch TV news shows when they're hunting a crook or they've thrown a net over one and got him under a thousand-watt reading lamp having a chat. They call him a 'person of interest.' There's a used-car lot near us that has a sign saying 'guaranteed credit approval.' A person of interest on the lam goes there looking for a getaway car. So does that make him a twofer person of interest, to the law and to the car lot while they're taking five minutes to approve his credit?"

Chuckles.

Buster drained his beer as he watched Carla and Tip Taylor toast each other with glasses of bubbly, Carla looking at Buster, hoisting hers.

Thirsty, knowing he'd forgotten something, he thought what the hell and ended with, "Okay, boys and girls, here's a homework assignment for you while I take a short intermission till tomorrow night. How come your fridge has a light but the freezer compartment doesn't?

"And for a higher grade, how come tarps are blue, even blue tarps?"

CHAPTER 3

Buster sat down with Carla and Tyler Polk (Tip) Taylor III. Formal introductions were made and Tip poured Buster a glass of bubbly. The glasses were tall and skinny, glasses Buster knew to be called, for whatever reason, flutes, even though they weren't musical instruments unless you counted flicking a fingernail against a side.

Carla held up her flute for a toast. "To a deserving driver who is finally insured when he travels our dangerous highways and roads."

"Hear hear," said Tip Taylor.

"Yeah," said Buster Hightower.

They clinked glasses and drank. Buster looked at the gold Rolex on Taylor's wrist. It was the size of an ingot and had to cost as much as—speaking of used cars—a late-model yupmobile with all the trimmings.

He wondered why this bubbly champagne didn't have a proper head on it like a schooner of beer. For all the money they charged over there in Paris, France, where they brewed the stuff, they could've added that touch of class.

"Don't drink so fast, Buster."

"A toast is an invitation to down-the-hatch, ain't it? It doesn't have to breathe like regular wine, does it?"

"Buster," Carla said, thinking: *you cannot take that man anywhere, even if he's already there.*

"Do you like it, Buster?" Tip said.

The comic shrugged. "It's awful sweet and it don't have that nice aftertaste that beer does."

Carla narrowed her eyes. "It is one hundred and sixty-five dollars a bottle and you complain about lack of aftertaste?"

Tip smiled, looking from Carla to Buster, enjoying the candor of his new friends.

Buster drank again and said quickly, "I changed my mind. There is an aftertaste and it's real nice. So you really got a policy written?"

Carla said, "As I said, it took a little doing, but we finally have full coverage on Tip's Aston Martin."

Tip Taylor smiled a white-toothed toothpaste-commercial smile. "I squandered the majority of my remaining trust fund on that baby, so I desperately needed insurance protection. Only Carla could step forward."

Buster thought of his own "baby," a red 1959 Cadillac Eldorado convertible, fire-engine red, white top, wide white sidewalls, and COMIC vanity plates. His uninsured and uninsurable baby.

Carla Chance's Last Chance Insurance Agency wrote auto policies for such spiffy, upstanding carriers as Mayhem Mutual, Angst Auto and Home, Crash and Burn Property and Casualty, and Precarious Insurance Group. Their home offices were in third-floor walkups and on offshore barges. State insurance commissioners had screaming nightmares about them.

"Yeah, well, hey, congratulations," Buster said. "Who'd you get him with, Carla?"

"Exotic Coach Collision and Casualty."

"Yeah? Where're they out of?"

"I'm not sure, Buster," Carla said. "They have a mail drop in upstate New Jersey and my Internet security program sends up red flares warning of viruses when I get online with them.

Thankfully, I managed to write Tip's policy without a crash or a virus."

"Give your computer a shot of penicillin if it's virused," Buster said. "Tip, that sports car of yours and the rest of those made in the Black Forest, they gotta cost a bundle."

Taylor said, "My Aston Martin DB9 is English. All-aluminum body, twelve-cylinder engine, one-hundred-ninety-mph top speed."

Buster snapped his fingers and said, "The JamesBondMobile. No sweat keeping up with the traffic."

"Bond, James Bond," Taylor said despite himself.

"Shaken not stirred," Carla said.

"Or stirred, not shaken," Buster said. "Gin's gin."

"Correct." When Tip Taylor gave two thumbs up, the look on his handsome puss made Buster think he'd seen too many 007 movies. Taylor was living the part, like a kid pretending he was some superhero, not necessarily a bad thing. You should never grow up.

Carla patted Tip Taylor's arm. "I know he's never driven that fast, but he's had minor fender benders."

Taylor sipped his champagne. "When you scrape a pole outside of a night club, it's not a thousand-dollar repair as it is with a Ford or Chevy."

"A couple or three bucks more, huh?" Buster said.

"Ten thousand dollars more," Taylor said. "It's the paint match. There are so many layers, it looks a foot thick."

Buster whistled. "Who else did you try to place him with, toots?"

"Little Bighorn Life and I had a dialogue. They've branched out into property and casualty, with an emphasis on auto, and were eager for new business. They kept us hanging before finally saying no, the jerks."

"They're the outfit that insured Custer and his merry band?"

"No," Carla told him. "Not Custer himself, but eleven members of the Seventh Cavalry."

"They had the *Titanic*, didn't they?"

"You're being silly, Buster."

"Didn't they?"

"They did write life coverage on twenty-some passengers. The payouts bankrupted them again."

Buster looked at Taylor. "Come to think of it, your name's kind of familiar. How come? Taylor's a common name."

"My father, Tyler Polk Taylor the Second, owns one of the largest law firms in Seattle, Taylor and Taylor, which was founded by my grandfather, Tyler Polk Taylor the First. Taylor and Taylor is high-profile, in the news frequently."

"Yeah, local robber barons as clients," Buster said. "Zillionaires in a jam with government agencies and other zillionaires."

"In numerous instances, I cannot argue with 'robber barons.' "

Damn, Buster thought, remembering what he'd forgotten. Without exception, he wrapped up a set with a stale lawyer joke or two or four. "No whiplash and ambulance chasing for your old man, huh?"

"Indeed not. Taylor and Taylor has never had a multimillionaire client who spent a day in jail or paid a penny in damages, aside from, that is, substantial legal fees."

"CEOs with their hands in the cookie jar," Buster said.

"You've made your point, Buster," Carla said.

Tip chuckled. "I could not have put it as elegantly."

"You're following in your daddy's footsteps?"

"I flunked out of Harvard Law."

"Sorry," Buster said.

Taylor shrugged casually and said, "In retrospect, I am not. Class attendance interfered with partying."

"Since you put it that way, congrats. Makes sense to me,"

Buster said. "You gotta have your academical priorities."

Carla said, "Tip is embarking on a new career."

"I have been disowned and, as I said, my trust fund is irresponsibly dwindling." Tip Taylor lifted his sweater, exposing a five-pointed badge that was clipped to his belt. It looked to Buster as if it came out of a cereal box.

"Appealing career choices were this and being a chef. I was and am in awe of the creative and delicious dishes served at the finer restaurants at which my family dined. It came down to a coin flip. Private investigation came up heads.

"By virtue of paying in advance the full tuition of nine hundred and ninety-nine dollars and ninety-nine cents for the Gumshoe Online Institute of Private Detection course with a check that did not bounce, I am automatically a GOIPD honor graduate, something that I have never been before, even in boarding school or prep school. A framed certificate and this badge are part of the package."

"Hey, that's great," Buster said. "Got any customers yet?"

"I have a single client. Mrs. Alvera Snails. I do not think Vera will mind me violating confidentiality as long as it does not go beyond this table."

Carla nodded, a finger to her lips. "You know it won't, Tip."

Buster raised his left hand. "Scout's honor."

"Well, Vera hired me to dig up dirt on her estranged spouse, Ralph, who is sowing what passes for wild oats. She is hoping for ammunition in case it comes to a divorce, which she is dreading. I had been reporting to her that there was nothing to report. Her Ralph wants to cheat on her in the worst way, but try as he might, he has been unable to score. Ralph Snails is not young and has a bowling-ball gut. He sports a spiderweb of a comb-over and an exceedingly tacky NASCAR jacket that is two sizes too small.

"I have surveilled Ralph to the customary singles venues.

Taverns, cocktail bars, bus stations, supermarkets, libraries, Laundromats, and coffee shops. At the last, he was the rare laptop-less patron and truly did not fit in.

"I observed as he drove a stake through his own heart with clever overtures such as 'Do you come here often?' and 'Seen any good movies lately?' and 'Sure feels like it's gonna rain' and the deadliest of them all, 'What's your sign?'

"His chances of getting lucky are slim. Or, rather, unlucky. None of the women he targets qualify as queen of the hop. Most have fewer teeth than I do and more tattoos. I am ashamed to bill Mrs. Vera Snails, but not ashamed enough not to.

"Two nights ago, I earned my keep. Ralph tried a different tack, an Indian casino. I trailed him north on Interstate Five for an hour and a half until he pulled into the parking lot of one that was right off the freeway.

"I waited interminable hours as he plopped from stool to stool at rows of slot machines. In an inversion layer of cigarette smoke, I watched him hit on his female neighbors. They were not the yuppie cuties you see on the television commercials and in newspaper advertisements, clutching large-denomination bills, and squealing and jumping with joy after a big winner.

"These ladies were of a certain age. Cigarettes dangled from their lips as they pumped their Social Security payments into the one-armed bandits. A smoker rolled an oxygen bottle along with her on her walker, a tube in her nose. I gave her a wide berth, then looked upward for sprinklers and fire alarms. For the most part, Ralph's objectives were hostile, blaming their foul luck on him interrupting their concentration at machines that demand scant concentration.

"Once, though, just once, a lady warmed to him. Her clothes were a bit too tight and her hair a bit too blonde for her age. If I may be permitted a vulgarity, she looked as hot to trot as poor, pathetic Ralph Snails. Then she hit a jackpot, the kind where the light on the machine flashes, calling for an attendant.

"In her screaming euphoria, Ralph Snails became invisible. He sulked out of there, thankfully calling it a night. I enjoyed four hours sleep, maximum, a liability of my new profession."

Buster was thinking of private eyes on TV and the movies, and the cases they had. They were solving murders and rescuing dames, wearing trench coats, fedoras pulled low, and using their dukes. Tip, on the other hand, was dressed like he was going to class at Yale.

Following a wandering putz of a husband who wore a stock car racing jacket didn't seem to fit the private-eye bill. He wondered if Tip packed a gun. A piece, a roscoe, a gat, a rod, a heater.

"Business will pick up, Tip," Carla said, patting his arm. "You're only beginning."

"I hope so," Tip Taylor said as his cell phone rang.

He cupped his ear as he spoke, then listened, writing on a bar napkin, turning the napkin over, and continuing to write.

Buster filled the time void by filling and draining his champagne piccolo or whatever they called them. The stuff was acquiring a nice aftertaste.

"Slow down, Mr. Piggy," Carla said. "*Slow* down. This isn't your cheap, rotgut beer."

"You and your discriminating prejudice against beer. That's injury upon insult." Buster raised his empty glass. "If you're gonna name these for a musical instrument, call 'em a harp or piano and make the glasses proportional-wise bigger."

Tyler Polk (Tip) Taylor III hung up and said, beaming, "I have my second client."

CHAPTER 4

"I am the only private investigator in town who is listed in the phone book, paper or online, under 'Private Eye,' " Tip Taylor said. "It cost me a small fortune to persuade the telephone companies to add the classifications, further depletion of my shrinking reserves, but that is how my new client, Judith Roswell, found me. The others like 'Investigators' sounded wimpy to her and my name sounded dignified too, the best of both worlds."

"Your financial gamble is paying off," Carla said.

They were in Buster's Caddy, headed toward Seattle. The comic was developing cold feet, thinking that he didn't want to be in the middle of something requiring un-wimpiness. He didn't know what to make of Tip either. A helluva nice, down-to-earth young guy, Buster thought, but one who didn't strike him as the type for a world of gats and hot dames and trench coats and flying fists.

Tip Taylor had said that Judith Roswell talked a mile a minute on the phone, and when he informed her he was with company, she said to bring them along if he could trust them. The sooner the better, as she was being stalked and could not take it anymore. Tip suggested the police. Roswell had quickly said that law enforcement was out of the question, but didn't specify why.

Carla had said she'd be happy to accompany Tip. Buster said him too, though he wasn't quite sure unless he knew if Tip was "packing heat."

So he asked, "Are you packing heat?"

"Buster," Carla said.

"What does 'heat' mean?" Tip said.

"Never mind," Buster said.

Tip said, "Oh wait. We covered that in a GOIPD chapter that addressed archaic and clichéd vernacular. Heat: a firearm."

"This stalker, did he strike her dangerous, like, you know, a *stalker*?"

"I have the sense that Ms. Roswell is bothered by the harassment, rather than fearing imminent physical danger," Tip said.

"So that's why no police?" Buster said.

"No, I think there is another reason, a hidden reason. But that is just a hunch."

Buster drove, thinking that they were headed in the dark in a bunch more ways than one.

Ask Dicky (Mad Dog) Coll if he was stalking and he'd tell you he wasn't stalking nobody. Not the old broad who lived in the old house. Nobody. Leastways, Uncle Randall never said he was. He was on *surveillance* was how Uncle Randall put it. Don't let her out of your sight but don't let her see you, he'd ordered Dicky, like he was talking to a retard.

Parked down the street from Judith Roswell's house in the old dirty-green shitbox Uncle Randall gave him to trail her around, he knew she hadn't spotted him. Just look to see where she goes, who visits her, anything and everything, was what he said. Uncle Randall, who didn't once visit him in the eleven long years he was locked up in the state pen in Walla Walla.

The *(A Family Business)* on the Coll's Jewelry and Loan: (A Family Business) sign was a sick joke. Dicky was Uncle Randall's only family who'd have anything to do with him, and only because he had to. They were a sorry-ass family of two.

So Dicky sat there, with a jug, hose and a funnel if he had to go and take a whiz, wishing to hell he had something to report so he could be out of this crappy car Uncle Randall had taken in at his pawnshop.

And get paid more than the nickels and dimes he'd given Dicky to live on. If you could call it living, being put up in that trailer park in that grungy trailer where you could hear the rats at night playing tag inside its walls.

No, instead, here he sat in a gutless wonder of an old junker that stank of puke and had a foot of play in the steering wheel.

Dicky looked at the old haunted house, perfect for Halloween, scaring the shit out of the kiddies, just two or three lights on behind curtains. This could go on forever, him in the car, but that's how his luck ran, a guy who couldn't catch a break. Never in a million years.

If you didn't believe it, Dicky could tell you his sad story, if it wasn't so unfair and painful, summarizing it out of news accounts and other bullshit, the honest-to-God truth:

Once upon a time, eleven-plus years ago, Dicky Coll was shacked up with a bartender he'd met in a dingy tavern. He was on easy street, but one day there was trouble in paradise. The barkeep said she was sick and tired of him being unemployed and sponging off her and laying around the house all day, while she was working her ass off serving beer to grabby drunks. She was ready to toss him out if he didn't help with expenses, so Dicky decided he'd better go and do his financial duty.

Dicky Coll ruled out gainful employment as too extreme and downright cruel. Unsure how else to contribute to household maintenance, he scouted a convenience store an easy walk from home. He'd planned on shoplifting or a quick reach into the till when the attendant made a trip to the back room, along those lines, in and out fast, with a minimum of effort and jeopardy to his own hide.

He was keeping an eye on the store, building up his nerve when an old boy with a quart of milk in a plastic bag shuffled out, a skinny coot needing a shave and a change of clothes.

Dicky had a record of petty crime dating to adolescence, although no crimes against person, but he had a brainstorm.

It was the first of the month, so Dicky figured the old guy carried a wad of rocking-chair money on him. He waited till the geezer was at the edge of the store's property, by shrubs separating it from a teriyaki joint. There were no cars in either lot and traffic was light. A perfect setup. Or it should have been.

Dicky made his move, coming up behind the old guy. He threw an arm around his neck, rammed a thumb hard in the small of his back, and snarled, "Freeze, motherfucker! Gimme all your money if you wanna live."

"I don't have any money. You're barking up the wrong tree," the would-be victim said, whining. "I get by on Social Security, that's all."

Dicky Coll, no dummy, told him that he knew how to read a calendar and that it was the first of the month. The old boy didn't have time before his seizure to inform Dicky that you didn't automatically receive Social Security on the first. He, in fact, collected on the second Wednesday of the month, so he really was almost broke.

Dicky jammed his thumb even harder and said, "Last chance to stay alive, Pops. It's your funeral."

The old-timer wheezed and grabbed his chest. His knees buckled and he crumpled onto the asphalt. Dicky thought he was playing possum and fumbled through his pockets and wallet, coming up with chicken feed. Cursing, Dicky stood up and for general principle was fixing to give the old phony a boot in the ribs.

But talk about bad timing, bad luck that was the story of his life. Just then a cop car pulled into the lot.

"I was stopping in for a cup of coffee and saw what the defendant *was doing,"* the police officer testified at Dicky Coll's trial. *"How lucky was that?"*

The coroner who autopsied the victim testified that he died of a massive coronary, probably dead before he hit the ground. The victim had $23.14 in his wallet and pockets.

"See, there you are," Dicky had contended to his court-appointed counsel, *"the guy shouldn't have been out on the street with that bum ticker of his. Him croaking wasn't* my *fault. It was just one of them things. Even without me, he'd of been dead before he got home, irregardless. That was a fact."*

Dicky Coll wanted to get that off his chest at his trial, to inject some common sense into the situation, but his lawyer told him that was the last thing he ought to say. *"Plead out,"* he advised. *"Throw yourself on the mercy of the court."* He was advising him that yet again and begging Dicky to remain seated and quiet, tugging on his sleeve as the police officer smiled as he testified how he wrestled the wild-man defendant into the shrubbery to cuff him.

Dicky was brutally pissed. They were ignoring him, listening to everybody else, and making fun of him too. He knew his Constitutional rights as he shouted over the police officer's testimony and the judge's gavel pounding, *"Fuck you, your dishonor, you and this shit-ass cop and your kangaroo court and that motherfucking shyster for the prosecution who's railroading me and must be running for dogcatcher and that incompetent shyster you stuck me with! I ain't no killer. That sick bastard should've been in a nursing home!"*

The media loved the show and made a circus of it. Dicky Coll was henceforth tagged Mad Dog by a TV reporter, named for Vincent (Mad Dog) Coll, a violent gangster from the Depression Era. The nickname seemed a natural. They ran Dicky's outburst endlessly on the news, him scuffling afterward with the bailiff and his reinforcements. They bleeped his cuss words on television. In the newspapers they used asterisks, as in f*** and m*****f*****, which fooled no one.

The hoopla didn't help his case, but Dicky knew he was screwed anyhow. There were no other witnesses. A confident prosecution rested. The defense (such as it was) had no choice but to rest.

Second-degree murder. Guilty. The jury was out forty minutes.

In his eleven years in the pen, Dicky Coll had plenty of time to think. A favorite topic was, compliments of the media, his new tag, Mad Dog.

"Mad Dog" grew on him. Dicky liked it. Dicky read all he could find on Vincent (Mad Dog) Coll. Read and read and read. He wasn't bashful giving interviews and telling reporters that the more he read, the more he admired "Vinny," as he called him. "Write me up as Mad Dog to your heart's desire," Dicky told them. Vinny had bigger balls than everybody in the cell block combined, balls as big and heavy as shot puts.

Dicky learned that the original Mad Dog Coll was born Uinseann Ó Colla on July 20, 1908, in Ireland. Coll and his family emigrated to New York in '09. Vincent joined a street gang in his teens and buddied up to Dutch Schultz, a big-shot mobster in the 1920s who kept Vincent on as an assassin.

In a parallel career, Coll kidnapped other gangsters and held them for ransom. A slick businessman, Dicky believed. A man hedging his bets and multitasking. A man far ahead of his time.

Before long, Coll and Dutch had a falling out and went their separate ways.

For sure, Vincent Coll was nobody to mess with. He was named Mad Dog by New York's Mayor Jimmy Walker for accidentally killing a five-year-old kid who got in the way when he tried to kidnap one of Dutch's underlings.

Why the hell wasn't the little shit home doing his homework, Dicky Coll thought after he read the account of the unfortunate child? It seemed to him that "Vinny" Coll, like himself, could never score any luck.

Thanks to the accident, Vincent had to go on the lam. Then he hooked up with Salvatore Maranzano, New York's boss of bosses, who hired Vincent to whack out Lucky Luciano, who Maranzano thought was muscling in on his action. Luciano was tipped off and whacked Maranzano instead.

Vincent Coll's luck got even worse. Owney Madden, boss of the Hell's Kitchen Irish Mob, put a big price on Mad Dog's head over a disagreement. On February 8, 1932, a gunsel tommy-gunned Coll while he was in a phone booth in a drugstore. Fifteen bullets were dug out of Mad Dog's body and more shots passed through it. Vincent (Mad Dog) Coll died at the tender age of twenty-three.

Dicky (Mad Dog) Coll was twice that old. He had not aged well in Walla Walla, as prison was wont to do to its guests. This jowly idolater of Vincent Coll was pale and paunchy, the shape of a rotting pear. Graying hair overhung his ears. It wasn't stylishly long; it was badly in need of a barber.

It was debatable whether he'd gotten educated in the can. If you asked Dicky, he had, although he hadn't finished the GED courses at Walla Walla. Too boring, too much homework. What he had done was take it upon himself to learn a word a day. He'd managed to learn and remember fifty or so words in the four thousand and some days he'd been locked up. You had to give the boy a D-minus for effort.

Today's word, as he sat, was: vigil. Maintaining a vigil meant being on surveillance, waiting for something to happen, which he was doing now. Easy word, vigil, but hard on the ass.

Dicky sat up straighter on account of a humongous red car pulling up to the Halloween house. It was a Cadillac from the olden days, with tail fins and more chrome than twenty Hondas. Out of it piled a big old couple and a younger guy who looked like the rich young lawyers he'd seen in court and the jailhouses.

They walked up to Roswell's door. She opened it for them and in they went.

Dicky Coll flipped open the cell phone Uncle Randall Coll gave him with orders to report anything unusual. He was still getting used to the newfangled gadgets that came along while he was away, like these phones that had grown smaller than a pack of cigarettes and had all manner of stuff on their baby screens, some with that Internet deal on it.

Dicky thought for a moment and flipped the phone shut. Maybe he'd just see what happened, try to see what this was all about before clueing in Uncle Randall, who did not once visit him during eleven long years in the joint.

CHAPTER 5

Capitol Hill, east of downtown Seattle, was an area of neighborhood shopping, dining and older homes. Some of the larger ones had been converted into apartments and condos. Some were rehabbed to the nines, some ramshackle. Judith Ann Roswell's fell into the midrange.

It was close to a century old, two stories of dormers, gables, leaded glass, and curlicue trim. Should Judith ever be inclined or able to sell, realtors would advertise it as Old World Charm, hoping that prospects were so enchanted by its *fin de siècle* appeal that they'd ignore the warts.

Introductions were made and Judith Roswell escorted them into a room she called a parlor, and asked them to take seats. They did, all three on an old, ornate sofa.

As Buster sat, he was thinking of flappers necking on it, them and their dates drinking moonshine out of mason jars. There were a ton of hallways and doorways in her place.

Carla said, "Your gingerbread house looks fantastic, inside and out. Your antique furniture and the rest."

Judith Roswell forced a smile and said, "Beauty that's skin-deep. I have wiring installed by Edison and pre-Columbian plumbing. Much is original, ninety-plus years of deferred maintenance. The house was built before my grandfather, Harry Spicer, was born, by his father, Jeremiah Spicer. That was in 1916, a year before Jeremiah went to Europe to fight in World War One. Jeremiah was gassed in the trenches, but survived.

"Paint is peeling on the siding. I spot-paint, chasing the latest flaking and blistering. I can't keep up. There are three layers of mossy shingles that have to come off before replacement. At the moment, there's just one big leak, in an upstairs bathroom. I make repairs or have them done strictly in emergencies. Knock on wood."

The wood Judith knocked on was a bookshelf, as if to draw their attention to it, and then offered glasses of wine. While she went to the kitchen for wine, red for Buster and Tip, white for Carla, they enjoyed the old-timey framed photos on the bookshelf. Many of the people had her features and eyes. Same with pictures hanging on the walls. In the outside shots, the house was the same, even those with Model T's in front, guys in neckties and suspenders beside them.

Carla was taken by the china cabinet. The centerpiece was a large plate mounted on a pedestal, a souvenir of the 1939–1940 New York World's Fair.

In the adjoining room, Judith saw Carla and said, "It was a gift from a friend of my Grandmother Ella who attended the fair. Ella glued it to that pedestal and displayed it there. I remember it as her proudest possession."

Judith Roswell looked to Buster Hightower to be forty-five, fifty tops. She had pleasant features and a nice body for her age. In loose-fitting jeans without makeup, making no effort to disguise her graying hair, she seemed to him to resist being attractive, but not getting the job done.

Judith Roswell looked to Carla Chance to be in romantic conjunction with Tip Taylor. They were alone and shouldn't be. She sensed an underlying loneliness in both, a depressing thing to have in common. Judith and Tip were an attractive May–September couple. No, make that June–September. Who knows what might develop with or without her help? Knowing herself to be an inveterate matchmaker, it'd be *with*.

Judith Roswell looked to Tip Taylor like an attractive older woman, a stressed-out client in immediate need of his services. Having noticed that a shiny, new dead bolt had been installed on the front door above the original skeleton-key latch, he remembered a line in the GOIPD curriculum:

When consulting for a client who fears clandestine entry is imminent, encourage great detail in recording current placement of personal property. A digital camera is an invaluable tool. If a desk paperweight has been moved a single inch, that may be all the proof required. An inch is as good as a mile.

Tip made a mental note to purchase a smaller, higher-resolution digital camera than the camera he kept forgetting to carry with him.

Carla first noticed two plump cats staring at him from a doorway, one orange and one white.

"They're adorable, Judith."

"When they choose to be. Meet Orange and Vanilla," Judith said, as she brought in a tray with the wine and glasses. "I hope you're not allergic."

Carla said, "We live with OC1 and OC2. Except for Vanilla's color, they could be quadruplets."

So what, Buster thought? There were a zillion orange cats in the world and two zillion white cats, he didn't say, valuing his own hide.

"They can be a comfort," Judith said, pouring the wine.

Buster sipped his red, picturing a tall cold brew in a frosted mug.

Tip sipped his wine politely, as he had the champagne at the bowling alley, which was fittingly celebratory, although he would've preferred a dry martini on each occasion, shaken, not stirred.

Despite hating gin, a martini seemed as if it certainly should be the drink of choice for a GOIPD honor grad who drove an

Aston Martin DB9. In a multiple flashback, he saw and heard his father, in his face, telling him to snap out of his fantasy world and perpetual adolescence, and grow up. This when he had flunked out or dropped out of one school or another.

An unusual trio, Judith Roswell thought. The older pair, a comedian and an insurance broker, made a darling couple. The handsome young man, her Private Eye, had just taken a notebook and pen from a pocket. She was unsure now of her choice. While likable and charming and attractive, even dashing, Mr. Taylor didn't strike her as an altogether serious person. She had visualized a Private Eye as being, well, not so collegiate.

Hoping she hadn't made a total mistake by giving in to panic and a hunch, not only hiring Taylor, but allowing him to bring his friends into a very personal matter, Judith said to him, "When I told you I was being stalked, I don't know if that's the correct term."

"How so?" Taylor asked.

"I do think he's constantly following me, but doing a terrible job of it. For instance, I went shopping yesterday. I came out with my cart. He was less than ten slots away. I looked over and he slouched down and turned his head the other way."

Buster said, "A superspy, he ain't."

Carla nudged Buster, her elbow advising him to stay out of it.

"Can you describe him?"

"I'd guess in his mid-forties. He's unkempt, overweight and flabby, with a pasty complexion."

As Taylor wrote in his notebook, she added, "He drives the same car, a small beat-up green sedan that's easily fifteen years old."

"When did you last see it?"

"Five minutes before I called you, Mr. Taylor. It was parked across the street near the corner. It still might be. I haven't wanted to look."

Tip Taylor got up and peeked through a curtain. The car was there, though because of darkness, he couldn't clearly see the person behind the wheel. "Any idea why you're being snooped upon. And please call me Tip."

"None whatsoever, Tip," Judith Roswell lied.

"How long has this been going on?"

"I first noticed him roughly a week ago. He followed me onto the freeway. I was visiting a friend in the north end for lunch."

Tip asked, "What do you drive?"

"A white Toyota Prius."

"Not an unusual car," Tip Taylor said.

"Is that important?" she asked.

Gosh-darned if he knew. "Perhaps. May I ask what you do for a living?"

She tensed. "I taught high school English."

"Taught as in past tense?"

"I'm on sabbatical."

On sabbatical. A mystery clue, Tip wondered?

A GOIPD-graduate should never take anything for granted, especially the obvious. Expand your knowledge base with our school-taught technique. If somebody wishes to speak, hear them out fully, and sift the wheat from the chaff later.

Bingo, Buster thought, also catching her body language. There are some ghosts in this place that she's confining to their closets.

"What is it you would like me to do?" Tip asked.

"Find out who it is."

"And?"

"And why he's there."

"There is no time like the present," Tip said, pocketing his notebook.

On their way out, Buster took his time, looking at the

pictures. One in particular held his interest, a thirty-something sport with his arms folded, leaning against the fender of an Oldsmobile that was a good ten years older than his Caddy. Grinning widely, his eyes—speaking of used cars—made Buster pat his pocket, to be sure his wallet was there.

Pointing at it, Buster said, "Who's that, Judith?"

"Harry Spicer, my paternal grandfather."

Going down the steps, Buster asked himself why his question had made her flush.

CHAPTER 6

The three ginks in the old red Caddy drove by Dicky (Mad Dog) Coll fast, tail fins slicing the night air. He'd slouched when they left the Halloween house, knowing he was unseen.

Buster drove by the green beater with a guy slouched behind the wheel, turned the corner, and said, "What next, Tip?"

"Hmm," replied the private eye. "The license number of that piece of junk is a sensible commencement of the case. I was able to catch the first three."

"Can you run the number by your daddy's law firm and have somebody check it out?" Buster said.

"No, Buster. I have been banished. I am the blackest of black sheep. For all I know, Father has a verbal restraining order if I go within a mile of the law office suite or the Lake Washington estate."

Estate as in home and abode, Buster thought. Be it never so humble.

"My family's a whole, entire herd of black sheep," Buster said. "A verbal restraining order? Can you pay them verbal money to order it unrestrained?"

Tip laughed. "It is not official, but Father makes his feelings abundantly clear. I can drop in on Mum—my mother—whenever I like. She tolerates me and Father is away frequently. He spends a great deal of time in Atlanta establishing a branch office for the firm."

"Do you see your mother much?" Carla asked.

"Well, I have been preoccupied setting up my detective agency."

Carla said, "You should always keep in contact with your mother, dear."

Tip sighed. "I know, I know."

"So how about that license number?" Buster said.

"I am remiss for not reading the complete plate."

"I did, and it's not your fault, Tip. Buster drives like a bat out of you-know-where," Carla said. "After a good night's sleep we'll go to my office and I'll see what I can do."

Judith Roswell had a second glass of wine, thinking that the private eye hadn't discussed money. Of course she'd have to pay him. But how much? However much it was, she couldn't afford it. And she couldn't afford not to have his services.

The collection agency hadn't badgered her since the call in that disgusting man's pawnshop. They certainly weren't giving up, not for the amount she owed. Judith believed they were going to take a different tack. They were going to escalate.

Tip Taylor appeared to lack confidence how to do his job, understandable as he was brand-new at it, but she believed he would put forth an honest effort. He looked prosperous, handsome and post-preppy, and you couldn't miss that gold Rolex. He was not her idea of a private investigator, whatever that might be. He didn't even wear a trench coat.

Should he? Or did the lack thereof disqualify him? Her experience with PIs had been on the large and small screens.

She certainly couldn't turn the stalker over to the police and be done with it. That man's appearance in her life could not be a coincidence, not with him materializing so soon after her visit to that creepy pawnbroker. She had selected Coll's Jewelry and Loan from the Yellow Pages, an impulsive move she hadn't repeated.

Judith opened the door to the basement and the source of her trouble. The can of worms she had opened.

She went down the steps, hanging on to a bare-wood handrail to avoid slipping, lighting the way by turning on pull-chain lightbulbs. As always, the basement smelled like mildew and old newspapers.

She knew from photos that the concrete floor was originally dirt. The walls had been brick, how foundations were built then when basements were intended for storage, not to be lived in. A section of the basement was framed in as a guest room. Judging by its brass-and-glass door hardware and Mini-Schoolhouse light fixture, in the 1940s or 1950s.

That room held secrets of its own.

From the timing of the pictures, Judith was certain her grandfather had the cement poured, not only the floor, but sections of the walls as reinforcement to the brick. Now she knew there was a second reason that had nothing to do with strengthening an aging home.

After her mother's funeral six months ago, she had braved the task of cleaning it out, spring housecleaning decades after its last spring housecleaning. For some odd and insistent reason—now not so odd, not a request driven by her worsening dementia—Mother had wanted the basement left as it was. Demanding it toward the end.

Mindful of the low joists and exposed plumbing, she looked at a coal chute that in the last sixty years had led to nowhere. There were cartons and boxes alongside it and against the walls. Her old bicycle, a girl's Schwinn, maroon like they often were. An ancient washing machine with the wringer on top. Suitcases and valises. Hanging from a wall hook was a sled that had been hers and Mother's. Judith remembered them sitting, daughter between mother's legs, gleefully racing down icy hills.

She looked sadly at cardboard boxes stacked next to the sled.

They were full of infomercial garbage, get-rich-quick-in-real-estate courses and overnight weight loss and the like. One of these days, they were all going to the dump, where they'd belonged *before* being mailed to the gullible. In her later life, Mother ordered everything she saw on TV.

What those oily pitchmen didn't get, her mother's "baby boy," Judith's brother, Gerald, had taken years earlier. The bastard took after their father, Doug Roswell, who walked out of their lives when they were teens. Good riddance, she thought: then as now. He'd been a loafer and philanderer. Like father, like son was never more apropos.

By the boxes were wooden milk crates from the days when glass bottles were delivered to the customer's door. Judith remembered a milkman in white uniform. His name was Brad and he was among the nicest persons she had ever known.

Atop a crate was a hardcover book the size and heft of a concrete block.

Judith knelt and opened the *1954 Seattle City Directory* to one of the four pages with its upper corner folded over. The first was easy. Page 1333 had a listing for Harry and Ella Spicer at this address.

She eventually doped out another: Pioneer Safe Deposit Vaults on 701 First Avenue, telephone MA 2080, on page 1577.

The third, page 998, covered part of the letter "M," Mullenbach to Munday. The fourth, 1315, was one of fourteen pages devoted to "Smith." She hadn't an inkling what their importance might be.

Then, beside the directory, she opened *The World Almanac and Book of Facts for 1955,* to a single page in it. *The World Almanac* was printed in hardcover then, and page 768 in this copy was also folded over. Near the bottom of the page, *Portraits on US Currency* was checkmarked with a blue fountain pen.

To Judith, the only significance to this was that bills were issued then above today's $100 maximum. They ran from $500 bills to $100,000 bills, Woodrow Wilson's portrait on the last. She wondered if President Wilson had been alive when the $100,000 bill came out, and what his reaction would have been. She studied the five marked pages in the books, wondering why she was repeating this ritual for the fiftieth or fortieth or hundredth time. Old Granddad Harry had bequeathed her a puzzle. And a nightmare in the making.

Judith stood, stooped, and slid the crates out. Using her fingernails at its edges, she pulled a brick free. Behind it was a steel plate. The brick looked like it was mortared with the others, but it wasn't. They fit so tightly, if you were searching, you'd have to use a magnifying glass.

Months ago, sweeping around the crates, she'd shoved one too hard, accidentally popping a brick loose. She soon realized why her mother had wanted the basement undisturbed.

She carefully removed a dozen bricks, careful to lay them out in proper configuration. She'd done this enough times so she could quickly and accurately replace them, as if pieces in a child's jigsaw puzzle.

Exposed, the steel was an end of a two-foot-by-two-foot unlocked door, a door to a box approximately five feet deep. When she first opened it, she thought of the mythical cornucopia. An elongated cubical cornucopia.

In reality, it was a twenty-cubic-foot snake pit.

Inside, on top of a manila folder, was currency. In envelopes and in bank wrappers. Circulated. Stocks and bonds were arranged in no particular order. Gems were piled willy-nilly, loose and in small jeweler's boxes and velvet pouches.

Harry Spicer, her grandfather, was a locksmith, a profession that could make one think the worst of people. Judith presumed he'd thought that burglars entering this house for valuables would ransack cupboards and dressers.

The box appeared to be waterproof. Her grandpa, whom she never knew, must have been thinking long-term.

Judith withdrew yellowed newsprint from the manila folder. Fragile from age, one piece was a front-page clipping from the *Seattle Daily Times*, Tuesday, February 23, 1954, edition. Its newsstand price was five cents.

The headline was *400 Boxes in 1ˢᵗ Av. Vault Looted.*

Below it was the photo of the scene, a mess of scattered debris and opened safe deposit boxes.

Skilled safecrackers over the weekend broke into and looted the Pioneer Safe Deposit Vaults, 701 First Av. The vaults had withstood the Seattle fire of 1889.

Frank J. Goodman, the owner, discovered the burglary when he opened for business this morning.

The safecrackers, using acetylene torches, cut through a steel wall one and a half inches thick to gain entry to safe deposit boxes. More than 400 boxes were opened and their contents removed. The vault contained 1800 boxes.

Goodman said it would be days before he knew how much was taken.

The safecrackers left in the vault two acetylene tanks and a foot locker containing two electric drills, concrete bits, goggles, gloves and crowbars.

Detectives termed the burglary a highly professional job.

The company, at street level in pioneer days, now is in a basement. The vault was built in 1884 for a pioneer bank. Goodman has leased the firm since 1949 from Dr. Al Sherman.

The safecrackers apparently picked a rear-door padlock and replaced it to leave no evidence of forced entry, said Victor L. Kramer, chief of detectives.

The safecrackers burned the locks off two steel doors to reach the vault.

Cracks around the firm's front door had been taped, appar-

ently to seal off the noise and odor from the burning.

The safecrackers first attempted to drill a hole in the front door of the vault, then moved around to the side, removed some bricks, and drilled through the wall.

Judith's research indicated that the burglars had thought it out well. The policemen's ball was that weekend, fortuitously a mile away from Pioneer Safe Deposit Vaults, so patrols were lighter than usual.

Later investigation theorized by the gear left behind that there were three burglars. It was traced to rental establishments, but the renters paid cash and could not positively be identified. A rumor had it that the burglars would have stayed longer and cracked all the boxes but for the racket one was making, a drug addict who sang in a loud voice, "Hi ho, hi ho, it's off to work we go."

The crime was never solved. Only a single piece of loot was ever recovered, a bond found years later in Nevada.

Grandfather Harry Spicer, the ostensible ringleader, died in early 1955 from a fast-acting cancer that could easily have been kept in remission now, a reason why the loot wasn't spent. Judging by what was here, she thought, little or nothing had been given to Harry's accomplices.

But why? The other two must have been antsy to go on spending sprees and Harry somehow persuaded them to wait until the take wasn't so "hot." Most criminals weren't long-range thinkers. Short-term gratification was the norm. Harry must have been the rare exception. The burglary was hard, physical work. There would be a sense of entitlement.

Or had Grandfather Harry double-crossed them, stiffing them with a phony name and address? Thus all this plunder?

Buster Hightower, the comedian, had zeroed in on Harry Spicer's photo, as if picking him out of a police lineup. Of all the people in all the generations on her walls, Buster read her grandfather as slick, as a hustler. He'd seen it clear as glass; she knew he had!

And why did Harry obviously finger himself? After he knew he was terminal, did Grandfather want his daring deed recorded for posterity? You couldn't arrest, try, and convict a dead man, a self-proclaimed master criminal. If he was eventually pinpointed and Grandmother Ella was served with a search warrant, a thorough police ransacking might uncover what she had. Harry would be front-page news again.

Guesses at the time on the aggregate loss ranged from $200,000 to $500,000. That was big, big money in those days. You could multiply each 1954 dollar by eight to approximate today's dollar, she knew.

Judith couldn't begin to estimate what the stocks and bonds were worth today. Not to mention the overall loss. It logically followed that some individual statements of loss were low because the box renters were hiding assets from spouses and the IRS. Other estimates were inflated for insurance claims.

She had counted the cash when she laid all the loot on the basement floor and organized it: $650,000-plus.

Mixed in the wealth was the oddest piece of correspondence she had ever seen. It was on flowery, dime-store stationery, stained as if it had been perfumed:

DEER HARRY,

I AWT TO GO CALL THE COPS ON YOU. I TELL THEM MY AGE, THEY WONNT LIKE YOU. YOU COME IN MY ROOM AND I GIVE YOU WHAT YOU WANT. SUK YOU OFF AND EVRYTHING AND YOU GO AND KICK ME OUT WITH THAT FAKE RUBY NEKLUS YOU GIVE ME. YOU CAN SHUV IT UP YOUR ASS. FUCK YOU HARRY. EAT SHIT AND DIE AND GO STRAIT TO HELL.

HARRIET H.

Who on earth was the youthful, charming and worldly Ms. Harriet H? She hadn't gone far in school, but did have a basic grasp of phonics, thought ex-schoolteacher Judith Roswell.

I tell them my age, they wonnt like you.

If she was pubescent jailbait then and alive today, Harriet H. would be in her seventies.

Judith looked at the framed-in room, imagining Harriet and her grandfather sharing it while her unsuspecting grandmother slept. Perhaps Mr. Harry Spicer had slipped his better half a sleeping pill. He seemed capable of it.

Her mother, Sharon Spicer Roswell, had been a teenager then. If she knew the sordid tale, she never let on to Judith.

She picked the necklace out of a gleaming, sparkling pile, a teardrop ruby in a flowery gold setting with a gold chain. The chain was broken and the setting that looked like two leaves or petals was bent. She closed her eyes and saw Harriet throwing a tantrum, ripping it from around her neck and flinging it in cradle-robbing Harry's face.

Judith held the ruby up to the light. It was three carats if it was a chip, and the most gorgeous and deepest red she had ever seen. No way could it be glass. Harriet H. may have had myriad talents, but jewelry appraisal was not among them.

She thought of her dear, devious brother, Jerry Roswell and of the home equity loan that had years remaining before payoff. She flushed with anger at the memory of him.

Judith Roswell had missed two house payments since Mother passed away. Mother died broke and then some. Unbeknownst to Judith, she lost all that the infomercial vultures hadn't taken to a telemarketer who said she'd won a large sweepstakes.

All they needed was her Social Security number and a bank account number where the money was to be transferred. They sacked it and drained her line of credit too. Judith negotiated with the bank to no avail. The police investigated and discovered that the bad guys were working out of Nigeria, so that was that.

She rationalized yet again that this loot will benefit nobody else. *Nobody.* She was deeply in debt and the 1954 victims had been compensated by insurance. The majority were deceased, almost seventy years later. Court battles among the descendants of the robbery victims and the insurance companies would rage for years, as the loot sat in a police property room while Judith worked until age eighty.

If she could find a job other than minimum wage. Past fifty, she'd be facing age discrimination, albeit good luck proving it.

Her options were limited to establishments with yellowed NOW HIRING signs in their windows.

Will you be having fries with that?

Judith picked out a piece of currency and asked herself, "What's wrong with this picture?"

Quite a lot was wrong with that picture. It was a $500 bill, with President McKinley's face on it. She looked at a $1,000 bill, adorned with Grover Cleveland's visage. The marked page in the *1955 World Almanac,* page 768, *Portraits on US Currency,* was mocking her, reminding her that there was nothing larger than a hundred in circulation these days.

Yes, there were smaller bills, fifties and hundreds, but they were crackling fresh, Series 1954. It might as well be Confederate money.

Judith had a small fortune in illiquid liquid assets.

She picked up the lovely ring she had almost pawned to that awful, seedy man. She held it, knowing that it was platinum, and put it on again. She had been a substitute science teacher and knew that the specific gravity of platinum at twenty-one-point-four-five was one of the heaviest elements, noticeably heavier than gold's nineteen-point-three. Far, far heavier than Mr. Coll's white-gold folderol.

Judith went to the milk crates and picked up a new manilla

envelope she had bought and left there, deciding to go through with what had been on her mind when she made the purchase. No further waffling. She would give away what she couldn't use of the accursed treasure in increments to charities she had researched as the most worthy. None were more so than one she knew firsthand. She had volunteered there on Saturdays while she was still teaching. It wouldn't solve her monetary woes, but she'd sleep better.

Judith Roswell put cash and jewels in the envelope, careful not to make the envelope too thick. Concealing it inside a lightweight jacket, she went out to her Prius. The green junker was still on the other side of the street. If the mysterious stalker set out after her, she'd delay her plan, go to a nearby convenience store for ice cream, return home, eat the ice cream, and try to sleep.

Out of the corner of her eye, she saw the man was hunched over the steering wheel. Asleep?

Dicky (Mad Dog) Coll was not following Judith Roswell, but not because he was asleep. As he maintained his vigil, he was indeed wide awake, hunched over, pants unzipped, taking a leak into the funnel just as the white Prius drove by. He had held his water as long as he could.

Dicky tried to stop urinating and start the car, but all he managed to do is piss all over his trousers and the floor of the car, thinking that his luck hadn't improved a bit.

Judith drove south on Seattle's Rainier Avenue South, a major thoroughfare. The neighborhood ran the gamut from recent gentrification to outright poverty. She stopped by a commercial building at a stretch on Rainier that rated somewhere in between.

Services for the Needy was a thrift shop between a dry cleaners and a pastry shop. Besides donations offered at a fair price, they contributed their meager profits to area food banks.

It was closed for the evening. The charity's lighted front windows displayed furniture and appliances.

Judith waited for several cars to pass, got out, and quickly pushed the manila envelope through the mail slot.

At the second red light on the way home, Judith yawned. She knew that a good night's sleep was in store.

CHAPTER 7

Last night, Buster Hightower had dropped off Carla Chance and Tyler Polk (Tip) Taylor III at the Westside Bowling Lanes and Casino to pick up their cars, Carla's Hyundai and Tip's "JamesBondMobile," which Buster needlessly said could be traded in for "a whole, entire showroom full of Hyundais."

Next morning, Buster and Carla started up the hill from their condo in downtown Kent to the Last Chance Insurance Agency. Tip Taylor was to meet them there. He'd said he lived in Tacoma, in a downtown apartment overlooking the water, nothing more specific than that.

Buster doubted if it was an estate like his daddy's, but it wouldn't be too shabby either. It'd be a deluxe pad with a swell view that'd be featured in the Tacoma Sunday paper, if Tip chose to have them over to do a story on it.

Tacoma was thirty miles south of Seattle and Tyler Polk Taylor II, aka Father. Distance wasn't gonna make their hearts grow fonder, so distance wasn't a bad idea for pa and son. The next time zone might not do any harm either.

As they rode, Carla studied her man, steering with one hand on his necker knob, reflecting that once upon a time she would have been classified as a spinster, an old maid. What her spinsterhood came down to was that the men she wanted to marry didn't want to marry her and she didn't want to marry the men who wanted to marry her.

She learned early on that her size considerably thinned her

dating pool. She was to most young adult males a sexual curiosity, a kiss-and-tell war story. Climbing Twin Peaks, she imagined the adolescent boasting around pitchers of beer. When she did acquiesce to a tumble in the hay, Carla Chance was neither easy nor grateful. That she went through life with the pickiness of an anorexic blonde yell queen thinned her dating pool even further.

Carla's standards for the opposite sex remained high into late middle age. She insisted on steady employment, no public nose-picking, no attempts to reach into her purse, no law enforcement anklets, and sanitary habits within the norm. It was surprising how many unattached men failed one or more of her criteria.

The older she became, the likelier her bachelor pool was to fall short in those areas and into dark niches such as outstanding felony warrants, voyeurism, alcoholism, bigamy, startling fetishes (with and without lace undergarments and whips), and unresolved issues concerning their mothers.

Several years ago, Carla had been sitting in her office reviewing stacks of policy apps and renewal requests. Her policyholders and prospective policyholders was a rogues' gallery. In the piles of paper were good people who had made bad decisions and bad people who made terrible decisions and people who were just plain scary. Carla believed that they all deserved the opportunity to purchase protection for their automobiles, homes, personal property, and lives that most Americans took for granted.

For no particular reason, Carla had had an epiphany. It came out of nowhere, blindsiding her.

She set aside the paperwork, stared into the middle distance, and vowed to henceforth cease searching for Mr. Right. At this stage in her life, Mr. Right was in the same category as the Tooth Fairy. He resided in Shangri-La and vacationed in Oz. If a flawed man attracted her and she grew to like him and he liked her, well, what were a few teensy little imperfections?

An enormous burden rose from her. Nothing outweighed futility. Carla experienced a giddy serenity. This state of euphoria lasted all of five minutes. It was interrupted when an automotive relic, a massive assemblage of chromium and red paint screeched to a noisy halt at her door.

Into Last Chance Insurance Agency shambled a large, silly-looking character with wild hair and a goofy grin. In a cockeyed and unexplainable way, he was adorably handsome. His eyes locked on hers. They became wilder than his hair.

Carla felt a mountain range of goose bumps on her arms. Maybe he wasn't Mr. Right, but he was Mr. Right Now. The applicant, one Buster NMI Hightower, had seen her Yellow Pages ad: LAST CHANCE INSURANCE AGENCY. TICK-ETS? ACCIDENTS? DUI? NO PRIOR OR CANCELLED INSURANCE? SUSPENDED LICENSE? NO PROBLEM!

Mr. Hightower's driving record was less than exemplary and his motor vehicle was an archaic oddity. He was denied coverage by all of her insurance carriers, every marginal and pathetic one of them. His request for a date was not denied. Three years ago, in what she considered a whirlwind romance, Buster moved into her condo in Kent, a city twenty miles south of Seattle.

The Last Chance Insurance Agency occupied a two-room suite in a strip mall ten minutes from home, east of downtown Kent, atop a hill where the original city of Kent gave way to Kent suburbia, a sprawl of housing developments and apartment complexes.

Last Chance shared a wing with a beauty salon, a dry cleaners, teriyaki, and a recent tenant, a payday loan outfit. Buster eased his tail-finned monstrosity into two slots. They got out and she unlocked LCIA's door, smiling, thinking yet again that Buster Hightower was a thousand times as likely to patronize the teriyaki as the cleaners.

He once did a bit at the Westside proving scientifically that teriyaki from Carla's neighbor combined with corn dogs and beer contained all the food groups, and increased life spans to boot, lowering bad cholesterol to minus zero. And it you ran out of cash before dessert, no sweat, walk across the lot and take out a payday loan. He'd been hilarious and oddly credible.

Carla stooped to pick up mail that had been dropped through the slot and tossed it on her desk as if it were diseased. She sighed, sat and opened some of the envelopes. A couple of her letters to policyholders had been returned, addressee moved to parts unknown. There was correspondence from some of the carriers she represented: Mayhem Mutual, Saint Carcinoma Health Plans, Unassured Insurance Associates, Angst Property and Casualty, Precarious Insurance Group, Incarceration Indemnity, Demolition Auto and Home.

The message button on her phone blinked. There was just one, from a largely incoherent client who rambled on about a sidewalk where it wasn't supposed to be, something new they must've just paved, then all of a sudden a storefront window flashing before his eyes and windshield, and a rigged Breathalyzer test. Carla recalled having him with The Pileup Group. She made a mental note to alert them. That is, if their phones hadn't been disconnected again.

She flipped through her Rolodex and said, "Here's a good candidate. Jack's a regional sales manager for Apocalypse Auto and Home. He owes me a favor and he knows somebody at DMV who will look up a license number for him on the spot."

"You wrote policies on his uninsurably uninsurable insureds? A serial killer or firebug or kamikaze pilot?"

She fluttered a hand. "You might say so. I wrote Jack himself with another company. He couldn't get coverage with his own. Don't ask for details. It's too soon after breakfast."

She dialed and said, "Hi, Jack, Carla. How are you?"

"Oh. Sorry to hear that. Uh-huh. Uh-huh. Well, you're out on bail, thank goodness. Count your blessings. And your wife's boyfriend did what to you? Oh dear."

Carla rolled her eyes as she listened to his tales of woe, then asked him to look up the license number, waited thirty seconds, wrote a name down, and thanked Jack.

"Coll's Jewelry and Loan, with a Seattle address in the Pioneer Square area," she told Buster.

"A pawnshop?" Buster said, puzzled.

"Apparently so. Judith Roswell doesn't seem the sort to do business with a pawnbroker."

"It ain't always the person," Buster said. "It's their situation. Every time I went to one, I wasn't what you'd call totally desperate, but I wasn't on easy street neither."

Buster watched out the window as Tip's Aston Martin DB9 pulled up. It was light blue; the paint job really did look like it was a foot deep. Cherry-looking set of wheels, he thought, almost but not quite as cool as his Caddy. Twelve cylinders, big deal. Under his hood was a V-8, but it had the power and torque to pull a supertanker.

He said, "I haven't figured out in my mind what sort of gal Judith is and isn't. We'll whip this new info on our private eye and let him figure out his client likewise."

"Whatever you said, Buster, I'm in agreement."

CHAPTER 8

A teary-eyed woman by the name of Brenda Hicks was blinking at the TV news camera, saying that thanks to a mysterious person or persons' generosity, Services for the Needy would be able to stay afloat indefinitely.

Trim, red-haired, and in her fifties, Brenda wiped her eyes and said, "If the money proves legally to be ours, our debts can be paid as well as operating expenses far into the future. We were in deep, deep financial trouble. Until now.

"Our attorney who volunteers her services for us said that because of the time that's apparently gone by, it'll be virtually impossible to know the origin of this gift. Money can be impossible to trace, so the assumption is that it was stored away for over half a century by our unknown benefactor, who decided to donate it. Maybe the gift had been written into a will and the giver wished to remain anonymous. Who knows? At this point, it's anybody's guess."

The news reporter was full-figured, pleasant and matronly. She said, "Yes, it is anybody's guess. The jewelry dates to the nineteen-twenties and nineteen-thirties and forties. The money is all old, much of it unused, bills of larger denominations no longer in circulation, series printed in the early nineteen-fifties, none later than nineteen-fifty-four. Can you think of anybody connected to Services for the Needy who might do this?"

Brenda Hicks said, sniffling. "I can't. All I know is that it's a miracle. Thank the good Lord, it could've been beamed down to us from Heaven or a UFO."

"A jeweler saw a piece you showed us on our morning eyewitness news program. Attracted to it, he raced over to appraise it for you," the newsperson coaxed.

Brenda Hicks felt comfortable with this woman. She was just plain folk, probably banished to the field, rain or shine, too old and too average-looking for the studio with its vacuous young anchors and their helmet hair.

Brenda held up a ruby pendant with a bent clasp. "Yes. This piece. He said it was a pigeon blood ruby from the Mogok Valley of Burma, the most valuable of all gemstones. Its deep red color is like no other ruby and it has to weigh in excess of three carats. He said it's worth tens of thousands of dollars. He wanted to buy it from me on the spot. Our attorney advised us to explore our options first and wait for her to confirm without a shadow of a doubt that the treasure slipped into our mail slot last night is legally ours."

Among those watching the noon news was Harriet Hardin Callahan Miller Kline Parker Jacobs Smith.

When she saw the ruby pendant portion of the report, the necklace dangling in the center of her television screen, her jaw and her dentures nearly dropped to her knees.

"Jesus H. Fucking Christ!"

"Now, now, Mrs. Smith," said the woman who had brought her meal. "A nice lady like yourself shouldn't be turning the air so blue and taking our Savior's name in vain. It is so lovely a story for that thrift store, isn't it? For all those folks suffering poverty."

Unable to summon a reply, Harriet took a deep breath, and clenched her dentures and bony fists.

"Mrs. Smith, you're wound up too tight. Maybe you should get yourself a cat. They do allow them in here, you know, and they're such clean and friendly animals."

"Cats. I hate the fucking things and they hate me. If you ask me, you can ship them all to the pound," Harriet said, thinking that the bent clasp was the clincher. There weren't two pieces of jewelry like it in the whole wide world.

Sighing, the meals lady said, "I give up."

The walls seemed even smaller now at Harriet's subsidized seniors' apartment in the city of Kent, Washington. For what that rock was valued at, she could buy this whole goddamn building, and buy and sell every geezer and geezerette on the premises.

Harriet Hardin had been a runaway, a fourteen-year-old school dropout who escaped a father who was abusive when he was around at all and a boozehound mother who wasn't there even when she was there. She bounced from friend to friend and onto the streets until she landed a job as a live-in housekeeper at the Harry and Ella Spicer residence.

She soon found out that she hadn't been hired for her housekeeping skills. She got the job ninety seconds into her interview with Harry because she was hot young stuff and just as cute as a button. Little Harriet Hardin was trained as a housekeeper by Ella. She was trained by Harry in other areas.

Harry Spicer, who came teepee creeping into her downstairs room at night.

Harry Spicer, who persuaded her to do tricks to him in bed that sweet and cold wifey Ella Spicer would not.

Harry, the lying bastard, had given the necklace to her, saying that if Ella noticed and asked, it was a gift from her boyfriend. Then Harry got sick, so sick he stopped sneaking downstairs and into Harriet's bed. He could barely climb the stairs.

This was just fine with Harriet, who needed her sleep more than she needed a filthy old man who liked to play rough when he'd had a few drinks.

Harry had gotten cranky over his cancer, blaming the world, Harriet included, like he'd caught it from her as if it was VD. Not that she could fault him for feeling sorry for himself. Cancer was a tough break. But that didn't excuse what he did to her.

Harry fired her over some no-no so trivial he'd concocted that she couldn't even recall what it was. What it amounted to was that he couldn't get it up and had no further use for her.

The stupidest thing Harriet ever did in her life, and she had done plenty of stupid things, was tearing the necklace off, snapping the chain and bending the clasp as she did, and flinging it in Harry's face, telling him to shove his cheap piece of rhinestone shit up his rotten ass. Then, when she was packing to leave, writing him a letter telling him what she thought of him, hoping that Ella would see it too. She was a nice lady who deserved to know what a shithead she was married to.

Harriet groaned at the memory as she listened to the TV gal say how odd the money was, old and odd. Series 1954 on the large bills, yet crisp and uncirculated. She'd hold up a Ben Franklin and say that none of the anticounterfeiting tricks were in use when it was printed.

"Are you all right, Mrs. Smith?"

Harriet nodded, staring numbly at the tube.

"Goodness, that is strange, though," the meals lady said at the door after microwaving Harriet's meatloaf, mashed potatoes, and green beans lunch for her. "If they're out there dropping manna from Heaven on those who do good, I hope they visit us. Me and all you folks in here, Mrs. Smith. We can use the money, can't we?"

Harriet Hardin Callahan Miller Parker Kline Jacobs Smith didn't reply.

At the meals lady was leaving, Harriet thought, yeah, she sure as hell could use the bucks. Nobody was entitled to a windfall more than she was. Her ex-husbands were all losers and snakes, so here she was, living on a pittance of Social Security, and subsidized meals, and lodging for the poor. Along with housekeeping, her own working career consisted of sporadic jobs as a bartender and cocktail waitress, low-paying jobs that didn't allow for savings even if she'd been so inclined.

Harriet was in nice shape and attractive for a woman in her seventies. When dolled up, she easily passed for ten years younger. Men in the complex frequently hit on her. The old duffers with a few bucks who took her out for a nice dinner, drinks and a movie had a shot at some nooky. The others, as poor as she was, dream on.

Harriet got out of her rocking chair and went to the tiny dinette to eat lunch, thinking that what she saw on the news maybe wasn't so strange, its connection to Harry maybe not so far out. It was the timing, the dates on those bills.

She knew Harry was a scalawag in more ways than one, more ways than what he was with his zipper unzipped. She sensed he had under-the-table income. The sleaze lived too high on the hog for a locksmith who didn't have a busy schedule, home as much as he was.

Harriet remembered a weekend when he went away, not long before he gave her the necklace, maybe a month before. Harry being gone overnight was unusual.

Ella had told Harriet what Harry had told her, that he was taking an advanced locksmith class in Portland, Oregon. It was sponsored by a lock company with a new line of hardware on the market. Ella gobbled it hook, line and sinker, like everything Harry told her.

Harriet knew better by then to believe a word the lying sack of shit said about *anything*. She knew for sure he was up to something when he spent so much time in the basement after his weekend away, being extra careful to lock the upstairs door when he was down there. Locking Harriet out of access to her own room while she was doing her housekeeping chores.

She finished lunch and decided two things. First, walk over to the library. It was under a half mile and it was a nice day for a stroll.

She'd snare one of those whiz kids there who were so smart on computers and spent half their lives playing on the library's. She'd sit down with the youngster and ask to be shown how to look up Northwest history.

See if there'd been a big robbery or caper in Portland or Seattle in February 1954.

The second thing she decided was that she was going by her maiden name from now on. Smith and her other exs, they can go straight to hell if they aren't already there with Harry.

CHAPTER 9

Tyler Polk (Tip) Taylor III called Judith Roswell from the Last Chance Insurance Agency asking to come over, that he had some information on the stalker's car.

The sooner the better, she said.

So off he went, Carla all but pushing him out the door, encouraging him to take credit for the discovery, beaming and waving at him as he left. Her support of his embryonic career was touching.

Per the manufacturer's specs, Tip's DB9 and its 470-horsepower V-12 and six-speed manual gearbox was capable of achieving a top speed of 190 mph and accelerating from zero to sixty in 4.6 seconds. Just last night, or rather very early morning, illuminated only by streetlamps and June twilight, Tip had verified the latter with a tire-burning, fishtailing shot onto Interstate Five, jamming through the gears like a Grand Prix champion.

He had been dying to do so, but wisely waited until he had insurance coverage (wisely being a relative term), until he was under the dubious protection of Exotic Coach and Casualty. Tip had set his alarm yesterday evening so that he'd be there at an hour of light traffic or police activity that permitted him to come to a full stop on the entry ramp and then rocketing onto Interstate Five. He continued accelerating before reluctantly taking his foot off the gas when the Aston Martin's speedometer needle effortlessly moved beyond 135.

And from 135 to a legal sixty in seconds, compliments of front and rear ventilated disk brakes the size of pizza pans. Nosing down, belt and harness tugging him, skidding, but decelerating as straight as the hackneyed arrow.

Lest anyone accuse Tip of having a James Bond fantasy, he'd keep that stunt to himself. Just because he'd seen every Bond flick multiple times and chose an Aston Martin over a Ferrari, Lamborghini, Maserati, or high-end Porsche or Mercedes, it'd be a false accusation. So he told himself.

Tip Taylor stifled a yawn as he sedately merged into freeway traffic, goosing it only when he had to. Drivers were rude when they had a chance to cut off a super-luxury car. *I'll show you, rich boy!*

He was in need of rest and if you asked his father, Tyler Polk Taylor II (when Father was speaking to him) and Claire Esther Jamison (Mumsy) Taylor, her Tippy badly needed to grow up.

On the first, he'd have a siesta this afternoon. On the second, well, there was ample time for maturity.

His phone rang.

"Oh, Mr. Taylor!"

"Mrs. Snails, how are you?" he said, knowing the answer.

"I'm terrible. Horrible. As miserable as I've been in my life."

"May I ask why?"

"My Ralphie has a floozy."

Ralph Snails had scored? It was a dubious miracle if he had.

"Are you certain?"

"Oh yes. Yes I am, Mr. Taylor. When he left me, he moved into the basement of his parents' home, you know. He just called me from there. Ralphie definitely wants a divorce. He said he's fallen head over heels. I heard the floozy in the background coaching him. She's seduced my Ralphie there, the filthy slut. The disgusting trollop. I know she has!"

Mrs. Snails broke down, unable to continue. For the first

time since hanging out his PI shingle, Tip Taylor had immediate professional requirements. He was multitasking.

Tip spoke soothingly to Mrs. Snails and said he'd fully investigate her Ralph and his paramour within two days and report back to her verbally.

Before parking, Tip took a couple of trips around Judith Roswell's block, doing a figure-eight. He didn't see the green Geo.

In the daylight, Judith's home's Old World Charm lost a substantial portion of said charm. The small yard was neatly clipped, but clogged with old-growth weeds. The roof was mossy and window-trim paint was peeling.

Judith Roswell was waiting on the front porch, door open. Tip Taylor smiled and shook her hand.

She was a nice-looking woman in daylight too, a refreshing antithesis of his usual Botoxed nightclubbers he could still keep up with, both having a ball until they realized he was not a serious person. Even the most bimboesque gold diggers came to that conclusion. A dilettante cum private eye did not qualify as a solid matrimonial candidate, A Serious Person.

As airheaded as the majority were, they did look forward to a ring in a man's nose and a five-carat beauty on their finger. He thought uncomfortably of his thirtieth birthday last month, how it was all downhill from there. How gray hair and a pot gut were imminent. He who had no marketable skills, no steady employment on his résumé, nothing beyond summer jobs at Father's firm while in school.

It was Private Eye or bust.

"Coffee, Tip?" she said as they went in. "It might be a bit early for wine."

Not necessarily, he almost said.

"No thank you on the coffee. I will get right to it, Judith. We do not yet know who the individual hounding you is, but the car he was in is registered to Coll's Jewelry and Loan, a pawnshop in the Pioneer Square area. Are you familiar with it?"

Judith Roswell hesitated. "Why, no."

"You have never been there?"

"I said no. I'd remember."

She said it looking at her cats, Orange and Vanilla, who were curled up on a throw rug, so she didn't have to look at him as she turned three shades of red.

He had known a multitude of girls and women accustomed to lying. Judith Roswell was not in their company. Tip waited, looking at her.

"Really," she said.

"Do you want me to dig deeper, Judith, and attempt to find out what their interest is in you? If it is indeed that pawnbroker or an individual associated with him?"

"Oh, I don't know. I don't think so. They might be keeping an eye on my neighbors. Don't you think?"

"You saw him ten slots away when you went shopping a couple of days ago, Judith. This might rule out a neighbor."

"Tip, I just don't know. You've been wonderful, but I think I'm just being silly."

"Okay, yes, well, I presume you will not require my services any longer."

"Can you bill me?" she asked.

Bill her? Good question. He hadn't the foggiest how to bill clients and how much to charge. He required forms, blank invoices, stationery like that.

Details, details, details. To the best of his recollection, the fictional shamus had no paperwork. The apocryphal PI's headaches were due to blows to the skull, the result of fisticuffs.

He had to set aside time to work on the details. The GOIPD manual that came with the badge and the certificate might have covered administrative procedures, but he'd glossed over the material. It was *so* boring. Perhaps he could just go to an office supply store or do it online. But to do it online, would he have to have a website built? The fictional shamuses led far simpler lives. Their worries were confined to life and limb, not accounting and office management.

"Do not worry about that for the time being," Tip said.

As he was getting into his car, Judith ran out and said, "Tip, wait. Please."

Sensing a breakthrough, a mystery clue forthcoming, Tip got out in a hurry.

They met halfway, Judith Roswell in an obvious hurry. She held out a ring and Tip took it from her. He rotated it in his fingertips: heavy, silvery, a nice-sized diamond.

"What do you think?"

"I am no expert, but it is obviously an antique and worth considerable money," he said, not saying that his Mumsy had similar pieces passed down from her MumMum.

"I wasn't truthful with you, Tip. I apologize for that. I was doing us both a disservice. I brought this ring to that pawnshop to sell and changed my mind. It's an old family heirloom. I'm pretty sure the pawnbroker was trying to cheat me, offering a fraction of what it's worth. He must have had my license number traced."

She needs the money, Tip thought. One does not hock a family heirloom unless one is desperate. He was not going to press her, though, but if he ever got a billing system in order, he planned to give her a twenty-percent discount on whatever he decided to charge.

Thinking of the new dead bolt on the front door, he said, "I agree. They must think it is very valuable to go to this trouble. And that there is more where the ring came from."

"Yes, they must," she said. "I'm doubly concerned what they

have in mind."

"Your shadow has gone away, maybe for good," he said, unconvinced. "Do you want to leave it as is?"

"Hoping they're really gone for good? Honestly, I don't know."

Every rule has an exception, including discretion. This is a rule that is meant to be selectively broken. The GOIPD graduate may find it advantageous to add fuel to the fire. The attention may prove inconvenient or worse. This is irrelevant to the client, who only wants peace of mind. On the other hand, a stitch in hand saves nine.

"Mayhap we should find out," Tip said.

"What do you suggest?" Judith said.

"That I pay a visit to Coll's Jewelry and Loan," Tip said. "Shake some limbs and see what drops."

"You and I?"

"No. Just the ring and myself. You wait in the car, please. We are counterattacking."

Counterattacking, Judith thought, with this man and his massive jaw in her corner. The pawnbroker would think twice before harassing her again.

"Stir the pot?" Judith said.

"Indeed. Without further adieu or cliché, shall we?" Tip said.

Chapter 10

Three time zones east of Seattle, Vance Popkirk, wannabe best-selling novelist, and prospective reality TV show producer, watched the intriguing Seattle charity story on cable TV news. Popkirk had once been chief historical and political affairs correspondent for the defunct *Weekly International Tattler,* another victim in the tragic demise of print journalism.

Half dozing in his recliner, half jotting notes for the start of his blockbuster literary opus, the woman and her *it could've been beamed down to us from Heaven or a UFO* caught Popkirk's attention.

Jerking upright, he was all eyes and ears. Flying saucers and space aliens had been *Tattler* mainstays. They had been what clouds were to a weather report.

Vance Popkirk was particularly fascinated by the old currency in bank wrappers. Some of the bills were $500 and $1,000 denominations, money that had been out of circulation for ages. He was conceptualizing an otherworldly context to the story.

His last assignment for the *Tattler* had been to Latin America, where he'd billed the paper for the trip he didn't take and wrote PROOF THAT ANCIENT ASTRONAUTS BUILT MAYAN PYRAMIDS. FRAGMENT OF CRASHED SPACESHIP FOUND AT RUIN. Stock photos of Chichén Itzá and Palenque sealed the scam.

The JFK assassination was another staple. Two utterances

could bring a *Weekly International Tattler* employee up on heresy charges:

"Lee Harvey Oswald acted alone," and "Elvis is dead."

Neither had or ever would pass from Vance Popkirk's lips.

Ah, but a long-enough stroll down memory lane.

He was itching to travel again, to explore the arcane and potentially lucrative. This time travel for real, to advance his new career.

A natty little man in his forties bordering on effete, Popkirk got out of his easy chair and fired up his laptop. Online, he booked airfare for the next flight to Seattle and a hotel room near the airport. Vance Popkirk was a confirmed bachelor, so there were no female encumbrances to hamper spontaneity and interfere with his career.

Popkirk missed his contribution to journalism, especially Your Correspondent at Large, the weekly column adorned with his picture. But his new career as a developer of reality television programming had limitless potential. The capacity of the American television viewer for dreck, for mind sludge, was infinite.

The working title of his first treatment was *Big Brides*. It offered to the unwashed masses what the title suggested, the poor whoppers trying to squeeze into their wedding dresses. The show encouraged stress eating to raise the poundage even further week to week, victory going to fiancées who made the scale creak the loudest. Grooms inclined to develop cold feet were encouraged to fulfill their obligations by the brides' fathers and brothers, no holds barred. That *Big Brides* was sub-moronic, appallingly cruel and decidedly unhealthy should make ratings soar.

Dear God was an even superior concept. The show played matchmaker, arranging blind dates, pairing atheists with drinking problems to evangelical Christians who were priggish to the extreme. *Dear God* promised an abundance of near-rape attempts, hilarious religious fanaticism, yelling and screaming, and outright physical violence.

Much blood and bleeping of language. Marvelous fun.

The competition was brutal. It seemed like every other show on the boob tube currently was of the reality genre, each more bizarre and vulgar than the next. Everybody wanted their fifteen minutes, so there was no shortage of recruits anxious to humiliate and degrade themselves.

Problem was, he hadn't been able to sell *Big Brides* and *Dear God* to producers, even the smarmiest of the breed. Fearful of litigation and backlash from health nuts, everybody he pitched *Brides* to passed on it.

Same reaction to *Dear God*. The prigs and weenies. You'd think he was burning a Koran and bringing on a fatwa!

Popkirk dug suitcases out of a closet, shaking his head at the trepidation and lack of intellect he was up against.

Vance Popkirk regarded himself as a Renaissance man, a polymath. He thought far . . . *far* outside the box. This windfall the thrift-shop charity enjoyed was speculated to be ill-gotten. *If the money proves legally to be ours.*

If he got to it first with a deal and set up an intermediate show, say, *Dead Man's Booty,* and claimed a share for his costs, well, a Vance Popkirk Production LLC smash hit was within his grasp.

Popkirk packed, whistling while he worked, blocking the concept out in his head, mulling the possibilities.

And looked forward to the time on the airplane to get going on his magnum opus, *Gone with the Wind: The Holy Bible.* The title was an automatic, a winner. So was the protagonist, a superhero who was a mirror image of himself.

If he could just get Chapter One going, off the launching pad.

If he could get past *Once upon a time.*

CHAPTER 11

Randall Coll made Dicky (Mad Dog) Coll wait in a corner of his shop, out of the way by a dusty coatrack, standing there with his thumb up his ass, until Randall was through with a customer, if you could call him that. Dicky was thinking that his uncle was no different than a fence. He'd known fences no slipperier than he was.

Dicky's word of the day: patience. Not his all-time favorite, as he had little of it, but patience was among the fifty or so he could spell.

The dummy was a jittery, sniffling, pencil-necked meth freak. He'd seen a jillion of them at Walla Walla. He was trying to sell Uncle Randall a hundred pounds of copper tubing he said he had out in his trunk of his car, reminding him for the fifth time that copper was going for upwards of four bucks a pound. He said he'd drive around in the alley if Uncle Randall wanted him to.

"I'll bet you inherited it from your grandma," Randall Coll said.

"Huh?"

"It was in her will, left to you," Randall Coll said with a sneer Dicky Coll had often seen face-to-face.

"Hey, man. It's legit. I bought it off this guy."

"Got a receipt?"

The freak patted his pockets. "Guess I lost it."

"I have a couple of problems with this. Didn't anybody tip

you that the price of copper's been dropping for the last year or so? Four bucks a pound is history," Randall lied, having some fun with him.

"It has? It is? When?"

"None of your colleagues have been electrocuting themselves lately snipping high tension lines. That should give you a clue. I'll pass on your copper. Come back when you find your receipt and the phone number of who you bought it from," Randall Coll said, gesturing to the way out.

At the door, the freak turned, flipped the pawnbroker the bird, told him to go fuck himself, and let it slam behind him.

The instant the mutant loser was gone, Mad Dog blathered a litany of excuses for losing the broad in the old house, which didn't include burning out what remained of the Geo's clutch getting out of the slot and U-turning to chase her.

"That shitbox you give me to use is on its last legs anyways and the old gal, she was going like a bat outta hell. You been in the thing? It smells of piss so bad you can't hardly stand it. Maybe a cat crawled inside through a window. That's what it smells like to me."

Randall Coll's headache began between his eyes and spread fast, as if via tentacles. "How did you let her spot you?"

"No way, man. I didn't."

"But you said she was going like a bat out of hell."

"She was but she couldn't of seen me, Uncle Randall. It was for some other reason, I guess. They act funny when they get to be her age, that change of life thing dinking with their hormones. I know how to tail without 'em knowing and how to park and watch without being watched."

"What spooked her? Did she have any company?"

"Nope," he lied. "Nary a one. She's one of these old tight-assed spinster ladies, is what I think."

"Then what did you do while you were forgetting that you

should be calling me?"

"I went back to the trailer for the night. Had to pay a cabby seventy-five bucks to get me there and here now," he went on, fudging by twenty bucks. "These cabbies, they're all dickheads, you know. It wasn't like that before I was sent up, not all of them anyways. Half of them don't speak English and they can't find their own asshole without a map, which none of them carry in these shitmobiles they drive."

"Where. Is. My. Car?"

"Where the clutch gave out on me for good, it was two blocks away is where it is if it's not been towed, Uncle Randall. It ain't my fault it gave up the ghost in front of a fire hydrant. It's there unless they went and hauled it off."

Randall closed his eyes as Dicky babbled on. Towing charges and the parking fine would exceed the car's value by a long shot. He must have been out of his mind for bringing the imbecile into this venture.

Coll had been uncomfortable around his nephew since he was a kid, him and his slouch and his breath that would etch glass, that and his shiftiness and unpredictable temper. Dicky's personality, if you could call it that, had a pulling-the-wings-off-butterflies aspect.

With his Vincent (Mad Dog) Coll fixation, Dicky was definitely funny in the head, no doubt about it. Considering his bloodline, a pair of useless drunks for parents, fetal alcohol syndrome was not to be ruled out.

Randall held up a hand to put a halt to the inane chatter. He opened his cash drawer and handed Dicky all his twenties. "I'll give you this walking-around money."

Mad Dog counted seven of them, a hundred and thirty bucks. Big deal, he thought. The last of the big spenders.

"How'm I supposed to get by on this with no wheels?"

Randall Coll sighed and said to wait a minute. He stepped

into the back room, picked up a small object, careful his nephew didn't see it, and went outside.

Dicky ran around the counter and grabbed a goodie out of the case he'd been admiring, which he had to have on him the way this clusterfuck was going: a Browning .25 automatic, a baby pistol that fit easily in his pants pocket, fitting like a glove.

Randall Coll returned and handed him a set of keys. "It's the gold sedan out back."

"What kinda car?"

"Surprise yourself. It's the only gold car and only gold sedan, so you should be able to narrow it down. Get going and do your job. Don't botch it this time."

Dicky went outside, pissed at Uncle Randall's tone, and saw the only gold vehicle, a faded-gold geezermobile that'd seen better days many, many days ago. He unlocked it and sat on a cracked leather seat. The car had a medicine smell, like from a cancer drug for the duffer who'd owned it before Uncle Randall screwed him out of it.

Dicky began to turn the key, but hesitated, continuing to pout on how Uncle Randall talked to him, like he was one of them Mongolian idiots. He fiddled with the .25, popping out the (fully loaded!) clip, popping it back in, back out, back in, and jacking a round into the chamber. That kangaroo court sent him up for eleven long years on account of what they said he did with a gun he *didn't* have.

Vinny (Mad Dog) Coll had liked to play with guns.

Dicky (Mad Dog) Coll did too.

A quarter mile north of Seattle's newish professional football and baseball stadiums was Pioneer Square, directly south of downtown. In the city's early days, it was known as Skid Row, and not just for the dives and houses of ill repute. Freshly cut timber was skidded down a hill to the waterfront for waiting steamships and sailing vessels. Pioneer Square was yuppified in patches, but a raffish quality remained. There were blocks in the vicinity where it was not prudent to walk at night.

At the core of Pioneer Square, between a tavern and a leather repair shop that might or might not be defunct was Coll's Jewelry and Loan: (A Family Business). In Randall Coll's window were the pawnbroker's three golden globes. The signage was fluorescent yellow. It lent authenticity and a traditional shadiness.

As Judith Roswell and Tyler Polk (Tip) Taylor III cruised by in the Aston Martin, searching for a parking spot, Tip wondered if the leather specialty was/is whips and thongs. It was in a prime location for prospective clientele. They were able to park on the same block as the pawnshop.

While Judith waited in the car, Tip went into the shop. A bell over the door tinkled.

The shop's interior was cramped and, at a glance, efficient. Guitars, rifles and shotguns, power tools and fishing gear hung on the back wall. Inside the glass counter were handguns, coins encased in plastic, cameras, video game systems, jewelry and watches.

A small man of indeterminate age in a gray cardigan stood behind the counter, examining a tennis bracelet with a loupe. Wearing a blank expression and wispy hair combed back, he fit Judith's description of the proprietor.

Randall Coll looked up and said, "Because there are fifty stones in these, everybody thinks they add up to twenty carats. I tell them, you're lucky if there are two carats, all chips, one step above those used as abrasive in polishing cloth. These 'precious' gemstones of theirs are a slightly higher grade than carbonados. They're mined by the ton. The people weren't happy, but I gave them an education and a fair price. How may I help you, sir?"

He's setting me up to be lowballed, Tip thought, as he had

with Judith. Was it standard operating procedure or did we look like easy marks?

Tip gave the pawnbroker Judith's ring and said, "We are thinking of selling this. Gosh, it has been in the family for ages. It belonged to a maiden aunt. Frankly, we did not care for Aunt Sylvia. She never had a kind word for anybody, God rest her soul."

Randall Coll wondered what a clean-cut young guy like this was doing in his shop. The gold Rolex on his wrist was worth more than every watch he carried and ever had carried. The guy was Ivy League and old money.

He focused on the too-familiar setting. Holding the ring to his loupe, he confirmed in an instant that it was the gorgeous diamond in the platinum setting the jumpy gal had brought in. Judith Roswell and this all-American boy were turning the tables on him. Trying to.

His piece-of-shit nephew had told him that Judith Roswell hadn't had a caller. In his words, nary a one. What else was Dicky keeping to himself?

Coll thrust it back at Tip and said, "Not interested."

"Excuse me?"

"Not interested," he repeated, returning to the tennis bracelet.

The private eye knew he had gotten a rise out of Coll. A vital mystery clue. What it meant and what Judith meant beyond the ring would require some advanced sleuthing.

A GOIPD graduate should never take anything for granted, especially the obvious. Expand your knowledge base with our school-taught technique. If somebody wishes to speak, hear them out fully. You can sift the chaff from the wheat later.

"I will entertain any offer you choose to make, sir. I have been asked by my siblings to cash out the estate."

"Read my lips. Not interested."

James Bond would tear the shop and this man apart to obtain an answer.

Tip said, "The family has money issues and are flexible in regard to a sale price and—"

"We're wasting each other's time," the pawnbroker said. "Do you need directions to the door?"

"If I have offended you, sir—"

"Out!"

Randall Coll peeked outside after the rich kid took the hint with a casual spoiled-brat shrug. He climbed into a fancy sports car. Coll was so intent on jotting down the license number that he didn't see the nose of a big gold car poking out of the alley, his nephew behind the wheel.

Dicky Coll saw that driver of the Ferrari or whatever the hell it was—one of the three who'd gotten got out of the old Caddy at the haunted house. When its door opened and the dome light went on, speaking of the devil, the old broad was in the passenger seat. Turning up like a bad penny, she was.

Yeah, he was definitely gonna see what this was all about.

CHAPTER 12

Unaware that a gold car well past its prime was in pursuit, Tip Taylor and Judith Roswell arrived at *Casa* Snails. Tip had mixed feelings inviting Judith along. He had to admit that he was fueled by bravado. Her opinion was becoming increasingly important to him, as a professional and as a man.

Judith had eagerly accepted, anxious to see the private eye in action on a case other than hers. She didn't know that Mrs. Ralph (Vera) Snails was his only other client.

Nor did she know he hadn't the foggiest what he was going to do.

As an outsider to the Snails' neighborhood, a stranger to lower-middle-class living, Tyler Polk (Tip) Taylor III observed and categorized the tract's homeowners into two distinct groups:

Those who park their cars in their yards.

Those who don't.

The elder Snails fell into the first category, with three vehicles in the driveway and two on the lawn. The Snails' residence was on a cul-de-sac two blocks off the four-lane arterial of endless strip malls. Tip imagined at night they were treated to a fast-food borealis. The home was a 1970s split-level that had not aged a fraction as well as Judith's dwelling. Hereabouts, it was dandelion season. The weeds and tall grass came up to the vehicles' hubcaps.

Tip pictured an interior of shag carpeting, avocado appliances, lava lamps and popcorn ceilings, all original and ultra-dingy. Dirty dishes heaped in the sink. A clogged garbage disposal. Six televisions on nonstop.

He called Carla and asked her to check on the license plates.

"Were you able to help Judith?"

"Thanks to you, we have hopefully made progress. She is with me."

"Oh, wonderful," Carla said.

What was *that* wonderful, he wondered? But Carla got back to Tip at what seemed like warp speed. Each registered owner was a Snails family member, four of five residing at this address.

Incest and inbreeding, he thought. Ralph's vehicle's address is shown as his conjugal home with Vera, a three-bedroom rambler in a similar neighborhood. If Ms. Floozy is inside with her "Ralphie," she had alternative transportation.

Deciding on a GOIPD-recommended tactic, he grabbed his clipboard from the floor behind Judith's seat and put on an unmarked baseball cap.

A proficient GOIPD operative quickly and readily adapts, blending into his or her working environment. Strive to become a two-legged chameleon. Be a fly on the wall.

"Dare I ask?" Judith asked.

Tip said, "The meter reader ploy, recommended and detailed in a Gumshoe Online Institute of Private Detection chapter. We shall see if an academic exercise translates into the real world."

He winked confidently and got out of the car. As the script scrolled through his head, Tip took a slow lap around the house, pausing to stare at the meter and doodle on the clipboard as little pointers circled round gauges. He felt Judith's eyes on him, unintentional pressure on him to get though this without being made the fool. Or worse, he thought queasily. A sizable percentage of people at this socioeconomic level kept an arsenal of firearms.

All blinds and curtains were shut.

Tip took a deep breath, thrust his noble jaw and knocked on the front door. Ralph Snails answered. He was unshaven, had booze on his breath, and the residue of meals past on a Seattle Mariners T-shirt, confirmation that he was no floozy magnet.

"The power company, sir. Your electric meter is running backward."

"It is?"

"Yes sir. You should be all smiles. Your photovoltaic solar collectors are doing their job. You are producing juice. Instead of paying a light bill, the power company pays you for your surplus. At this moment, you are on the plus side to the tune of six hundred and eighty-four kilowatt hours at the rate of twenty-three cents per."

"Yeah?"

Tip ballparked the ersatz numbers. "Which adds up to a hundred and forty bucks."

Ralph Snails frowned, puzzled. He was a warehouse picker. His comprehension of technology began and ended with the hydraulics of a forklift.

"This is my folks' house. They're getting up in years. I didn't know they had these roof collectors you say they got."

Tip shrugged. "Parents do not tell their kids everything. Mine did not either. Do not blame yourself."

His attempt at camaraderie failed. Ralph wasn't entirely fuzzyheaded. "Yeah? Prove who you say you are. Where the hell are they? Is this a come-on to sell me some door-to-door shit?"

"On the roof, at the rear of your house. You would have to be standing at your fence to see them. Come on, sir. I'll show you."

Ralph Snails came out and gaped at the roof. "I don't see nothing."

"Hmm. They could be in the shop for repairs. There is no other woman, is there, Ralph, a new lady for whom you are divorcing Vera?"

Ralph stepped rearward and stumbled, catching himself with a railing. Although hours from normal cocktail hour, it had been a long, liquid day for Ralph Snails. He worked swing shift this week and must spend a fortune on aspirin and breath mints.

"Who the hell are you?"

Tip presented a business card. "I am the person Vera cannot afford to hire whom she hired nonetheless to keep tabs on you because she desperately wants your marriage to endure."

"You're a private eye, like it says on this card?"

"I am."

He looked at the card again and at Tip. "Do you pack heat?"

Pack heat. Shades of Hollywood and the small screen.

"I am not packing heat, Ralph. It is not like in the movies. A real-life shamus is as often as not a paid voyeur."

"A who-zit?"

"A professional peeping tom, a person on an infidelity hunt. Do you want to know how many night spots I trailed you to? How many Laundromats? That smoke-filled casino."

"I never seen you."

Tip shrugged, a suave lifting of a shoulder.

He shook his head. "That goddamn casino you're talking about, I damn near scored at the slots and I don't mean what was spinning away on the screens. Then this broad got lucky and I didn't. She was a babe too."

Tip cleared his throat. "Yes, I saw her. A babe. A living doll."

"Want some advice?"

"I am all ears, Ralph."

"You go in a casino looking to get lucky, see, stick to the floor and the machines. The martini and cigar bars in them places, forget it. The gals in there are snooty. Their noses are a mile in the air."

"I shall keep that in mind. Who was that woman in the

background when you asked Vera for a divorce, Ralph? I am betting it is not who you wanted her to think it was."

He jabbed a thumb at the house. "My sister, Peg. She's been living with the folks after her husband up and left her. Peg, she hates Vera's guts. The whole shebang, it was her idea in the first place."

"Ralph, is that any reason to ruin two lives? I would love to have a woman as devoted to and as concerned for her man as Alvera Snails is."

"Yeah?"

"If just one of my young lady friends had been as devoted to me as Vera is to you, loving you strictly for yourself, I should be the happiest man on Earth."

Ralph Snails replied with a nod. He turned quickly so Tip couldn't see his eyes moisten. He went into the house and slammed the door.

Tip left, knowing that he had throttled his cash cow.

He was mightily pleased that he had.

Judith's window had been down. She touched his forearm, their first physical contact. Her arm tingled as she did.

She said, "I overheard much of it, Tip. I know I hired the right man."

Tyler Polk (Tip) Taylor III avoided his mirrors. Her fingertip to his arm had generated an erection. He did not want to see himself blushing.

Dicky (Mad Dog) Coll was parked in a convenience-store parking lot across the arterial, taking it all in, knowing he was invisible in this car nobody younger than the age of eighty ever drove.

What was this rich swell with the fancy sports car doing in a dumpy neighborhood talking to some loser? With the old broad from the haunted house riding shotgun? He'd stick to them like glue till he could dope out the situation and have hisself a payday.

CHAPTER 13

"I don't know about any of you out there, but once when I was a young whippersnapper, I wanted to be a fireman when I grew up," Buster Hightower told his Westside Bowling Lanes and Casino audience. "I wanted to be a bus driver for a while. You too? Fireman, bus driver, anything like that? C'mon, show of hands."

Those over fifty, roughly half the crowd of eighteen, raised their hands, smiling. The younger people looked at them and at Buster, mystified. A couple of them had been playing with their electronic gizmos.

"I gave up on fireman when they said you had to go out and fight fires. I grew out of the bus driver hang-up too when I decided I didn't want to be anything when I grew up. But, you know, back then in the kind-of-good old days, you didn't need ten years of college for those jobs and you could apply in person, not on a damn *computer*. I was looking through the want ads the other day. The computer and hardware and software and medium-ware jobs out there, if I applied, they'd ask me if I was qualified and I'd have to say how the hell should I know? I haven't the foggiest what this job of theirs is. They give you puzzles in the ads with initials you gotta solve before you know what the job is. Like TCP, DNS, HTTP, LAN, SOA, ETL, ASP, OOAD, AEIOU, SNAFU and SQL. What's this SQL short for, Squirrel? You oughta bring acorns along with you on the interview? Fuhgetaboudit. This ad, they wanna hire you to do data mining. Huh? You gotta wear a helmet with a flashlight built into it and keep a canary in your office, which if it goes feet up, you get the hell out of there? Same with these outfits that are looking for wizards at C plus and C plus-plus. My high school GPA was C minus."

Buster had a bottle of beer in one hand, a newspaper's classified section in the other. He swigged the beer, waved the newspaper, and said, "Like for instance, this company wants a software developer that knows Java. Huh? They want to hire a computer nerd or they want a barista? Which is it?"

Laughter from most, Carla and Tip included. Judith too, but hers seemed strained as she was obviously uptight. To everybody in the solar system except Tip and Judith, Buster thought, it was crystal clear that Carla was up to her old matchmaking tricks. Carla had the knack, but she tended to push too hard. Maybe that was making Judith fidgety.

"Here's some others, a bunch of them, real head-scratchers. They're asking for Cloud Computing whizzes. C'mon, if you're looking for a weather forecaster, just say so."

Chuckles and clapping, mostly from the younger people.

"This is the best one yet and it hits close to home. 'Perform end-to-end software engineering and algorithm development and systems as a member of a team.' People ask how I got started as a comic. It's on account of I flunked algorithm. They called algorithm algebra way back then, when I took it. I walked out of high school algebra class that day and never returned. All these numbers and letters the teacher was putting on the blackboard every single day was giving me a chronological headache that aspirin didn't cure, so I did what I did for a valid medical reason. Sorry to make your arms sore, but a show of hands again. Anybody ever use algebra for anything. Anything at all? Just one single time?"

No response beyond smirks and mild laughter.

"Me neither. I couldn't figure why it was so important what x equaled. Far as I knew, x was in between w and y in the alphabet, which is what you're taught in English class not math, ain't it? Last I checked, x is still in between w and y, whether algorithm class has an unhealthy alphabet hang-up or not.

"After I barely graduated from high school without honors, I knew college was out of the question. Colleges have got the mother of all nasty algebra courses, plus other brutally tough and useless classes like Ancient History, which teaches you the lives of dead people and various happenings that are long gone and not coming back. Like Socrates and Attila the Hun and Guy Fawkes and Julius Caesar. Trust me, you ain't gonna bump into them on the street and what's done is done. Underwater Basket Weaving and Advanced Playground Management, okay, I could probably handle them, but every opening in the classes is filled with football players.

"Speaking of football, the next season's coming up pretty soon. I watch a lot of football, so much that I get an earache from the commentators saying 'situation' every other word. It's a punting situation. It's a crucial third-down situation. The quarterback calls a time-out to talk over the situation. One game, I counted eight hundred and twelve 'situations.' Don't believe me? Try it. You won't be two minutes into the first quarter before you run out of fingers and toes to count on.

"And if they're not saying 'situation,' they're saying 'issue.' As in 'preparing for the Green Bay game next week is an issue they'll have to deal with before next week.'

"So, educationally deprived as I was, I drifted from place to place, job to job. Even joined the circus. I was a skinny pup then and got volunteered to be shot out of a cannon. Don't know if it was a coincidence, but it was always on payday. By the time I was blasted out of the thing and hitchhiked back to where the circus was playing, they'd folded their tents and moved on to the next town.

"Anyways, how I got to be a stand-up comic is this. One night I was tending bar, filling in for a friend who'd got sick on their happy-hour food, which had been sitting out since the last happy hour, and had got unhappy in his lower GI tract.

"This drunk I'd over served while I was chewing the fat with him . . . he said I was funny. Hilarious was the word he used and he had trouble saying it. Some other drunk at the bar said I was funny and that a nearby tavern was having a comedy competition and I oughta enter it, so I did. And won because it was also full of drunks. Unfortunately for civilization, the rest is semi-ancient history.

"Hey, remember that saying 'words can't hurt you'? Don't believe it for a minute. My second ex-wife clobbered me in the head with a dictionary. The doc said I might've had a concussion, but he couldn't tell if I was goofy like I was anyway even if I hadn't been conked on the noggin.

"Speaking of relationships, you know how you know you're in a relationship? You're in a quote-unquote relationship, when your significant another is in your dreams all the time. You can't get away with nothing even if you're sound asleep."

Buster ran his hands through his hair and said, "Like my Carla out there, she don't even mind this mop of mine, which I can't do a damn thing to fix. I once broke a mirror in a beauty parlor and got seven years of bad hair.

"These are hard times for the ol' pocketbook, you know, so I feel it's my duty to pass along my financial prowessness, my investment tips. The secret to my success is how I invest all the money they pay me here. Just last week, I swapped out my shares in the Brooklyn Bridge for a big chunk of Enron stock. Made me a killing."

Rolling eyes, applause.

"Okay, boys and girls, time to obey tradition here at the Westside that goes back beyond ancient history to the beginning of time, I gotta wrap up with some stale lawyer jokes."

Buster waited out the good-natured booing and said, "It's a cold day and this guy's walking down the street. How do you know it's a lawyer? Easy. He's got his hands in someone else's pockets."

Applause.

"Here's a couple more coming at you rapid-fire as well as super fast. Just a couple. Then I'll stop abusing you. Scout's honor.

"How come lawyers in fourteen states banned lawyers from walking on the beach? Answer. Cuz cats keep trying to bury them in the sand.

"Speaking of the beach. Whadduya call five thousand lawyers on the bottom of the ocean? Answer, a good start.

"Okay, one more. Yeah, I lied when I said just a couple. You don't like it, go find yourself a lawyer and sue me. It'll be easy. There's umpteen thousand of the rancid putzes listed in the phone book. Question. How can you tell when a lawyer's lying? Answer, his lips are moving.

"This here is technically not a lawyer joke. It's a state law on hunting lawyers. Yeah, there really is that law, but it ain't open season. Like elk and mooses, lawyers have got their rights too."

Buster took a piece of paper from a pocket and read, "It shall be unlawful to hunt lawyers within a hundred yards of a BMW dealership."

The most laughter and applause yet.

"Okay, by popular demand, one more. Killing attorneys with a motor vehicle is prohibited. If accidentally struck, move dead attorney to the roadside and proceed to the nearest car wash."

Buster waved his beer bottle like a semaphore. "Here's some food for thought to take home with your leftovers. We got the Motel Six and Super Eight all over the place. And people are dressed to the nines one time or another with the exception of me. So how come no number seven, you know, like the Bates Motel Seven?

"And how come kamikaze pilots wore helmets?"

When the crowd was done putting their hands together for Buster Hightower, he sat down with Carla Chance, Tip Taylor, and Judith Roswell. After kudos from the threesome, Judith took an embroidered cloth napkin and another piece of paper from her purse.

She laid the napkin on the table, and asked, "Does anybody know her or recognize her name?"

Scrawled on the napkin:

I KNOW WHO YOU ARE AND WHAT YOU GOT.
SINSERELY YOURS.
HARRIET HARDIN

"No, but she ruined a lovely napkin," Carla said.

"It's my mother's favorite set too. Anybody?"

After lifted eyebrows and head shakes, Judith said, "Tip, when you dropped me off, I went inside and found this on the armoire. I smelled cheap perfume, and Orange and Vanilla were huddled on the stairwell upstairs."

Buster said, "I couldn't help but notice you had a new dead bolt installed. You been expecting company you don't want? Namely that stalker?"

"I don't honestly know who or what I've been expecting. That horrible man in the pawnshop or whoever was watching me in his car? I don't know."

Carla said, "Dear, it was none of our business until you brought us into it. Now it is. I feel free to give you unsolicited advice. If you're in peril, you need to call the police."

"No."

"You've left gobs and gobs unsaid, haven't you?" Carla said.

Judith didn't reply.

Tip said, "You hired me, Judith. I would like to remain on the clock. But you do have to open up."

Judith bit her lip, then said, "Very well. Did anybody see the noontime TV news today?"

Buster said, "I had it on. Those talking haircuts, they're a gold mine of material."

Carla said, "I was home for lunch. The lady reporter with the microphone was nice. She was older and well-spoken and actually listened to the thrift store lady. You were snoring in your recliner, Buster."

"I absorbed it subliminalistically, but you'll have to refresh my memory."

Judith said to Carla, "So you did see a feature on a Rainier Avenue thrift store receiving an anonymous gift of old currency and jewelry."

"Oh, that was such a sweet story. The ruby necklace was breathtaking."

Judith laid on the table what else she'd taken from her purse. "Please read this and try not to be offended by the language."

DEER HARRY,
I AWT TO GO CALL THE COPS ON YOU. I TELL THEM MY AGE, THEY WONNT LIKE YOU. YOU COME IN MY ROOM AND I GIVE YOU WHAT YOU WANT. SUK YOU OFF AND EVRYTHING AND YOU GO AND KICK ME OUT WITH THAT FAKE RUBY NEKLUS YOU GIVE ME. YOU CAN SHUV IT UP YOUR ASS. FUCK YOU HARRY. EAT SHIT AND DIE AND GO STRAIT TO HELL.

HARRIET H.

"Yikes," Buster said.

"Goodness," Carla said. "If she speaks that way, she needs

her mouth washed out with soap."

"Both authored by our Ms. Hardin, one must assume," Tip said, looking at Judith, thinking mystery *clue*.

"I'm certain she's one and the same. The printing is nearly identical," Judith said. "Please, all of you, come to my home. I have a long story and something to show you. I have to do this before I burst. With people I trust."

Dicky (Mad Dog) Coll stood outside the cocktail lounge, watching the bowlers, guys and gals with shiny shirts, half of them rolling the ball like spastics, while he watched the lounge out of the corner of his eye. The comedian was done doing his act and had sat down with the others. They were talking, looking at some papers, serious as all get-out.

Dicky saw the old broad and the others stand up, in a big hurry. He boogied on outside to the car, ready to keep on the trail, the way it was done. Him and Vinny, they'd make a helluva team.

CHAPTER 14

Judith plainly had apprehensions. Her "long story" did not immediately commence. Her guests did not rush her.

She served wine. Carla sipped hers, looking at the pictures on the walls.

At one, Harry Spicer sat on a couch his arms around a smiling woman. He wore a cockeyed grin, and the woman's smile seemed to Carla to be for the benefit of the camera.

"Harry's wife?" she asked Judith.

"Yes. Ella. Ella Hitchcock Spicer."

"You're too young to remember the TV program, dear, but she's a spitting image of the actress who played June Cleaver in *Leave It to Beaver*. It was a sitcom in the late fifties."

"I've seen *Leave It to Beaver* on telethons. Was life that idyllic?"

Carla shook her head. "Not for a soul I ever met. What became of Harry and Ella?"

"I'd bet the farm Harry wasn't any Ward Cleaver," Buster said. "Like the picture of him leaning against a fender, he's got a rascally look to him."

Judith said, "Grandfather Harry died of cancer six years before I was born. My mother, Sharon Spicer Roswell, was fifteen when he passed away. Grandmother Ella died in a one-car accident in 1970. She ran off the road in Pierce County, a mile from the Narrows Bridge. Suicide was suspected, although unproven.

"I was old enough to know and remember her. She was a sweet person, often sad for reasons she kept to herself. She had a serious drinking problem, which had gotten worse toward the end. Her blood-alcohol count was in the stratosphere when she crashed."

"I'm sorry," Carla said.

"It was inevitable, I'm afraid. She never worked outside of the home and had too much time on her hands to brood and stew."

"Troubled by her husband's death?"

"Yes. I can't prove it, but I think it may have gone beyond that. Grandmother Ella never opened up to me or, to my knowledge, anyone else in the family. She sold Harry's locksmith shop and tools. She must have had other income because my brother and I didn't lack for anything."

Carla said, "Where is your brother?"

"I don't know and I don't care."

End of topic.

Judith said, "I am going to burst unless I cease procrastinating. We're going to the basement. Please watch your head and step."

"I'm not speechless a whole big bunch of the time," Buster Hightower said. "But the cat got my tongue at this point in time."

"You aren't speechless, Buster," Carla Chance said.

"I am now. I'm not saying another bleeping word and that's the truth."

"Buster."

"Hear me say a word?"

The exchange released no tension.

In Judith Roswell's basement, after she told her story, removed the brick false front from the wall, and pulled out a portion of the Pioneer Safe Deposit Vaults loot, Tyler Polk (Tip) Taylor III was speechless too, busy on his knees, notebook and pen in hand.

Carla said, "That necklace on the news has to be the mysterious Hardin woman's, doesn't it? Broken clasp or not, it's absolutely beautiful."

"That's my guess," Judith said. "I sort of wish I still had it."

"She'd be seventy-three years old," Carla said. "Give or take a year."

"And obviously amongst the living, though not a spring chicken," Buster said.

"She did not keep the ruby, but she must have kept a key to the house," said the private eye, as he finished taking notes from the marked pages in the *1954 Seattle City Directory.*

"When I realized I was being followed, I wasn't thinking when I had a dead bolt installed only on the front door," Judith said, shaking her head. "The back and side door can be unlocked with a skeleton key. It didn't occur to me because, according to the locksmith, the locks are the coded kind that won't work with a standard key and I didn't think there'd be an actual break-in. I'll remedy that at the first opportunity tomorrow."

"From what we could see of him, that bum in the pawnshop's car doesn't exactly fit the description of a little old lady," Buster said. "Maybe they're in cahoots, the putz and Harriet Potty Mouth. And answer me this, how come Harry didn't put a match to that letter? It's mighty incriminating."

Judith didn't have an answer.

Nor did Tip Taylor. He asked himself why he had opened the clichéd Pandora's box by visiting Coll's Jewelry and Loan. An easy answer that went beyond "counterattacking." To impress Judith. It had been a James Bond stunt lacking the requisite car chases and violence. He hoped it wasn't going to backfire.

If Randall Coll wasn't actively in the hunt then, he was now. A continuation of bad choices, Tip thought, from the Harvard Law fiasco to who knows what.

"In the meantime, dear, you shouldn't be alone," Carla said.

"Thanks, Carla, but I'll be fine. I'll have my cell phone with me. If I hear a peep, I'll call nine-one-one."

"C'mon, Judith," Buster said. "They didn't find the pirate treasure. You gotta think they'll be back. And it wouldn't knock me over with a feather if the news story set Harriet Potty Mouth off like a Roman candle. My nose'd be outta joint too."

"Double-check the doors. We'll put chairs against the knobs of those with skeleton key locks," Carla told her.

As they prepared to leave, Judith said, "I changed my mind. I don't want to stay here tonight. I can still smell her perfume."

"I was hoping you'd say that, dear. We have a spare bedroom with its own bath."

"Thank you, Carla, but no. I'll feed the cats and get a motel room."

"Buster and I won't hear of it. You come home with us. And, Tip, you're invited to breakfast."

"Well," Judith said.

"It's settled," Carla said. "We'll roll out the futon. The only visitors you'll have is OC1 and OC2."

"They don't wear cheap perfume," Buster said. "Eau de Catnip's their bouquet of choice."

After saying good-byes, Tip drove home to Tacoma, thinking about Judith alone on the Chance-Hightower futon and him alone in his bed. Sleep, he knew, would not come easily.

CHAPTER 15

Meanwhile, Dicky (Mad Dog) Coll sat in the geezermobile half a block from the old broad's haunted house, wondering what the hell was going on. First her and her three pals come visiting. They go in and the basement light goes on, then it goes off. Now all four of them, they're leaving, the old broad with a bag like you'd carry groceries in instead of a suitcase.

Five minutes later, sitting there, trying to sort out his next move, wondering if he should of followed their car, the situation got even goofier. This beat-to-shit Ford Pinto he'd seen parked up ahead a few cars when he'd circled the block, the dome light came on and this *really* old broad climbed out. She was older than dirt. That was all he could tell of her face. But she had a nice bod, slim without any bulges and sags that he could noticeably see.

Dicky watched her go on up the steps and around to the side and—holy dogshit!—she let herself in with a skeleton key after shaking the door, shaking it hard and cussing a blue streak. Playing it cool, he watched some more and waited. No upstairs lights went on, but pretty soon on came those basement lights.

Okay, time to rock and roll. Dicky climbed out too. He walked on the sidewalk side of the Pinto, recalling that when he was railroaded and sent up the river, Pintos were old. These days they were ancient, like the driver of this one.

He went around to the side door of the house the gal had gotten in, and dug a lock pick kit out of his pocket. A Walla

105

Walla cellmate had been a three-strikes-and-you're-out burglar. There wasn't diddly-squat to talk about, so the guy taught Mad Dog all he knew of the trade, except how not to get caught.

Dicky easily snicked the skeleton key lock, smirking. Who said you didn't get rehabbed in the pen and learn yourself a trade? To hell with a high school GED. Get yourself an education. Half the guys in his cell block were B and E pros.

There was a chair on its side by the door. Like the chair had been jammed up against it before the old lady shook it loose. She was feisty and had a temper.

He felt his way around, concentrating on a sliver of light cast on the floor and a sliver on the wall. It led to a door that was cracked open a hair. On the other side of the door were basement steps. He smelled strong, cheap perfume, like the gals in a cathouse wore.

Taking the stairs a careful tiptoe step at a time, he reached the landing, saw the Pinto gal looking into an empty room that'd been framed into the basement.

Proud of being quiet and sneaky, he'd slip up behind her and say "boo." She'd shit her britches. Mad Dog proceeded to slip on the next step. Down he went, bouncing, landing flat on his ass on the basement floor.

"Ow, shit!"

"Who the hell are you?" Harriet Hardin Callahan Miller Kline Parker Jacobs Smith demanded, turning and edging backward, hand inside her purse, holding a can of pepper spray.

"Who the hell are *you?*" Dicky (Mad Dog) Coll said, up on his feet, rubbing his backside.

"I'm the young girl who lived in this room fifty-some years ago when I kept house for the folks who owned the place."

An old hag in loose blouse and slacks. She had short, gray hair and nice eyes set wide apart. She had her share of wrinkles, but might of been a looker in the olden times.

"Yeah? What's this, like a family reunion?"

"None of your fucking business," she said. "What's your story?"

It kind of turned him on, how the old prune and her toilet mouth was looking him in the eye, hands out of her purse and on her hips, unafraid.

"I'm the insecticide exterminator."

She laughed, showing loose yellowed teeth. "You're a hoot and a cutie pie to boot. How'd you get in?"

Cutie pie? Coll didn't recollect his mother or any other gal ever calling him a cutie pie. "They give me the key."

"I'll just bet they did, whoever they is."

"Yeah, how'd you get a key to get in here?" he said, trying to keep up with her. "You inherit it?"

Harriet had been in the house earlier when the lady of the house and others pulled up out front. She was able to get out the door and into the alley and back to her car without being seen, after leaving the napkin that scared the lady of the house out—what it was supposed to do. But she hadn't counted on all those others with her, and this wild card she was facing who was anything but a cutie pie.

Harriet Hardin pegged him as a shifty bugger, slow-witted but useful. She reckoned she'd be needing help. The guy was a loser and a slob, but he had that look in his eye that said he'd do whatever she told him to do if she played her cards right. All men were alike; unless they were light in their loafers, their brains were in their shorts.

Harriet had to hope that there was some loot left and it was actually tucked away in Harry Spicer's house, over and above what a nutcase gave away to that charity junk shop.

She lifted a single skeleton key and cocked her head. "It's for the side door off a porch where milk used to be delivered. I don't imagine you remember when dairies came to the door, left bottles of milk. Glass bottles. They had paper lids, you know. Cats could pick them off and lick the cream off the top. Homogenized milk came along later."

Mad Dog decided she wasn't kidding about her history here, whatever her point was. "How come you came back?"

"You tell me first why you're here. The truth."

Those eyes. It'd be damn hard to bullshit her, make it stick. "Okay, I'm not real sure."

"You're not a burglar who just picked out this place?"

"Nope. I sort of know these people."

She reached into her purse again and withdrew papers. "I got these at the library. I think we're here for the same thing. You just aren't sure what it is, are you?"

"I'm not?"

"Well, I *am* and I have to have help getting it."

"What's in them papers?"

Harriet figured she'd get out of here, at least for tonight, and take this dipshit along. No telling when they were coming back.

She put the papers back in her purse. "You invite me out for a drink, honey, and we'll have us a chitchat."

In the wee hours, Harriet and Dicky Coll sat in the nearest neighborhood bar. They were squeezed together in a corner of a booth. He'd been drinking shots of bourbon chased with beer, piss on the parole rules. Rules were made to be broken.

The old hag was on her third or ninth sidecar, a fruity drink Mad Dog couldn't remember the ingredients to no matter how many times she told him. She was looking younger by the drink, the wrinkles ironing out.

Their hands were on each other's leg and Mad Dog had a boner that wouldn't quit. He hadn't had any loving he didn't have to pay for since getting out and the night seemed young, all kinds of possibilities lying ahead.

It'd taken her time to get to the point, all the while going on and on what miserable douche bags her six ex-husbands were, each and every lousy one of them, serving time in jail or dying of alcoholism and AIDS, Number Four being a switch-hitter, thank God she found out before he stuck his dick in the wrong rear end, the one who gave him the incurable disease.

She sure did have a toilet mouth on her, a turn-on and a half. Not that Mad Dog didn't get a dirty word or two in edgewise. He told her about Walla Walla, telling her war stories how you survived in stir, but not giving the specifics of his crime and why he was tagged Mad Dog. He recited Vincent Coll's biography, how him and Vinny were blood brothers, all of the above turning her on, lighting her fire.

"You believe in reincarnationing?" he said.

Except for what she needed this make-believe Mad Dog for, thanks to the sidecars, Harriet's train of thought had derailed. She was just sober enough not to mention the ruby necklace that was eating at her craw.

"That's where a dead person's ghost goes into a live person?"

"Uh-huh. That's it. Me and Vinny, I'm thinking that me and him, we been reincarnationed."

He was getting too weird about this old-time gangster he idolized, going on like a broken record. Harriet had to get to the nitty-gritty while she could, so she brought out the papers.

For better light, they slid the table candle almost close enough to set the papers on fire. She read the highlights aloud, in a whisper to his ear, tonguing it between paragraphs.

Distracted as she was making him, squinting and shutting an eye to focus, he eventually got the picture.

Mad Dog knew Uncle Randall was holding out on him big-time. But then again, maybe he didn't know the whole story. Damned if he'd hear it from his nephew, who he treated like a retard.

He said, "The crooks, way back when, they stashed the loot in the haunted house?"

Harriet laughed at the "haunted" and told him why she thought they did. She went on and on about her ruby necklace given to her by Harry Spicer, a locksmith and a no-good, lying, scumbag, two-faced, cradle-robbing bastard pervert.

Mad Dog couldn't keep his mouth shut either, not with her hand moving farther north on his leg. He spilled all on Uncle Randall and the people he'd ordered him to keep a close eye on without telling him why.

"I'll be go to hell, it's them!"

"Sure is," he said, shaking his head. "Me, his own flesh and blood, my uncle. The old boy figures to ace me out of everything except the peanuts he pays me. I gotta wonder how much he knows the scoop on this undertaking back there in 1954."

"Somebody sure as shit does, Mad Dog. If those people don't, the remains of the Pioneer Safe Deposit Vaults job are right under their noses. We gotta get it."

"Goddamn straight!" Mad Dog said, slamming his glass on the table, earning glances from customers and the bartender.

"If they know what we know, we'll get a cut."

Mad Dog looked at her, a Greek goddess. "A big *big* cut."

"Mad Dog, are you my man?"

He moved her hand to his pocket and the Browning .25. "Me and my itty-bitty buddy are all the help you need, Harriet."

"You gotta have balls, Mad Dog." She reached between his legs and honked him. "You got them for what's lying ahead? If you do, you follow me home."

"Oh yeah, baby," he said, moaning. "Gonads like shot puts."

CHAPTER 16

Next morning at Carla Chance and Buster Hightower's condo, in bed, OC1 and OC2 at her feet in loaf-of-bread configuration, Judith Roswell said, "Your noses were twitching last night. Orange's and Vanilla's scents are on me, aren't they?"

They yawned.

"I wonder if you'd like to meet Orange and Vanilla. You'd hit it off."

They replied with nose twitches.

"Or not. Mr. Taylor, our detective. I believe you met him here briefly. Your candid opinion, please. Professionally and personally."

No reaction, but Judith thought she detected smiles.

"Me too."

Just before Judith was out of the futon room and Tip arrived for breakfast, Buster asked Carla, "Picked out your maid of honor dress yet?"

"What on earth do you mean?"

"Yes, you do. I mean you, matchmaker of the year."

"Me. Matchmaking?"

"You might as well be emcee of a reality TV show where that's what they do to boy and girl, toots."

"Goodness, no. It's just professional, isn't it, their arrangement? Client-detective, you know. I don't know what you're seeing, Buster."

"You firing your Valentine's arrow is all. You hit a bull's-eye. Her, I don't know."

After a leisurely and pleasant breakfast, the foursome caravanned to Judith's place. Orange and Vanilla had to be fed and she wanted company.

There was an unfamiliar car in Judith's usual parking spot, a large, oxidized shoebox, 1980s vintage. On the porch, they smelled cigarette smoke.

"Our new pals and their pals?" Buster asked.

Judith Roswell unlocked the door and threw it open. "No. There's only one person in the world who's this much of a jerk and has access to my home. Unfortunately, he has skeleton keys."

They walked in to find a man seated on the sofa smoking a cigarette, using an ornate cut-glass dish as an ashtray. He had a pot gut, receding hair, pouches under his eyes, GGR tattooed on the middle fingers of his left hand, and a silver Rolex on a wrist.

Judith yanked the cigarette and makeshift ashtray out of his hand and headed toward the kitchen to dispose of the cigarette and rinse the dish, saying, "Same old baby brother Jerry. You know very well that's part of our great-grandmother's wedding china that you're using for your filthy habit."

The guy smiled. "Big Sis was also hard to please as a kid. Why'd you change the front door lock? I had to go around to the side."

"This is Gerald G. Roswell, my prodigal drifter of a sibling, who I haven't seen for years, which isn't long enough," she said as she came back in the room.

"Must be the wrong time of the month for Judith Ann Roswell," Jerry Roswell said, swiveling his head and winking. "Call me Jerry."

Nobody spoke or returned his wink. Carla made fists, picturing the creature's neck in her grasp.

Judith's arms were folded. "A typically classy remark. Well?"

Without visible emotion, he said, "I saw Mother's obituary in the paper. I'm grieving. I'm here for you."

"I know you're distraught, Jerry, but you're hiding it nicely. You're holding up bravely. You must have been living close to Seattle to see the notice."

"I've moved around from time to time for professional reasons. I've been in Everett the last few years."

Judith Roswell closed her eyes and shook her head. "Thirty miles away. You bastard. I didn't care if I ever saw you again. Mother did. She worshipped you. At the end, she asked about you every single day. She made apologies for you from the moment you slithered out of her life with her money."

"You were always jealous of me." Jerry Roswell jabbed a finger at her. "I want my half, what I got coming from the will."

"Oh, you do need to get what's coming. For instance, the home equity loan you skipped town with. What happened to it?"

Jerry Roswell looked at Carla, Buster and Tip, swiveling his head again.

"This is a private family matter, gang. Why don't you go take a hike around the block?"

The GOIPD operative resorts to physical violence as a last resort. However, he or she will surely lose the client's confidence by turning the other cheek and, irrevocably, by turning tail.

With JamesBondian cool, jaw jutting, Tip said, "We shall let the lady of the house decide."

Carla said to Jerry Roswell, "You have awful manners, young man. You couldn't have possibly been raised by the same mother."

Buster said, "I'm with the majority, pal. What you call your quorum."

"They stay if they want to stay," Judith said. "Thanks to the money you stole, Jerry, your half of the will is a pipe dream."

"Lousy luck. Business downturns. Shit happens." He fluttered a palm. "I had every good intention of giving it back to her with interest, but the situation was out of my control. You can't blame me for the economy. It's those bigwigs who—"

"Buy high, sell low. That's how your typical get-rich-quick scheme ends, doesn't it? Don't talk to me about a will until I see some of the money you swindled her out of, you weasel," Judith shouted.

Jerry Roswell plugged his ears, then changed the subject. "Father died four years ago. Did you know?"

Startled, Judith asked, "How do you know?"

"I got lucky on the slots in Vegas on a weekend and hired a private detective with some of my winnings. Found out the old man was living in Tucson when he croaked."

"Are you telling me the truth for once in your life?"

Jerry Roswell said, "I swear to God. Word was that Doug Roswell had an attack while in the saddle with his fourth or fifth wife or a gal he was cheating on a wife with. The way all us guys want to go, right?"

"You and them winks," Buster said. "You got winkitis. You oughta go find yourself an eye doctor before you wear out your eyelids."

"And I want you to go," Judith said, gesturing to the front door.

In case her shameful brother did not get the message, Tip went to the door and opened it.

"It doesn't matter if there wasn't a red cent in the will, Judith. What would this old dump bring on the market in this neighborhood? A cool half million, I'll bet. You living here on your own, Sis, it ain't healthy. We'll sell and you can sink your half into one of those upscale downtown condos."

"Give me your house keys, Jerry the Weasel. You're trespassing and I'm having them all changed anyhow."

Gerald (Jerry) Roswell sighed, stood, and handed them over. Too compliantly, Tip thought.

"You haven't heard the last of this, Judith Ann. I got my rights."

Jerry paused at the door and told Tip, "Whoever you are, man, talk sense into her. We don't need lawyers in the situation."

"Have a nice day," Tyler Polk (Tip) Taylor III said, not meaning it.

CHAPTER 17

Dicky (Mad Dog) Coll stirred in a strange bed, his head throbbing as if it'd been clobbered by a sledgehammer. Daylight came through a space between curtains like a flamethrower.

Where the hell was he?

He smelled powerful odors, a mix of sweat, bad breath, and whorehouse perfume.

Dicky heard snoring and soon came to the realization that he wasn't alone. With effort, he raised up on an elbow and looked over at a shriveled, toothless, old witch. He flinched, stifling a cry. Whoever she was, she looked like she'd climbed out of a casket.

He gingerly eased back onto his pillow to spare himself more pain.

Word of the day: catastrophe.

Staring at a ceiling he'd never seen before, it was beginning to come back to him. She was that old gal he'd met in the haunted house. He'd taken her to a bar or she'd taken him, one or the other or both. He'd had a few drinks and then some, and as time passed, she'd looked to him like Miss America of 1895 or thereabouts. How the hell had he ever thought she was a raving beauty?

Dicky slipped out of bed, every tiptoeing footfall a blow to his skull. He looked at whatshername again, Juliet or Helen or something like that, and cringed. She had drool on the side of her wrinkled lips, her mouth all sucked in on account of her teeth were sitting on the nightstand, aimed right at him.

Dicky thought of a joke a Walla Walla cellmate had told him. The guy had an endless supply of them. He was doing time for rape and sexual assault, so Dicky regarded him as an expert on chicks.

The joke went like this: *A guy in his condition wakes up in bed next to the ugliest woman in the whole wide world. He's got hisself a killer hangover and no recollection of nothing the night before. He creeps out of bed, dresses as quiet as he can, starts for the door, and thinks, okay, maybe it was a business deal. So he takes a ten-spot out of his wallet and lays it on the dresser. Then he feels a tug on his cuff and looks down at the second ugliest woman in the whole wide world, who says, "Nothing for the bridesmaid?"*

Mad Dog sure hoped it hadn't gone that far last night, but he couldn't be sure of anything. He breathed deeply to keep from puking his guts out. Backing toward the door, he almost tripped over the hag's purse that was right in the middle of the floor. Since it was there, no harm in a quick toss. He wasn't gonna leave her money, like in the joke. It oughta be the other way around.

Folded papers were on top, sticking out. He opened them to copies of old newspaper pages on a 1954 burglary of the Pioneer Safe Deposit Vaults in downtown Seattle.

It was dawning on him, her story of the haunted house, how she used to live there as a young girl, how she was kind of certain that a long-dead guy named Harry Spicer was the safe-cracking ringleader, him who'd stashed the safecracking loot. Her and them in the old red Caddy. Maybe they were in cahoots. Lots of questions had to be answered.

Answers he had no intention of sharing with Uncle Randall.

"Get out of my purse, you thieving son of a bitch!" he thought she said, as it was hard to make out the words when her teeth were out of her mouth.

The hag was sitting up, a bony finger pointed at him. "Put them back, goddamnit!"

"Shut the fuck up, Granny."

She put her teeth in her mouth and yelled, "I will not shut up, you sneaky little dog turd."

He winced at the noise. "Keep your voice down."

"I will not keep my voice down. Don't forget. We're partners."

"We are?"

"You don't remember, do you?"

"Remember what?"

"You hold your booze like a twelve-year-old, you know. You're gonna help me with the dirty work, whatever we gotta do. You're a tough guy. You put my hand on your little gun you had in your pocket. It's little, like your needle dick."

Needle dick?

You don't insult Dicky's manhood no more than you did Vinny's.

"You take that back, Granny."

She cackled. "You gotta enroll in lessons on how to take care of a lady and you need those pills guys take to get it up and keep it up."

Dicky Coll was shaking his head.

"Get away from my purse, you moron, and sit down and listen."

Dicky lost it.

He lunged and slammed her onto the bed, then pushed his pillow over her face. He considered just holding her there like that till she passed out. Then he'd pull his .25 and finish her off.

Nah. This'd be funner and less noisy anyway.

Straddling her, he pushed and pushed. He liked how she was

fighting, hitting him on his sides, punches he barely felt. He pushed and pushed and pushed until he heard nothing, including breathing.

At the very instant of Harriet Hardin's last audible breath, Randall Coll drove into the parking lot of a subsidized elderly housing complex in Kent and confirmed the location of the green dot on his laptop screen. This complex was only a few blocks from the trailer park Dicky had been overseeing in his own shiftless way.

Randall had placed a GPS transmitter in the trunk of the car he'd given Dicky. He'd taken it in for fifty bucks from a down-on-his-luck yuppie. The gadget had performed flawlessly.

And there the car was, on the next row, parked cockeyed, taking two spaces, by a Ford Pinto, a model he hadn't seen lately. Last night, Randall had tracked it to a dive of a watering hole, and after several hours on to here. He imagined his nephew had tied one on. Why here, though, rather than the trailer park?

Flying out of a door, walking fast, trying to play it cool, but looking guilty as hell about something, here the dimwit came, looking for the car, then stumbled to it.

Randall Coll got out of his, a pawned Hyundai Dicky didn't recognize, and called out, "Hey, by golly. By gosh, what do you know? It sure is a small world."

The younger Coll froze. His eyes were big and they were bloodshot. He looked like death warmed over and over.

"Uncle Randall?"

"In the flesh. What's up, Dicky boy?"

"Nothing's up, Uncle Randall. How come you're here?"

"How come you're here?"

"I know someone. I just dropped by to say hi."

"Who?"

"You don't know him," Dicky said. "He was somebody I

knew way back before Walla Walla. A solid citizen."

"Gee, I'm really sorry. I thought you were up to no good. This guy you knew in there, was he a close friend?"

"Sort of."

"Sort of?"

"He's gonna help me find a good job, not that I'm bitching about what you got me doing in the trailer park."

"Speaking of the trailer park. How's it looking?"

Dicky said, "Damn good. I'm on my way there now to do them weeds."

"Are you wondering how I located you?"

Mad Dog was clutching rolled-up papers, as if a relay baton. He nodded.

There was no global positioning system available to the average consumer when Dicky was sent up. It was prohibitively expensive. GPS was in the vernacular then, but Randall doubted that the nincompoop kept up with technology, in or out of the can.

The pawnbroker said, "I'm clairvoyant."

"Claire who?"

Lord help me, Randall Coll thought. He tapped his forehead. "I have ESP. I read minds."

Mad Dog offered his uncle the papers. "Then I reckon you already know what these are."

"Well, let's you and me have a discussion on your documents. My magic has its limits."

CHAPTER 18

"Amazing luck," Buster Hightower said as he piloted his 1959 Cadillac Eldorado convertible to the subsidized-housing complex's parking lot.

"As you recommended, Buster, we let our fingers do the walking in the White Pages," Judith Roswell said.

"Who needs computers and the phone books that ain't books at all that they have on their screens," the computerphobic comic gloated once more. The telephone directory was his idea to locate Harriet Hardin. "You got a kind of book that's been around since the Model T and when Al Bell invented the telephone and you got your eyeballs. It's simplicity personized."

"Yes, Buster. You are a practical genius," Carla said. "But enough, please."

"Nice work indeed, Buster. Sound detective work starts with the basics," Tip Taylor said. "Among the first lessons in the GOIPD course."

"She signed her cryptic note as 'Harriet Hardin' and she's listed as capital h-a-r-d-i-n, comma Harriet," Carla said. "She isn't in hiding. Or if she is, she's doing a poor job of it."

"Women list by their first initial to avoid obscene calls, myself included," Judith said.

"Considering her history, perhaps Harriet welcomes them," Carla said.

"Heavy-breathing strangers whispering unsweet nothings in her ear," Buster said. "Could well be she's that kind of gal. Not that I'm criticizing. It takes all kinds."

They were antsy, killing the morning after breakfast, waiting for the locksmith Judith called to finish changing her door locks.

Too anxious to wait for the elevator, they took the stairs to the third floor, where the directory stated that "Hardin 305" lived.

The door was ajar.

They heard hacking and loud coughing from within and entered.

"Yoo hoo. Hello," Carla said. "Friend, not foe."

An elderly woman in a bathrobe sat at the edge of the bed, a wad of facial tissue in a trembling hand, a glass of water in the other.

"Who the hell are you?" she said, rasping. "I've had enough company for one day."

"Among others, the person to whom you left a note," Judith said.

"To *whom?* Now isn't that special."

"I taught English."

Barely above a whisper, Harriet Hardin said, "At least you're not him. I'm having a flashback. Shut the fucking door."

Carla closed it. "Him?"

"I can't even remember his name, but if you'll give me a minute it'll come to me. Last night was drunker than seven hundred bucks worth of loose change on the bar. He's rough between the sheets and thinks he's God's gift. That I do remember. The bastard tried to kill me this morning before he scrammed."

"Who did, Harriet?" Carla said.

"Never saw him before last night."

Judith reached in her purse for her phone. "I'll call the police."

"No you won't!"

"They can protect you," Carla said. "They can find him."

"Police or no police, he'll come after me and get me sooner or later if he thinks I'm alive. I want him to think I'm dead. Oh wait," she said, clapping her hands. "He likes to go by Mad Dog. He acts like this old gangster he's named after is Jesus H. Christ Almighty."

"Coll," Tip said. "Is his last name Coll?"

"Yeah, how'd you know, Cutie Pie?"

"A hunch," Tip said casually, with a hint of a smile, the way Sean Connery did it.

Harriet tossed a pillow across the room. "Here's his murder weapon. Good luck finding fingerprints. My third ex, Jackie Bob Kline, he tried it with a pillow. I learned to fake passing out when he slapped me around. I learned to fake croaking when he thought he'd smothered me. He got twenty years for it and other offenses and died in the can, shanked in the shower by his lover boy, may Jackie Bob rot in hell."

Harriet went into a coughing fit.

Carla refilled her water glass and sat with her on the bed, feeding her sips.

"Thanks, hon. I smoked till I was sixty-three, so my lungs aren't exactly in the swellest shape."

"Can you tell us why this Coll fellow tried to kill you?" Tip asked.

"You don't wanna know, sweetie. Hey, are you dating anybody?"

"He was in my house, wasn't he?" Judith said. "You too."

"Okay, you're way ahead of me on that count. It did get kind of crowded there. What's that old saying? One's company, two's a crowd."

"Describe him."

"Mr. Right he ain't. Pale, big gut, overdue for a haircut. Funny eyes. Foulest foul breath."

"Is his first name Randall?" Tip said, puzzled that he didn't fit the pawnbroker's description.

"Nope, not Randall. The creep bragged on and on and on he was called Mad Dog. Real name's something. Ricky, Dicky. That's it. Dicky Coll." She looked at Judith. "I'll never forgive you for giving away my ruby if you're who did it and I'd bet even money I don't have to bet that you were."

Judith said, "I don't know what you're talking about."

"You're a shitty liar, hon."

Nobody responded.

Harriet Hardin Callahan Miller Kline Parker Jacobs Smith smiled, displaying ill-fitting dentures and looked at her visitors, one by one.

"That rat's ass was gonna be my partner in crime. Now you four sweethearts are."

CHAPTER 19

Buster and company had left Interstate Five southbound at the Kent exit just as the Colls entered northbound. They missed each other at Harriet Hardin's by half an hour.

Randall Coll drove to Seattle in the pawned Hyundai, tailgating and changing lanes. He'd been in the car far too long. He couldn't wait to get out and on his flat feet. His hemorrhoids were acting up and he knew he'd be miserable for days. The sting of flat feet was the lesser evil.

After ordering Dicky into the car, Randall hid the GPS transmitter and receiver in the trunk, to be used again. His bird-brained nephew sat like a dazed child who'd been up to no good and caught at it, convinced that his uncle did possess black magic.

Randall wasn't letting Dicky out of his sight until he had important answers. He figured to leave the car in that parking lot and pick it up later.

Or not. If it wasn't on its last legs before, in Dicky's custody, it was now.

"What else do you know, Uncle Randall?"

He tapped his temple. "Everything about everything."

Mad Dog was having his doubts concerning this mind-reading shit, but he wasn't gonna take any chances. This whole situation was downright creepy. Answers poured forth from him, with and without questions. Might as well spill his guts as Uncle Randall knew it all anyhow already, if he had beamed into his skull.

Dicky did leave out the old hag, jumping her bones, then polishing her off. She was out of the picture for the grand prize, so it didn't matter. The *catastrophe* was all hers.

Randall Coll took the next exit and pulled over at a gas station to read the documents on the February 1954 burglary. His nephew was yakking nonstop, all over the board, some things making sense, some not, making it difficult to concentrate on the papers.

"Part of the stolen jewels and bonds and stocks and money remain, and the woman in the old house has it?"

Mad Dog nodded vigorously. "I think so. Odds are pretty good she does, Uncle Randall, her and her pals. Dunno where they hid it, but I know the old broad what lives there, she's got it in there somewhere unless she took it to a bank."

Meaning the Roswell woman who didn't seem all that old to Randall Coll. She had that heirloom ring and had brought the swell with the gold Rolex into the mix, to play games. Randall had given his license number to his DMV acquaintance: Tyler P. Taylor III, an Ivy League moniker if there ever was one. Every answer raised another question.

That story about old-time loot donated to that charity had been all over the news. It couldn't be a coincidence; the old bills and antique jewelry were clinchers. If the goody-two-shoes was Roswell, was the insane woman going to give the kit and caboodle away?

Coll tingled at the thought of that incredible platinum and diamond cocktail ring. How it was the tip of the treasure iceberg. How if he didn't make a move fast, he could forget luxurious retirement. Or any retirement. He'd be operating his ongoing garage sale until they carried him out on a stretcher.

"And too many people, more and more people, know what you're telling me? Is that correct?"

"Uh-huh."

"We have to go into the old house and find out what they have and what they don't have."

"We do?"

"You've been in there before. Don't tell me you can't."

"I won't tell you that, Uncle Randall. I can do it."

"And you did things inside there you didn't pass along to me."

"You know that, huh?"

"I do."

"We go in," Dicky said. "Right?"

"If she's gone, yes. If she isn't, no. We go in there at first opportunity."

"I know that, Uncle Randall."

Randall Coll looked at him. "Except you'll go in alone. I wait outside in the car."

"So you can haul ass if the cops come?"

"Don't let that happen and you'll have no worries. One more thing. That old red car that's turning up here, can you give me a thorough description?"

"I can do you one better. It's got one of them vanity plates, like I used to make in Walla Walla. It's like 'comics' or 'comedians' or 'comma.'"

CHAPTER 20

"Hey, a show of hands out there, those of you like myself that are of a certain age. How many of you are happy that Watergate and the Watergating crooks are done and long gone, out of the news long long ago? Getting to be ancient history, they are."

"I'm counting fifteen or twenty hands, which is counting the show of both hands and my own. Okay, you're exercising your constipational right to cast a voter's ballot in this great nation of ours. Me, I'd be sitting on my hands if I wasn't standing up, mike in one hand, ice-cold bottle of beer in the other.

"Know why? I'll give you a clue. You know what today is? June seventeenth. It's a gargantuanal anniversary for yours truly and me too. A whole bunch importanter than my three wedding anniversaries, which I always forgot, more nails in the coffin of connubial bliss.

"Back in the very good old days, on Saturday June seventeenth, nineteen-seventy-two, five rancid putzes who couldn't break into their own homes with the front door wide open got nabbed by a Watergate Complex security guard as they were busting into the Democrats' National Committee office. To do what, who knows? Don't think they even knew.

"Simultaneous-like, I broke into the stand-up comic profession at a motel lounge in Toledo, Ohio. So I got a soft spot in my heart and head for the scandal. I'm only sorry it isn't going on today.

"Watergate was a cash cow for me and a kazillion other comics. A pasture of cash cows. Yeah, it really and truly was. Had me a partner back then by the name of Blinko Potts. We broke into stand-up around the same time and teamed up, one of us playing a snarling Senate subcommittee interrogator and the other a slimy unindicted coconspirator. We'd switch roles in midstream and had 'em rolling in the aisles. We were frisky young pups then and had great fun.

"Blinko was a runt half my size. He had a cowlick and—you guessed it—blinked like crazy. We were Mutt and Jeff, a sight gag before we opened our big yaps. Blinko burned himself out and went straight, bailing out of stand-up. Went to work in a library, not as a libarrian but in the back room, sorting and cataloging. Last I heard he met a gal who was visiting from Panama and went down there with her to Panama City and bought a bar. Sorry about the reminiscing, but Watergate and Blinko, for me they go together like gin and tonic.

"Compared to Watergate, it's kinda dull these days in the news. Sure, you got your wars in Africa and Asia and those other countries over there and everywhere else. You got your floods and your droughts. You got your national overthrows and play-off sports teams overthrowing their opponents, and your corporation bigwig CEO and bank president hanky-panky. Where the hell's a good juicy government scandal when you can really use one? A humungous commotion with the pizzazz of Watergate? A smoke-filled room deal you gotta organize a Senate investigating committee for? I get so nostalgic, I wanna cry my eyes out.

"I know these current and uncurrent events I'm lecturing you on are glazing your eyeballs. That gent in the back under the beer sign, he's snoring in his nachos. Somebody rescue him so he doesn't sour-cream and guacamole hisself to death. It's not a horrible way to go, but it's kinda messy.

"Speaking of nachos, they're as American as beer and apple

pie and beer and prime rib and beer and eggs and beer. And speaking of eggs, we all know that potato salad's got eggs in it, right? Maybe you can help me out and tell me how come eggs are sold by the dozen. Why not by the ten or fourteen or twelve or some other number? Does the potato salad know or care?

"Doughnuts come by the dozen and that I can understand. A dozen doughnuts is a satisfying appetizer. But eggs? A dozen is an even number is all I can figure. Do chickens lay eggs in pairs? That explains part of it, but not my whole entire question.

"I'm not seeing any raised hands or anybody piping up with the answer. That's okay. This is a bowling alley lounge. It ain't a quiz show or a research laboratory.

"Hey, you know those childproof containers that damn near everything seems to come in these days? Anybody else have trouble getting the things open? Yeah, you and you and you. Know what I do? I hire a child to open them. They're the only human beings who can. The tykes work cheap too, charging me just a few pills out of each bottle. If I object, they threaten to hire lawyers and sue me if I don't pay up.

"Speaking of the legal profession, I know of a lawyer who billed twenty-eight hours of work a day, eight days a week. He's a sure thing for the Lawyer Hall of Fame. Like that sports hall, he'll be eligible to be voted in five years after retirement. He's spending those five years in federal prison. The disbarred lawyer gets out with a new suit and twenty-five bucks. The hall of famer will have a certificate and a trophy waiting for him too.

"Speaking of the hall of fame, why ain't Moe Mentum a member of the football hall? Moe's played in every game I ever seen on TV. He plays both ways, offense and defense, for both teams. He's all over the place when a team's able to move the ball and score. Poor guy never gets a rest. Is that unfair or what?

"Us comics gotta be careful what we say, you know. We got political correctness hanging over our heads like buzzards every time we open our big fat mouths, if we make a boy-girl remark that ruffles feathers. Especially if a guy comic don't obey the PC rules, he'll have the feminist police swarming all over him.

"So how come manhole covers get a pass? Why don't they have to be person-covers? It's discrimination against cast iron is what it is.

"Likewise with manhunt. You're a gal on the run from the law for a quadruple murder, it's gotta be insulting. It has to hurt her feelings.

"Manure, the ladies might be okay with that. Mansion, the ladies won't care if they're living in one.

"Not so with mankind, management, mandatory, manacle, mango, mandarin, manhandler, manicurist, maneuver, mandate, manatee, man-of-war, mannequin, maniac, managed care, and manic depressionive. If I was a gal, my nose'd be seriously out of joint. Any of you out there, chase them PC violators and leave me alone.

"You know, there're shopping malls here, there and everywhere. I know this's not the season to be jolly, but malls remind me of Christmas. They're intertangled, right? You may not know this, but Santa and his elves do not begin manufacturing and woman-facturing Xmas presents on the day after Thanksgiving. Blackbeard Friday, I think they call it, where shoppers attack the stores like pirates. No way could they go into mass production that close to Xmas and meet the demand. They're hard at work as I speak to meet this year's orders.

"I gotta wonder about them elves up there at the North Pole. I really gotta worry about them little guys. You know damn well they're making less than minimum wage and get no bennies. They oughta go on strike and get themselves unionized.

"And don't even think about workplace accidents in Santa's

factory. They punch the time clock and walk home after a long day. I have it on good authority that they come down with frostbite all the time. The frostbite-medicine pills they get, they can't open the bottles as they're tiny adults, not kids.

"You think Watergate was a big-time cover-up? It's same-same and then some with Santa's elves being eaten by polar bears. It didn't just happen in 1972. It's been going on annually as well as yearly for who knows how long.

"You know that old ad slogan you'd see on commercials long ago, Better Living Through Chemistry? Forget medicine and chemical warfare, if chemistry is such a red-hot deal, how come they can't have themselves a breakthrough that's important, like geneticalistically engineering celery to taste like chocolate. There's a Nobel Prize in Betty Crockering waiting to be had."

As Buster wrapped, pausing for applause, preparing to assault the crowd with stale lawyer jokes, his three companions applauded.

So did a new member of Buster's audience, a non-bowler by the name of Randall Coll who sat by the threesome by the door. Coll was in disguise of sorts—thick-rimmed glasses and Seattle Mariners cap. He wasn't amused, but he didn't want to stand out by sitting on his hands.

Coll had called his DMV acquaintance with his birdbrained nephew's "comics." For once in his life Dicky had done something right. They played with combinations and came up with COMIC, which was registered to one Buster NMI Hightower. Further research brought Coll here tonight, to this downscale venue, to watch and listen and wonder how the comedian and his pals fit into the equation. Especially the rich kid who brought the ring into his shop, and why him and Roswell were jerking his chain.

He continued to puzzle over all this when Buster Hightower

ended his set with, "How come blue tarps aren't any other color?"

CHAPTER 21

Meanwhile, Dicky (Mad Dog) Coll, as ordered by his ungrateful uncle, had arrived at the haunted house a hair after nightfall, which came awful late this time of the year. After eleven years locked up, days and weeks and months all the same, the change of season was hard getting used to.

And what did he see but some loser trying to get in the side door? His only saving grace that Dicky could see was that the mook had Dicky's physique and good looks. None of his cool and class, though.

Using a skeleton key, twisting it, trying to jam it, having a fit, then throwing it to the ground, he went out to a turdmobile from the olden days, built like in 1985, a large square rig. Despite being parked two cars ahead of Dicky, he didn't look at him or both ways crossing the street. A loser, pure and simple.

The guy lurched from the curb, pumping a rooster tail of blue smoke. Dicky accelerated none too smoothly, cursing the Datsun pickup, latest in the parade of Coll's Jewelry and Loan beaters. Nissan hadn't been called Datsuns since like forever and Dicky had to listen to a lecture on being careful with it, Uncle Randall's lectures a broken record.

Unaware that he was being tailed, Gerald G. (Jerry) Roswell drove to a tavern that wasn't far. Thankfully it looked like it hadn't changed a bit in his absence. This neighborhood of his bitch of a sister, *their* neighborhood, it was going ritzy left and right.

An old machine shop was a fancy restaurant where you could see the original brick walls and ductwork from the old shop. Menus were posted outside with prices out of sight. It was a chore to find a joint that didn't have wine tastings, sushi, jazz combos, phony-swanky bullshit like that. He had to park three blocks away, there were so many Benzes and Beemers and SUVs the size of locomotives.

Inside, the tavern was the same too. Your choices on the menu were Jerry's idea of comfort food—hardboiled eggs from a jar and franks in a Crock-Pot full of beer. Bags of chips and pork rinds hung on wire racks, perfect side dishes. The jukebox played shit-kicker, and a coat and tie was as rare as hen's teeth.

What did bug him about the tavern and every other bar and restaurant in the state and too many other states was that law outlawing smoking inside and within twenty-five feet of the door. The twenty-five-feet rule was ignored by everybody, but any way you cut it, standing five or ten feet from the door, you were outside in any weather conditions.

On his second beer, after returning from a smoke in the alley, a new guy was on a stool one down from him. Wasn't the guy sitting at the end before? Guy with funny eyes and a slouch? Jerry didn't think he was coming on to him.

It didn't matter and no way was this dump a fag bar. Make a move and you'd be tossed out on your ear.

"Nicotine Nazis," the guy said.

"You got that right. Making folks go outside if they want a puff. If the weather's bad like it usually is, these summers Seattle can have with the rain and shit, you could catch your death of pneumonia. Far as I'm concerned, that'll kill you a helluva lot faster than lung cancer."

"Big Fucking Brother," the guy said, shaking his head.

"Everybody takes it in the ass for everything except the fat cats."

That got Jerry Roswell going. On how The Little Guy trying to do an honest business deal hasn't a prayer. On how you're screwed from the word go. On how your relatives turn on you for no reason.

"I'm what you call your independent entrepreneur," Jerry went on. "I've been out of town on various business ventures for a few years."

"How'd it go?"

"I had a run of bad luck? Who the hell hasn't at one time or another? I go out of my way to pay my sister a visit and it's like I have leprosy."

"Damn straight it ain't your fault. Like I said, the average guy, he gets it in the ass. Try as hard as you want, you're always wrong. If you don't mind me asking, what happened?" Dicky Coll coaxed.

Jerry Roswell didn't mind him asking.

He leaned closer and said, "I borrowed money from my mom who's now dead, which nobody even told me about. Missed the funeral and everything. See, I'd hooked up with this guy. He'd been in the restaurant business for years, working as a cook and a chef. There was a closed post office and Uncle had the building for sale. We bought it, fixed it up, and called it Going Postal. Get it?"

"Yeah. Right."

"We had specials like the Forever Stamp Cheeseburger and the Express Mail Cosmo."

"Cool. Sounds different, sounds like a winner," Dicky said, thinking it sounded stupid, dorky.

"We closed down inside of two months. There were too many other restaurants close by, I guess, and my partner couldn't cook for shit. Put a couple of customers in the hospital with food poisoning, which got wrote up in the local paper.

"Then I hooked up with this other guy. He was a mining consultant who was on the ground floor of this nickel mining company down there in Guatemala. His specialty was foreign mining, the import-export aspect. He had all kinds of contacts, and had all these charts and graphs.

"The company's stock price was rock-bottom and the metal itself was undervalued, selling for less than it was worth, ready to move on up. Nickel's used for all kinds of stuff. Plating other metal, batteries, the five-cent coins in your pocket, you name it.

"So I sunk every red cent I had to my name in it. I don't see the guy for a while and when I run him down and ask him what's going on. He goes, somebody went down there and found out that the nickel reserves were overvalued by two thirds, and the stock's in the toilet.

"I go, how come you didn't find that out when you were there? He goes, why would I wanna go down there? Guatemala's a dangerous country. I liked to of ripped his fucking heart out, but if I give him what he deserves, who's in a jam? Me, that's who. They'd lock me up for performing a public service.

"After all that, I come home to what's my house, half my house, and my sister treats me like a criminal. She comes unglued, like I'm a pile of dogshit. She made me give her back my house keys. The only reason I did was she had all these other people there who'd be witnesses if her and me got into it. She called me a *weasel*, even. Fuck her.

"Judith, that bitch, she's so uptight, it's like she has a steel rod up her ass. She's over fifty and I'd bet even money she's a virgin."

"Man, I know what you mean," Mad Dog said, unsuccessfully trying to keep his eyes off the silver Rolex on the mook's wrist. It was silver, not gold like that rich swell's, but worth a bunch irregardless. He had to ask, "That watch on your arm is nice. It's a Rolex, ain't it?"

"Sure is. The genuine article. This gal I used to go with, Mary Ann, I forget her last name, she gave it to me. Mary Ann said she was born into high society, but was disowned, so that's how come she was working as a barmaid."

"Getting back to your sis, I got my share of them kinds of relatives. They got it going good for them and they don't tell you diddly shit and then they go and ace you out. You can't control bad luck neither and I had my share too. Like once when a guy had an accidental heart attack and died, and I got blamed for it. Long story."

Jerry Roswell shook his head and said, "My sis, she had a guy there who looks like a male model and I think he's nosing into our family business. He's lucky I didn't kick his ass just out of general principle. I could of with a hand tied behind my back. Don't know what their story is, but something's going on."

"What do you mean?"

"I don't know for sure. I think they're hiding something. Judith, my sis, she couldn't get me out of the house quick enough."

"What do you think they're hiding?"

"Don't know, but whatever it is, I think it's in the basement. I didn't have time to check things out, but I know that house like the back of my hand. I took a quick look down there while they were gone. Things've been moved around and cleaned up, not the way I remember how it used to be, dust an inch thick."

Dicky clapped him on the back. "You'll come out of it okay. I got confidence."

"Yeah, I wish."

"And like they say, if you got your health, you got everything. You look healthy enough."

"I guess so."

Dicky thumped his chest. "Your ticker's good, right?"

"I guess so. They say smoking's bad for it, but what do they know?"

"No heart attacks?"

"Nope."

"No chest pains?"

"Nope."

"Then you're in the pink, man," said Dicky. "Hey, it's time to go out and light up. I'm gonna have me a nicotine fit."

Jerry Roswell agreed. They went into the alley, Dicky to Jerry's rear. It was totally dark, tall buildings on each side blocking even the streetlights. They had the alley to themselves, so Dicky Coll wasted no time.

Vinny Coll sure as hell wouldn't of either.

In a repeat of eleven-plus years ago, Dicky threw an arm around the jerk's neck, jammed a thumb hard in his back, and said, "Stick 'em up. Gimme your wallet if you wanna live."

"You gotta be kidding."

"Right fucking now!"

As Dicky pushed, the jerk fought him, trying to spin around. No danger of a heart attack here. Dicky pulled the .25 automatic pistol out of his pocket. It was tiny and cute as a button and had a price tag tied to the trigger guard. There was a full load of seven cartridges in the clip, one round in the chamber.

The jerk was starting to get the better of Dicky, turning himself around. Out of self-defense, Dicky jammed the Browning against Jerry Roswell's right ear and pulled the trigger.

There was a small pop, a fraction as loud as a backfire.

A guy he knew in Walla Walla had used one. He called it a peashooter. He'd said that the auditory canal was nature's silencer. The slug would blow the brain into porridge and wouldn't come out the other side. No muss, no fuss. Lock picking and brain physics, all the education you could ask for from the pen.

★　★　★　★　★

Mad Dog lowered Jerry to the ground, dead or soon to be. He took the jerk's keys, Rolex and wallet. The wallet contained thirty-eight bucks and credit cards under three different names. His driver's license and other ID had him as Gerald G. Roswell.

Playing it cool like Vinny would, Mad Dog slipped on the Rolex, pocketed the cash, and walked out to the sidewalk. He dropped the wallet and keys in the nearest sewer grate. Uncle Randall would screw him on the Rolex, but he'd have to pay him semi-mucho for it.

He turned around and had a last look. Anybody else coming out for a puff would think the guy was passed out, dead-ass drunk.

Mad Dog went to the Datsun, thinking, hey, I done the time. It's only fair that I got to do the crime. That old hag he smothered was on death's door anyway, so she didn't count. He was even steven with the legal system and he was having fun.

CHAPTER 22

It was a tale of three cities or suburbs thereof: Seattle, Washington; Atlanta, Georgia; Atlantic City, New Jersey.

Simultaneously, as Buster Hightower's set ended three time zones to the west and the nouveau Mad Dog Coll evened the homicide ledger, Tyler Polk Taylor II stared at the darkened ceiling of the home he owned (on paper) in Dacula, Georgia, a suburb of Atlanta, forty miles north-northeast of the city.

Trixi, who dotted the "i" with a bubble when she signed her name, sat cross-legged beside him on the bed, channel-surfing, hunting for Plutonium Gecko, one of her favorite hundred-decibel rock bands, volume already cranked that high.

At Tyler's shouted request that accompanied his patting her naked upper thigh, Trixi stuck out her tongue at him and muted the sound. Since he could hear her bubble gum popping and snapping, televised silence was a mixed blessing.

Pop snap pop snap pop snap as he wondered yet again how he had gotten himself into this hopeless imbroglio.

Without question, Tyler II was a victim of circumstance. He had come to Atlanta for the grand opening of his firm's first branch outside of Seattle. They had set it up first-class in every facet, from the best local and Seattle-transfer talent to the two-floor aerie in one of Atlanta's finest office towers. Taylor and Taylor opened its doors as Atlanta's twenty-seventh largest law firm.

As at the home headquarters, their clientele was distinguished

141

and their legal problems were complex. Taylor and Taylor was renowned for aiding large corporations in fending off the tax man. Mergers and acquisitions were fortes also, burying opponents in an avalanche of paper and motions and hearings. There was to be an obligatory smattering of heavily publicized pro bono, assisting the downtrodden, police brutality against a homeless person and the like. No criminal law, thank you, nor were there Whiplash Willies on their staff.

To further celebrate after the swank reception that numbered as guests prominent business and civic leaders, Tyler II and the senior partners in charge of Atlanta flew to Atlantic City.

One drink led to another and one thing led to another, which led to another and another. They ended up at a private strip party and Tip had somehow gotten cut from the distinguished herd.

He awakened in bed with Trixi and a trio of no-necks in chairs, who proved to be associates of hers. They were laughing, drinking coffee, and smoking cigarettes. She awakened, at which time they told her to get lost.

Sleepy-eyed and yawning, unsurprised by their presence, Trixi dressed immodestly and obeyed.

His memory of the past evening an alcoholic blackout, Tyler II dressed in the bathroom after a bout with the dry heaves.

Their impatience apparent, they ordered him to sit the fuck down and pay attention. They ran a video they had shot. It starred Tyler, Trixi, and her bodily orifices.

The no-necks informed Tip II that Trixi was sixteen years old, a Georgia peach who came up north to seek her fame and fortune. As Taylor sat, head buried in his hands, they became kindly and sympathetic, patting his back, commiserating that, yeah, she did look older to them too. With the vitamins kids take nowadays, you never know.

Unfortunately, the law and Claire Esther Jamison Taylor,

Tip's humorless prude of a wife, would not understand.

So there he was in Dacula, in the mini-Tara of a home he had purchased for Trixi, after he had generously paid off the three no-necks, business associates of hers (i.e.—pimps). Their ship had come in—the SS *Tyler Polk Taylor II*.

Mini-Tara was the abode Trixi had without his permission invited her white-trash family to share, six members of whom were active members of the Ku Klux Klan. The home was not small. It featured pillars, gables, and a full-width porch with rocking chairs and a proudly flying Confederate flag.

Tip visited the home and Trixi whenever he was in town on branch business, so often he feared, that the home folk might be growing suspicious.

He could not help himself. He was addicted to her. To her blue eyes and naturally blonde hair. And her freckles. Oh Lord, those freckles! It didn't even matter that she was figuratively doing her nails while they—or at least *he*—made mad passionate love.

As per usual, bankrolled by Tip, Trixi's nightmarish family was out for an evening of drinking and whoring and driving badly.

He lay there, thinking of Tyler III, the worthless son he had disowned who should be a junior partner of what he eventually planned to christen Taylor, Taylor and Taylor. Instead, at age thirty, he indulged in playboy behavior and childish superego fantasies that were exacerbated behind the wheel of his ludicrously extravagant Aston Martin. And the depth of it all, his "career" as a private detective!

But who was he to talk in this impossible predicament? Like son, like father, he thought, oh so mortified.

Simultaneously, Vance Popkirk, rolling his suitcase at the Seattle-Tacoma International Airport terminal, was unconcerned that he had made scant progress on the airplane with *Gone with the Wind: The Holy Bible,* beyond increasing his mirror-image protagonist's physical, analytical, crime-busting and sexual prowess. Although there was nominal progress blocking the novel out in his head, the overall concept, no words met paper or laptop screen.

He could think of nothing but *Dead Man's Booty.*

Vance Popkirk was on his way to a car rental counter. From there to that thrift shop where the manna from Wherever had landed.

It could've been beamed down to us from Heaven or a UFO.

The possibilities were dizzying.

CHAPTER 23

"Don't get the wrong idea, dear," Carla Chance told Harriet Hardin Callahan Miller Kline Parker Jacobs Smith. "We are not partners in anything. We are your companions and temporary protectors. We couldn't let you stay at your home. You refuse to notify the police and your attacker might return."

Pretending to ignore her, Harriet picked up a framed photo on Judith Roswell's armoire. "Not much has changed in this house. I remember these. The pictures of Harry and Ella on the walls, it's like it was yesterday."

During this impasse, Tip Taylor had gone into the basement and brought up the *1954 Seattle City Directory.* In quest of a mystery clue, he turned to the folded pages.

"Harriet, we realize it has been a long time, but are any of the names on the pages familiar? Any of them dropped by Harry Spicer?"

"Good luck on the Smiths page," Buster said. "It's the population of Delaware."

"Leamy Monday or Munson or Monson," Harriet said. "The name popped into my head. I think he was a shit-ass pal of Harry's."

"Your language, young lady," Carla said. "Please watch your mouth."

"The grandpappy of the lady of the house, he didn't mind my mouth in a variety of ways," Harriet told Carla.

"You leave me speechless," Carla said.

"Almost," Buster wisely didn't say.

"A colleague in his locksmith business?" Tip wondered out loud.

"In on the caper," Buster said. "Yeah, that makes sense."

Harriet shook her head. "I don't remember. It's that unusual name that stuck in my head."

"Yeah, Smith," Buster said.

"Can anybody get a drink in this place?" Harriet said.

"I'll go for wine," Judith said, heading to the kitchen.

"The other marked page, page nine-ninety-eight, Mullenbach to Munday," Tip said. "There is no Munson or anyone with the first name of Leamy."

"It's a shot in the dark. I'm drawing a blank. It's been, Jesus Christ, close to sixty years," Harriet said, then turning to the kitchen. "Don't be stingy on the pour, hon. I'm not driving."

"Nor are you, Tip," Carla said, patting his arm.

"I know. I am riding with you."

"What I meant is, you're on bodyguard duty," Carla said.

"I have oodles of room," Judith said, setting a tray, wine bottles, and glasses on the dining room table.

Deep in the heart of Matchmaker City, Buster thought, scanning the tray in vain for a cold bottle of suds. Sour grape juice was happy hour here.

"I don't need babysitting," Harriet said. "You wanna make sure I stay out of the basement, don't you?"

"Do I have to remind you that you were this close to being a murder victim?" Carla said, holding thumb and forefinger a millimeter or two apart.

"I don't like sleeping in a strange bed," Harriet said, smiling at Tip. "Alone."

Judith looked up the stairwell. Orange and Vanilla sat at the landing, staring. "Be nice to them and you can have company."

Harriet made a face at them and said, "One of my ex's was a

cat lover. No matter how many of them I took for a ride, he'd replace the damn things. He was the fudge packer."

Carla rolled her eyes and said, "I give up. Buster and I will be running along. Judith, is there a main-floor bedroom for Tip so he can hear attempts at entry?"

"No, but I have sleeping bags and an air mattress. If that's okay?" Judith said, looking at Tip.

The GOIPD professional does not seek trouble, nor does he or she back down from it when a client's personal safety is at stake. It's all in a day's work.

"Absolutely," he said.

Thirty seconds after taking a glass from Judith, Harriet's wine was half gone and she said to him, "You get lonely, Cutie Pie, you know where to go."

Judith blushed. Tip forced a wan smile. To be a polite guest, Buster forced down a half glass of spoiled grape juice.

Carla took her man's arm and said, "That's our exit cue."

Seated on the air mattress and sleeping bag, leaning against a wall adjacent the front door, Tyler Polk (Tip) Taylor III was in darkness but for the screen of his laptop, which was on his lap.

The only sound in the house was loud snoring coming from the direction of Harriet Hardin's room, a guarantee that Tip would not be sexually accosted. Her four glasses of wine was a good sign that the snoring would continue.

Tip wondered what Judith was wearing in bed.

Using every Internet trick he knew, Tip hunted for Leamy Monday or Munson or Monson. No luck.

He was giving up for the night when his cell phone rang. Its ring was the chiming of the noon bells on Harvard Yard.

"Tippy?"

"Mumsy!"

"Are you doing all right, Tippy?"

"In the pink, Mumsy. You?"

"I have been better, I have been worse. This, um, private investigator endeavor of yours, are you sticking with it?"

"I am, Mumsy."

"I trust it is providing an income."

He hesitated and said, "An income that continues to improve."

"That is disturbingly ambiguous. Your father and I disagreed that it was the proper career track for you, Tippy, as you well know. I felt it was an imaginative and venturesome choice, but you are an adult."

"Technically an adult, Father often said. I do appreciate you speaking your mind to him, Mumsy, on the occasions when you took my side."

"For what good it did."

"You did try, Mumsy. Father had long ago washed his hands of me. That was a foregone conclusion."

"It is nice to speak to you again, Tippy, but this detective activity of yours is also why I called. Do you and your fellow detectives work jointly?"

"Not as a rule."

"Are there times when you can gain assistance from colleagues in other parts of the country?"

"As a matter of fact, yes. The GOIPD has an alumni referral and networking program."

"Those initials, Tippy. Please tell me again what they stand for."

"Gumshoe Online Institute of Private Detection."

"How quaint. Do you suppose this school, this institution, has matriculated private detective graduates in the Atlanta, Georgia, area?"

Atlanta, where Taylor and Taylor launched a law-firm invasion of D-Day proportions, Tip thought. He had harbored suspicions about his father's fidelity since he worked summers at Taylor and Taylor. Tyler II's personal secretaries were often young, with dubious office skills.

But Mumsy would clarify her request on a need-to-know basis. At an early age, he had learned that it was fruitless to probe her.

"I can check and give you an e-mail address for the alumni referral program."

"Do they have a telephone number, Tippy? I am more comfortable speaking to a real person than communicating via a computer. Your father and I were raised in a world where people did our typing for us."

"Give me a second, Mumsy."

Tip signed on to GOIPD's Web site, located a phone number for the alumni referral program, and gave it to his mother.

"Thank you so much, Tippy."

"Not at all, Mumsy."

"Good night, Tippy."

"Good night, Mumsy."

Tip hung up, thinking that this was as close to family intimacy as it got. He closed the laptop, and got into the sleeping bag.

Wondering what Judith was wearing in bed.

Chapter 24

"You keep pushing them together like you are, toots, squeezing them in a vice, they're gonna consommé their relationship without benefit of clergy or even a first date. Is that what you really want?" Buster asked Carla the next morning.

She was touching up her lipstick, ready to leave for the Last Chance Insurance Agency. "Don't be silly and melodramatic. I encouraged Tip to stay strictly for protection. Besides, what could possibly happen with that—woman there with them?"

"She was knocking down that rotted grape juice with both hands and it's a big house," Buster said. "Ask Harry Spicer's ghost."

"If there's a twinkle in Judith's eyes when hers meet Tip's and vice versa, am I to be credited or blamed?"

"You emptied your whole entire quivering of Cupid's arrows into them is all I'm saying."

"This debate is pointless, Buster," Carla said at the door. "Have a nice day."

"Likewise on the nice day and the pointless."

Waiting at the door for Uncle Randall to open up Coll's Jewelry and Loan, Dicky Coll followed him in and laid Gerald Roswell's watch on the counter.

"Whadduya think, Uncle Randall?"

The moron couldn't wait until he got his jacket off and counted out his till. He'd changed in a small way Randall couldn't put a finger on, and it wasn't an improvement. The watch must be hotter than midsummer on Mercury at high noon. Randall picked it up and pretended to scrutinize it, but he didn't even need a magnifying glass or to remove the back. It was garbage, the cheapest, cheesiest, made-in-China Rolex knockoff he'd ever seen, the kind of trinket he'd take out of pity for a few bucks, hoping the schmo was so grateful he'd return when he had an item of value to hock.

"Remember my mom, Uncle Randall?" Mad Dog said.

How could he forget Sophie? She was a shrew and a drunk just like her sister, Glenda, Randall's ex. The fishwife gene ran in their family.

"Is that a question?"

"Mom left it to me, Uncle Randall. It belonged to a boyfriend of hers who was killed in Vietnam while he was dying as a war hero. It was her most valuable and sentimental possession."

Inscribed on back was *to GGR from MAJ*. Try as he might, the kid was a bullshit artist who could never get the knack of the art. He placed it on the counter.

"What'll you give me? I'm running low on cash."

"What's going on at where you're supposed to be?"

Dicky feigned a yawn. "I was there all night long. Zilch was going on. I went for breakfast just before I come here. The price of gas, these A-rabs, they're robbing us blind. Shit, it was like a buck-fifty a gallon when I was sent up. Gas money's what I gotta have if you want me to keep playing private eye."

The pawnbroker glanced at the empty space inside his counter case, where the Browning .25 mini automatic had been. He knew damn well what had happened to the .25 the day before yesterday and was tempted to tell his goofball nephew to take the pistol up the street to a competitor if he wanted quick cash. Or stick somebody up, more his speed.

Instead, he unzipped his change bag and gave Mad Dog five

twenties. "This is for your priceless Rolex."

"That's all?"

"It was made in the Third World, not Switzerland. If you don't believe me, take it to every jewelry store and pawnshop in town. They'll laugh you out the door. A hundred bucks is a gift. Merry Christmas. Happy Birthday to you."

Dicky couldn't summon a word, even today's word of the day: unethical. Which was exactly what Uncle Randall was doing to him. Unethicaling him. Then again, maybe it was a fake. Roswell was a loser, the kind who wouldn't know the difference. But only a hundred bucks?

Mumbling unintelligibly, Dicky picked up the money.

"Head back there and keep an eye on things. How many times do I have to tell you? Check in with me every few hours."

Dicky Coll pocketed the hundred and skulked out the door. Randall Coll thought it odd he gave in so easily. Randall had guessed the whack job carried his own agenda. Now, there was no question.

"We're old news, Mr. Popkirk," said Brenda Hicks, director of Services for the Needy.

Vance Popkirk, would-be novelist and former historical and political affairs correspondent for the defunct *Weekly International Tattler,* had been looking around the store at the pathetic flotsam for sale. How sad that people were reduced to such frayed merchandise, furnishing out of a 1980s sitcom. "Excuse me?"

"News, these days, people watch it and it's gone. I swear, the adult public has a shorter attention span than an infant."

Half listening, projecting the story beyond merely an isolated incident of time travel and aliens, Vance Popkirk recollected a classic headline of his: ALIENS PREPARE FOR CONQUEST BY BRINGING THE WORLD ECONOMY TO ITS KNEES

BY OLD-CURRENCY CASH INFUSION.

An old woman in a flowered dress audibly gasped and limped to him on a cane. "Sir, are you Mr. Vance Popkirk?"

"Yes I am."

"Mr. Popkirk, sir, I remember you from your picture when you were a news columnist. Every week when we went grocery shopping, I picked up your wonderful newspaper in the checkout line and Your Correspondent at Large was the very first thing I read."

Popkirk smiled modestly.

"I loved your piece on President Nixon. Say what you want about the Trickster, I liked him. He kept the Commies at bay. I'll take him instead of what we have now. I'm so sorry your newspaper folded. Every time I go up to pay for groceries I can't afford, thanks to all those crooks in office, and your newspaper isn't there, I want to break down and cry."

NIXON HAUNTS OVAL OFFICE. SECRET SERVICE FINDS UNEXPLAINABLE INSTALLATION OF TAPING EQUIPMENT, Vance Popkirk recalled.

The hopeful producer of reality TV smiled condescendingly. "Well, thank you. I'm honored."

"Will we be in the news again?" Brenda Hicks asked. "Can you bring the story back to life?"

"Oh yes," Vance Popkirk replied, unsure if he would've portrayed her as an alien or not. A red-hair linkage to the Red Planet was over the top, even for the *Tattler*.

"Sincerely, Mr. Popkirk. Until you told me, I hadn't the foggiest you were a reality TV executive."

He'd told them of *Dear God* and *Big Brides*, speaking vaguely and deceitfully of their imminent launch dates. But not of *Dead Man's Booty*.

"Mr. Popkirk, sir."

Popkirk turned. Facing him was a balding man dressed in the

storm trooper uniform of a rent-a-cop. He held out the final issue of the *Tattler* and a pen. "I called home and had the missus
bring it from home and drop it off on her way to work when I
saw you here. We keep our back issues of the *Tattler* for the missus. She belongs to a UFO support and research group. Could
you autograph this here piece for me? It'll be a collector's item."

Vance Popkirk obliged, signing over his column, under his
photo: STARLET CONFIDES TO FRIENDS, JFK INSA-
TIABLE AT AGE 90.

"You speak the truth where these so-called real newspapers
don't. I know you gotta catch a ration of crap for some of your
articles. Like Saint Patrick's Day, your article claiming
leprechauns were homosexuals. I don't care who it pisses off,
the way they dress in those tights, it's pretty obvious they're
fags."

"Indeed it is obvious," Popkirk said. "One must stand up for
one's beliefs and bring the truth to the public."

"Once again, Mr. Popkirk, thanks for your John Henry on
this here paper. Who knows, maybe it'll be worth a bundle in
ten on fifteen years. I can sell it to help finance my retirement."

Eager to be free of these bores, Popkirk glanced at his watch
and said, "Evidently the general public is unfamiliar with the
First Amendment and the legacy of journalism in a free society.
I really must run."

"People are speculating this magic treasure came from an old
unsolved crime here in town."

"I gather that."

"Sir, when the envelope was dropped in the door slot, I was
on duty and saw who did it."

He had Popkirk's full attention. "Can you describe this
person?"

"I can do more than that, sir. I know her."

★ ★ ★ ★ ★

"I am a tad gamy," Tip Taylor said, seated at the dining room table. "I should be running along."

Judith Roswell rather liked the sight of him in the morning. She had had trouble sleeping, fantasizing him coming up the steps, not the gentleman he appeared to be. "How do you like your eggs?"

"Over easy, please."

"Harriet, how do you like your eggs?"

Harriet Hardin was coming down the stairs slowly in a tired-looking bathrobe, her hair askew, clinging to the railing. "Eggs? It's the middle of the fucking night."

"It is nine-thirty in the morning by my watch," Judith said, opening the oven door, trying to ignore the sight of the woman and her profanity.

"The bacon's ready. Toast? Coffee?"

Harriet slowly sat at the table. "Do you have a Bloody Mary?"

"Sorry."

"Toast, I guess. Black coffee."

Tip stood and filled a cup for her from a pot.

"Thanks. Chivalry ain't dead, Cutie Pie. Did we have us any intruders?"

"Not that I am aware of."

"Since you're not gonna let me hang around Memory Lane here without a babysitter, you can run me home. I'll be safe, so long as I'm careful who I bring home from bars," Harriet said.

"I wish you'd reconsider."

"Thanks, but no thanks."

"Immediately after breakfast, I will," Tip said.

"You keep one thing in mind, if there's loot lying around here, you ain't acing me out of it. I got my rights."

Tip and Judith exchanged looks as the doorbell rang.

With tongs, Judith had been laying strips of bacon on a paper towel in a plate. "Tip, would you, please?"

Tip opened the door to a blubbery fellow in his forties with a mullet. He was Tip's height, had beady eyes, and was busting out of a wifebeater.

"Lady of the house in?"

"May I ask who's asking?"

"If you aren't the man of the house and my records say there is no man of the house, you may not ask, Slick."

Tip closed the door, aimed his impressive Bondian jaw at the man, and said, "That will not do."

The GOIPD offered postgraduates an optional video entitled *Fight Dirty and Live.* That and annotated material on the art of violence cost $139.95. Promos depicted a small man defeating a big man with various tricks. A swift kick to a shin and a swifter kick to an area above the shins. A thumb poke to an eyeball. Most creatively, grabbing a finger with a hand cupped over the other, then jerking it backward, vertically, until a bone or joint snapped.

Tip had watched the intro with interest, but did not purchase the postgrad course. He had not gone face-to-face physically with an opponent since fencing class and the lacrosse team in prep school. If bluffing and diplomacy did not win the day, he would do what he had to do to protect his client and his honor, however he might prevail.

The visitor spread his hands and said, "Look, Slick, it doesn't mean shit to me, you playing sentry and impressing her, and it doesn't change the lady's obligations, her and her problem with her senile Ma being bamboozled by those Nigerians and her worthless brother with his hand in the cookie jar and her losing her job and maxing out credit cards and the rest, running up a tab that'd choke a mule and the credit card outfit turning it over to us, a situation by the looks of you you never had to face, and it also doesn't change things that you think credit card companies and collection agencies are lower than snakeshit, so you go tell the lady of the house that we're losing our patience her ignoring us when we're calling, making us drop by, the third trip for me, her not answering the door, and when we're totally out of patience which will be soon, they'll be coming after this old house.

"These folks I work for, they get their money, and if the lady of the house doesn't want to lose her home and be living under the freeway in a cardboard box that was once home to a home-entertainment center, she has to resign herself to fucking work with us or cough up one hundred and eighty grand in a big lump sum."

Tip Taylor was immobile and speechless as the bill collector lumbered off to his massive SUV.

One hundred eighty thousand dollars was the base price, before options and tax, of his Aston Martin DB9.

He went back inside, doubly, if not triply, protective of Judith.

CHAPTER 25

Buster Hightower, underemployed stand-up comic, was short of any number of goods and services, but not time. With a surplus of it prior to his Westside Bowling Lanes and Casino set in the evening, he drove in to Seattle to check on Judith Roswell.

Yeah, Judith and her basement bankroll were none of his beeswax, but he was feeling kind of like a big brother to her. Not feelings like Carla had, Carla who wanted to attend her wedding to Tip Taylor and fling rice at them, but just to look out for her. You got that much dough in your cellar, you're gonna attract the wrong sort of boys and girls, and she already had. If this kept up, the bad folks would have to take a number.

As he pulled up in front of her old house, a spiffy little guy was on her stoop, waving a business card and talking loudly at the door.

When Buster reached him, he said, "She ain't in the market for pots and pans or encyclopedias, pal."

"Are you a resident?"

The guy's cologne was higher octane than Harriet's perfume, pricier but still potent enough to kill mosquitoes. "I don't live there either, but I ain't selling anything."

"Nor am I."

He gave Buster the card:

Vance Popkirk
Novelist and Independent Television Producer

"Yeah? What kind of novelist? You wrote a book?"

"My editor and agent insist that I reveal nothing before its release."

"I can see where you're coming from there. My lady friend likes the paperbacks where there's a pirate and a hot babe on the cover. Is that what you write?"

Popkirk looked at him. He had paid the security guard for his discretion, but had not expected to encounter this bizarre gauntlet.

"Okay, fine. TV Producer of what?"

"Reality television of the highest quality."

Buster laughed. "Reality TV and highest quality, sorry, but that's the mother of all oxymoronicals."

Vance Popkirk ignored the cretin's remark. "Are you acquainted with Judith Roswell?"

"A whole bunch better than you ever will."

"Perhaps you are familiar with me from my column in the late, lamented *Weekly International Tattler*. It was a feature column called Your Correspondent at Large."

"I'm not. My lady friend and me, we love them supermarket rags. So do our kitties when we line their litter boxes with 'em. Crop circles and kinky aliens, you're the world renowned experts."

Popkirk wrote a phone number on the back of the card he'd given Buster. "That's my cell. If you're granted entry, please have her contact me. It is of great importance to her."

"Why?"

"Just say these four words that I called through the door. Services for the Needy. And further, sir, her name, Roswell, it's destiny that we collaborate."

"Yeah? How come?"

"Roswell, New Mexico. Nineteen-forty-seven. Hint hint."

"Gotcha. Your little green men."

Popkirk started down the stairs.

"Hey, is Elvis alive?"

Popkirk ignored him.

"If he is, is he in Area 51?"

Judith let Buster in.

Popkirk was so loud, Buster knew she'd been listening to every word. He'd keep his trap shut. If she was of a mind, he'd let her do the talking.

Dicky (Mad Dog) Coll was no fool, just like Vinny (Mad Dog) Coll was no fool, Vinny who wouldn't of been a goner at age twenty-three except for rotten breaks and bad people he had to work with and for and against.

Dicky finished leaning on the steering wheel, trying not to hit the horn while pissing in the funnel. He got out of the Datsun truck, zipped up, and started on a stroll, a physical fitness walk if anybody asked. He'd go through the alley and around the block, having a look at the haunted house from different angles, different ways to bust into the place when nightfall came.

There was a toolbox built into the pickup's bed, the stamped chrome kind. Stuff shifted and clanked around in it when he was driving. The box was padlocked, so Dicky didn't know what was in it and didn't care. Toolboxes meant tools, which meant work, which wasn't for Dicky. Hadn't been for Vinny neither. Work was for losers, for suckers. He'd be all business if anybody asked, a guy sent out to do a repair. These old places, they'd have no shortage of breakdowns.

He could of chased after that weird little dude who was at the door shooting the shit with the big old comedian who drove the big old red Caddy. But the guy getting chased off hisself, he had to be a door-to-door peddler.

On his second trip around the block, doing a figure eight at the next street and the alley, about to give up from fatigue and lack of solutions, lo and behold, there the door-to-door peddler was, parked. His car was a tin can, almost brand-new, with a car rental agency license frame.

Dicky walked up from behind, and saw that the guy had both windows partway down because of the heat. The little fella had a cell phone to his right ear, not talking, just listening to somebody on the other end or to it or making a call, listening to it ring.

He opened the passenger door and got in with him. "Didn't your mama tell you you oughta lock your car doors?"

Vance Popkirk yelped and lost his grip on the phone, which landed on Dicky's lap. "Ain't your day, is it? Can't sell shit to nobody on foot and now you got me."

"Give me my phone and get out of my car!"

"Whew," said Dicky (Mad Dog) Coll. "No wonder you got your windows rolled down. That French whorehouse perfume of yours, you smell like this old lady I knew for a night of fun recent-like, who's dead from the excitement, God rest her soul."

"Out! Now!" Popkirk shouted. "Or I'll scream for help and you'll be sorry."

A hand around the cell phone, Dicky fished the Browning .25 out of his pocket with the other, pointed it at Popkirk's side, and said, "You're the one who'll be sorry, you don't shut your fucking mouth till I say to open it back up. Drive up a coupla blocks where nobody heard you here, yelling like a girl. Park, so me and you, we can have us a talk."

At sight of the slob's gun, most of Popkirk's tan blanched. He did as he was told, parked, and removed his wallet, saying, "I am not a door-to-door salesman. If you want money, please take it and what's in there and let me go. I won't tell anybody."

"They all say they won't tell nobody." Dicky did take his wallet and pocketed the sixty bucks in it, thinking all that plastic he had, doesn't anybody carry cash? Looking at Vance Popkirk's driver's license, he said, "Okay, Poopkirk, "I wanna talk about old broads and haunted houses and what you were doing there."

"It's Pop-kirk. And you are, sir?"

"Ever heard of Vinny Mad Dog Coll?"

"The nineteen-thirties gangster. I have."

"I'm a di-rect descendant of Vinny Coll, you might say. My name's Dicky, but you can know me as Mad Dog."

Popkirk didn't reply.

"Talk to me, Poopkirk. Or else me and my peashooter, we're gonna give you a second belly button."

Popkirk thought he was going to lose the lunch he hadn't eaten. Not knowing what this malodorous mental defective knew and didn't know or if he did intend to use his pistol, he told all, ending with, "Her name, Judith Roswell, her and I, given my previous profession, it's fate."

"How is it fate?"

"Because of the UFO crash in 1947 near Roswell, New Mexico. It was a staple in my *Weekly International Tattler* column. This is a natural, copacetic bond."

Dicky squinted at Poopkirk, not understanding his flying saucers and shit. "So this old broad, you wanna do a reality TV show with her on dead people's money. Me, I'm after the money if there's more where that come from. I got these papers back in the trailer about this old safecrack job. The old Roswell gal, she knows the score. You and me, we're working as a team. We blackmail her if we got to. We get the dough."

"I—I don't like that b-word."

"Call it what you wanna call it. That's what we're gonna do. Pull her fingernails out one by one if we got to. Find out if there's anything left and get our hands on it before the crazy old bat gives the rest away to bums and winos."

"An alliance?"

"Yeah, an alliance. Call her up and tell her you gotta talk to her."

"I was trying when you so rude—joined me. Her phone rang and rang."

"They had answering machines before I went away, but she don't? You and that charity, that should of got a rise out of her."

"I presume so."

"Okay, this is what we're gonna do, Poopkirk."

Randall Coll read the GPS signal, perplexed. It was absolutely motionless.

He doubted if Dicky would have or could have gotten into the toolbox and discovered it. His pathetic excuse for a nephew was where he was supposed to be. Doing what he'd been told was extremely suspicious behavior.

It was beyond time to learn what was cooking inside his pea brain.

CHAPTER 26

Tip Taylor, Harriet Hardin, Buster Hightower, and Judith Roswell drank coffee, small talking, sharing nothing they didn't have to share with Harriet, who rested cup on saucer harder than necessary and said, "That boy at the door had high-rent pimp written all over him."

Buster said, "The world's second-oldest profession. Without ladies of the first, they'd be drawing unemployment."

"Services for the Needy," Harriet went on. "How'd he know?"

"I'm recollecting his column. That boy's a crack journalist and the *Weekly International Tattler* knew all," Buster said. "Popkirk was the only reporter who told the truth about Martians making those crop circles. He should have been nominated for a Pulitzer or an Oscar. Too bad he's sunk down into unreality TV. A sad career move."

Tip looked at him and smiled, "How do we know if you are serious or not, Buster?"

Buster shrugged. "You don't and I hope to hell nobody ever does."

"What did he want with you, hon?" Harriet asked Judith.

Who shook her head.

"Next time, if there is a next time, let him in, and don't let him back outside until we know what you're dealing with," Harriet said, then to Tip, "That whale you sent off, sweet pants, what did *he* want?"

A GOIPD graduate must accept the fact that a falsehood is ac-

ceptable if it is in the client's best interests. Deem it a constructive lie.
Practice in front of a mirror. It'll be as easy as pie.

"A meat salesman who claimed he had sold some meat to a neighbor and had prime cuts left over. He could not name the neighbor or the neighbor's address. A routine scam."

"We got suckered by one of them once. You couldn't cut their tenderloin steaks with a bazooka," Buster said.

Judith was aware she was crimson. She hoped nobody else noticed. She had recognized the bill collector. This wasn't the man's first attempt to persuade her to open her door.

How much had the bill collector told Tip?

Bless him, he wasn't letting on as he spooned sugar into his cup. He was a special man.

"Let's talk turkey here," Harriet said. "Judith, hon, any of that loot left?"

"I'm sorry. I'm afraid not."

Harriet stood. "Your nose is growing, but I'm throwing in the towel. For now. Meeting adjourned. Cutie Pie, wanna run me home in that Eye-talian hot rod of yours? I'm in need of a change of clothes and to be there for my meal lady when she brings lunch."

"It is an English car."

"Same difference. Yes or no on the lift?"

Tip stood. "It will be my pleasure."

At the door, Harriet wagged a finger at Judith. "If you're fibbing, don't forget, charity begins at home."

Alone with Judith, Buster said, "Are you giving the rest away?"

"What would you and Carla do?"

Carla shook her head.

"That's the sixty-four-zillion-dollar question."

CHAPTER 27

The patio of Tip Taylor's apartment overlooked Tacoma's Commencement Bay and downtown skyline. Seattleites looked down on their smaller neighbor thirty miles south. Seattleites came up with bad jokes, such as Velveeta being in the gourmet cheese sections of Tacoma markets.

Tip knew better. He lived within walking distance of Washington State's highest density of art and history museums. He lived within walking distance of a restored waterfront, and a nice mix of restaurants and bars.

He brought dinner out to the patio: a carton of hummus, a bag of pita chips, and a bottle of a smoky Argentine Malbec he'd uncorked to breathe the moment he walked through the door.

He looked forward to the Malbec. Unloading Harriet Hardin at her seniors facility had not been easy. She did everything to ensnare him in her apartment but do so by gunpoint.

How often did the male of the species plead a headache?

Tip brought out his laptop, to continue researching the enigmatic Leamy Whomever. At least until sunset, when it would be him, the Malbec, the view, and speculation on what Judith Roswell was or was not wearing to bed.

His cell phone announced noon at Harvard Yard.

"Tyler P. Taylor?"

"Speaking."

"Robert Clounse here. Fellow GOIPD alum working out of

the Atlanta area."

"My, that was quick."

"Quick because it was so easy," said Robert Clounse, with no trace of a southern accent. "The subject of my investigation might as well have been shooting up red flares. A vital mystery clue was irrelevant."

"Excuse me?"

"Mrs. Claire Esther Jamison Taylor, my client. She asked me investigate the activities of your father, Mr. Tyler Polk Taylor the Second, when he's in Atlanta on business. He owns a home free and clear in Dacula, an upscale suburb north of the city. And no, y'all, we don't all have an accent."

Tip laughed and said, "At the end of the day, a good GOIPD interviewer anticipates all reactions and responses."

"I vividly remember that lesson. Listen with Your Ears," Robert Clounse said. "Mr. Taylor is an occasional visitor, who tries to be subtle and secretive. Yeah, it's an okay neighborhood, but stretch limos are rare except on prom and graduation nights.

"A pack of rowdies occupy it full time. They're loud, dirty and abusive. There have been multiple police complaints, not the least of which concerns the Confederate flag flying on the front porch and them on that porch wearing KKK uniforms as they drink beer and play 'Dixie' full blast on the stereo. The police come and they settle down. Temporarily.

"There is also a young woman, a very young woman, in their company, who they treat with what passes for them as respect. She's a family member of these savages. I interviewed several neighbors. They're most scandalized by her and Mr. Taylor together. They're lovebirds, the elder member of the couple obviously smitten. I'm sorry to have to break news as unpleasant as this to you and your mother."

"Regrettably, it is not a complete shock. You do excellent work, Robert."

"We're all excellent. It's the result of our training. The GOIPD should have school colors and a fight song."

"Boola boola," Tip said. "Does your client know you are reporting this to me?"

"Did the GOIPD cover ethics and detective-client privilege?"

"I can check my study material."

"Irrelevant. My client asked me to forward what I uncovered to you too."

"Does Mum—your client wish me to contact her?"

"She didn't specify. I think she simply wanted you to know."

"Please stay on the line, your call is important to us?" Buster Hightower said. "Anybody here who ain't heard that a thousand times?"

Patrons of the Westside Bowling Lanes and Casino's cocktail lounge uttered a collective groan.

"If our call is so important to them, how come they ain't taking it? How come you're listening to elevator music or you're listening to a pitch for their company's gizmo, which you're calling to complain about what they're pitching, which turned out to be a lemon?" Buster yelled.

Laughter.

"Your important call finally is answered, the answerer is this guy or gal who sounds like a maharaja or maharaja-ess from an old Khyber Pass movie, locked in an echo chamber. You tell them your problem, that the Widget Master Turbo Two Thousand X you bought doesn't shred veggies like it's supposed to. It vaporizes them and short-circuits power in a three-block radius.

"They tell you to take it on back to the store you bought it from for a refund unless, sir, the warranty ran out. You ask how long the warranty is. He or she asks you what day and time it is where you live, and what time zone you're in, then asks you to do a short customer service survey. If it's a he, you whip a four-letter word on him he can use to fill in every blank. If it's a her, and you're a gentleman, come up with a three- or five-letter word.

"You hang up and hurry on down to the store where you bought the thermonuclear device. The store's in a mall, as one hundred and seven percent of each and every store in this day and age are, but you've been on the line so long waiting for your important call to be answered, it's so late that the whole entire mall is closed for the day and your warranty expired five minutes after they locked their doors.

"Speaking of malls, I had me a dream the other night that I went into a mall, through a big humungous entrance with gold doors, floors made of turquoise and jasper, and harp music. I did my annual shopping, buying a pair of socks to replace the pair I wear every day, but I couldn't get out. The mall had no exit."

The women in Buster's audience of seventeen clapped and cheered. The men drank faster.

"A last word on malls. Do outlet malls have their own outlet malls? If they don't yet, they will.

"No, make this the last word. I hear there's a law in mall parking lots that if you run over someone walking into a mall, it's vehicular homicide. If you hit 'em coming out, it's a misdemeanor. If they're not carrying shopping bags, you get a verbal warning."

Far more male applause than female.

"Television. A favorite topic for many of us. Sundays are 'specially interesting. You get up in the morning, turn it on as you're making breakfast. There's nothing on but preachers. The richest ones have their own TV equipment and cathedrals as big as Saint Peter's. Some of those old boys are faith healers. Call in your credit card number and they fix what ails you, everything but how to pay off your credit card when the bill comes next month.

"I had one of those foaming-at-the-mouth Bible-thumpers on, Bible in hand, one-eight-hundred number on the bottom of the screen, but my eggs ain't frying. The reason for that is our stove don't work.

"So I dialed that one-eight-hundred number which by then I know by heart. My call was important to *them* cuz they picked up on the second ring. I asked if the Reverend can heal stoves. The sweet, syrupy southern gal on the line said no problem so long as I add a twenty-percent surcharge to my generous donation. I asked how come. She said the Reverend was trained by God to heal souls, not major appliances, so it takes a skosh longer.

"I hung up and ate cold cereal, and tuned in the weather. Forecasting weather is alchemy, not science. Anybody disagree? No? My question is, if they say it'll be eighty and sunny, and you look out the window and it's fifty and monsooning, do you still have to slather on sunscreen?"

Buster waited out the applause and said, "After the Sunday weather, there was football. I love pro football. I hate halftime, though. Answer me this, is there anything tackier in the whole wide world than the Super Bowl halftime show? All them floats and bands and singers in shiny clothes and blinking lights and smoke. They give overkill a bad name. You'd think the weight'd ruin the turf, killing the plastic crabgrass."

The women booed Buster. The men cheered.

"Okay, I see we're split down the middle and center on demagogueraffic and girl-boy lines here. Technology is taking over football, you know. NFL quarterbacks and the radios in their helmets for one, the radios the coaches use to send in plays. What if the other team's listening in? What if they can talk into his radio, huh? If it was me, I'd be calling in a stale lawyer joke.

"Like I'm gonna do, wrapping up this set. Sorry, stop boo-ing, it's in my union contract, okay. Just one, I promise.

"Why did the lawyer cross the road?"

Mild laughter.

"To get to the car accident on the other side."

Less mild laughter.

"The last one, I promise. I swear on the stack of Bibles I bought from a TV preacher. What do you get when you cross the Godfather with a lawyer?"

Puzzled silence.

"An offer you can't understand."

"Okay, I lied. How do you get a lawyer out of a tree? Answer, cut the rope."

Moderate laughter.

"Speaking of spitting. You know which NFL coaches were former players and those who weren't? The ones who have the ath-e-letic coordination to spit without lifting their mikes, they were the players, the top-notch spitters all-pro.

"NFL quarterbacks and the radio helmets. What do you call the lawyer who crossed the wires and was able to talk into the quarterback's helmet?

"Answer. The lawyer's also his agent. What's he saying to his client?"

Several smiles, but no response.

"He's telling him he's been traded to the other team."

CHAPTER 28

Good morning to Vance Popkirk, wannabe best-selling novelist and independent producer of reality television programming. He had been unable to sleep a wink. Inside a filthy sleeping bag on a filthy floor in a filthy trailer in a ghost town of a filthy trailer park, listening to rats frolicking throughout the night, and listening to and smelling his stench-ridden captor pass gas and snore. Without a shadow of a doubt, this was the worst experience of his life.

He did try to be positive, though. The experience might be useful fodder for *Gone with the Wind: The Holy Bible.* His protagonist/doppelgänger, whoever he may turn out to be, would make mincemeat out of a self-styled Mad Dog Coll.

Good morning to Dicky Coll, who awakened with a snort. Blinking and yawning, he looked up at daylight coming through a crack in a seam joining a wall and the roof. He looked down at Poopkirk, who had his thumb in his mouth. A sissy and a queer by the looks of him, but he hadn't made a move. Dicky had learned to be on the lookout for them at Walla Walla, learned to avoid them in the shower room, learned never to drop his soap.

After getting up, the two of them, they'd head out for breakfast, on Poopkirk, paying for it with plastic, then running him over to an ATM for extra spending money. They had a lot on the plate today, things that'll get them closer to the pot of gold in the haunted house.

Dicky thought of the old hag he'd snuffed not three blocks from here. Kind of a turn-on. He had a boner. Not a needle dick of a boner neither, like she said. She'd still be alive if she hadn't dissed his manhood.

The pot of gold. All his.

Word of the day: optimism.

Good morning to Randall Coll, home at his apartment. At daylight, Coll got up to urinate for the eleventh time. His GPS screen served as a night light. No movement whatsoever by the target. His sub-mental nephew was home at his trailer park, a good boy. Randall climbed back into bed, thinking that the only time the loser behaved was when he was asleep.

Good morning to Carla Chance, who was pulling out of the garage when Buster Hightower awakened with a start. He was dreaming that his feet had been amputated.

He had lost feeling to his feet because OC1 sat on one calf, OC2 on the other. They stared at him, as only cats can stare.

"Good morning, boys. I know what you're thinking. You can con me into believing your mama forgot to feed you, so I'll feed you again. Huh?

"No comment? Now tell me this. How the hell can I follow through on this con job of yours if my feet don't work?"

The cats stood, stretched, yawned and jumped off the bed.

"They understood every word I said. They understand every word either of us say when it pertains to food," Buster told the ceiling. "That is eerie."

Good morning to Judith Roswell, who awakened with a smile. She had been sleeping on her side. Orange and Vanilla were curled against her back. For a few foggy seconds before she was completely awake, she thought she felt Tip Taylor curled against her back.

It was a nice feeling.

Good morning to Tyler Polk Taylor III, who awakened with a

smile. He had dreamt that Judith Roswell wore *nothing* to bed. He awoke with an erection that bordered on painful. He wished he had researched what she wore and did not wear to bed. In person.

Good morning to Tyler Polk Taylor II, who was three time zones to the east, at Atlanta's Hartsfield-Jackson Airport, in the first-class line, having his ticket processed for a nonstop flight to Seattle.

God help him, he already missed Trixi, who dotted the "i" with a bubble.

Trixi, who snapped her gum and blew bubbles in bed.

Trixi and her freckles.

Good morning to Claire Esther Jamison Taylor, who had not awakened because she had not slept.

She was not grieving because of the absence and infidelity of her husband. The Atlanta private detective's report came as no great surprise. Tyler having a lover in the State of Georgia, far from Seattle, was no great surprise. That she was almost young enough to be their granddaughter was no stunner.

She had had the detective inform Tippy. She could not bear to do so herself, but as an adult, at least in years, he had a right to know what sort of man his estranged father was, if he did not already.

Claire Taylor had been awake all night planning her next step. Not whether she would divorce Tyler or not. That was a given.

Whom to retain for the sordid task, that was the question. As one of Seattle's most prominent law firms, Taylor and Taylor had made powerful enemies throughout the years, enemies that neither forgave nor forgot.

She would retain the barracuda with the longest memory and the biggest and sharpest teeth.

Would Tippy be at his mumsy's side?

Good morning to Harriet Hardin, who awakened, wiped drool from the side of her mouth, put in her dentures, and—

Bingo! It came to her. *The Three Musketeers!*

Leamy Smith and *Mutt Mullins.* Harriet had gotten the names backassward and wrong besides. She'd seen them singly and together with Harry, drinking beer, making goo-goo eyes at her and smirking.

No doubt Harry had told all. He was the type. A chippie chaser too, she believed. Cheating on Ella was as natural to him as breathing.

Harry Spicer calling the threesome the Three Musketeers—how could she have forgotten?

She wondered if that was important for any reason and how she could use it to her advantage.

CHAPTER 29

Tip drove to Judith Roswell's uninvited to check if she was A-OK. She was a client or a former client. The arrangement was nebulous and ethereal. And tingly whenever he thought of it and her.

Carrying a feather duster, Judith came to the door. She was wearing *the* ring and a pink T-shirt printed in large black letters: SYBFM.

"I should not barge in, but I wanted to check if you are safe and sound. A client follow-up to see if you have had unpleasant and unwanted visitors."

"I'm in the pink, pardon the pun. Come on in, Tip. I'm cleaning house and you're a perfect excuse to procrastinate."

She held the door for him, then grinned as he sidled past her. "You're curious about the T-shirt?"

He smiled. "Who, me?"

"You're looking at it."

And what was inside the T-shirt. "Yes. Mildly curious."

"When I said I was on a teaching sabbatical, that's not the truth. It was a white lie and then some. I'm on permanent sabbatical. If that isn't an oxymoron, I don't know what is."

"You resigned?"

"I was fired."

"Oh?"

"I know, I'm the quintessential old-maid schoolmarm."

"I do not see you in that regard. No I do not."

She liked the way he was looking at her, affirming his words. "Thank you, kind sir, but the kids did. The atmosphere in public schools is different than when I attended. I remember in the first grade a classmate who wouldn't keep his mouth shut, talking to his classmates, regardless what the teacher told him. She ran out of patience and taped the kid's mouth shut. That solved the problem.

"Try doing that today and you'd have lawyers and the board of education all over you and perhaps even the police for assault.

"In my last class, I had a major, major problem with a young man. He was a little sneak, a poor student who copied homework. He was suspected of selling drugs too. I don't know what compelled me to react as I did. I was fed up, burned out, sick of playing politics.

"I snapped. I marched up to him while he was chattering away to the student across from him and yelled—not said but yelled—'Shut your big effing mouth.' "

"Wow," Tip said. "Effing or the actual word?"

"The real McCoy, the F-bomb, a word I use three times per year or so and only when I'm absolutely at my wit's end. 'Shut your big effing mouth' spread throughout the school and beyond. This repressed old schoolmarm became a folk hero to some and the Great Satan to others. SYBFM T-shirts and bumper stickers appeared overnight.

"The notoriety didn't endear me to the school board. The brat's parents said their baby boy was traumatized by me and my foul mouth and was entering counseling. They said I was so loud I gave him tinnitus too. The parents sued the school district and that was the end of me."

"Next in the life of Judith Roswell?" Tip asked.

"That man you sent away outside yesterday, you know he was a bill collector," she said.

"I do."

"What did he tell you?"

"In excess of what I deem ethical."

She laughed. "Those people have ethics?"

"A point well taken."

"The collectors that've been hounding me have no ethics I'm aware of. The amount I owe, I'll concede that they do have an incentive. Did he tell you how much?"

"One hundred and eighty thousand dollars."

"That was yesterday," Judith said. "The interest accumulates."

Tip said nothing.

"I know what you're thinking."

"You probably do."

"The solution to my problem is in the basement."

"An accurate guess," Tip said. "How attached are you to that ring? If we can connect with a reputable jeweler, you will have a down payment. I will volunteer all the help you feel you wish and require."

"Thanks. That's sweet." She turned the ring on her finger. "I am attached to it. Don't ask me why."

A GOIPD graduate does not necessarily regard money as the root of all evil, regardless of its source. Nor does he or she allow it to blind him or her. Be flexible. Money doesn't grow on trees.

Tip gestured to the downstairs door. "Shall we?"

Judith looked at him, undecided.

"My recommendation is this. Organize the loot by type. Sort out what you require to reach debt breakeven, plus an additional amount to live on until you secure new employment. If you choose, we can disburse the remainder to worthy charities. This is your home, Judith. Your grandfather and his mysterious confederates may have been safecrackers and thieves, but the statute of limitations on their daring Pioneer Safe Deposit Vaults caper has surely tolled."

Nodding, Judith said, "I have rationalized and rationalized that it will benefit nobody else. The majority of the nineteen-fifty-four victims were compensated by insurance. Most are deceased anyway, almost seventy years later. If there are legal challenges by the descendants of the robbery victims and the insurance companies, the loot will sit in a property room till I'm eighty years old."

"Permit me to lead the way," Tip said, doing so.

Halfway down the steps, eyes adjusting to the dim light, Judith slipped on the edge of a tread. She caught herself with one hand on the railing, but fell forward. Agile and cautious on the old, ill-lighted stairs, Judith Ann Roswell would ask herself for years to come if this lapse was intentional or accidental.

Tip wheeled, set his rear foot, and caught her.

She released the railing and left her safety in his hands.

Because of the ensuing pawing and smooching, miraculously, neither party fell.

"Believe it or not," Judith said. "This is an all-time record for me, for shortest amount of time between 'how do you do' and where we are now."

Tip replied by kissing a breast. If he had said the same, she would indeed know he was lying, and their relationship would flame out before it began in earnest. No elements of a playboy lifestyle were omitted in his.

"How long has it been?"

Using her fingers to calculate, she said, "Three and a half days. I won't break it down any closer."

"It seemed like three and a half months to me."

"Mister, what are you doing?"

"A grand old bed," Tip said, sitting up.

"It's known by the shape of the footboard and headboard as

a sleigh bed. I'm told by Grandmother Ella that it was designed and built by my great-grandfather. Father of Harry Spicer, who slept in it when he wasn't sleeping downstairs with Harriet. Poor, naive Ella."

"Sleeping downstairs in the basement with Harriet, where we were headed before we headed each other off at the pass," Tip said.

Judith said, "The day isn't still young, but we can."

"After we shower," Tip said.

"Personal hygiene is important," Judith said, out of bed and into the bathroom.

He followed, saying, "Two people, one shower. In the interest of water conservation."

It was her idea, but he did the work, spray painting the basement windows so no light was visible outside. The threadbare curtains weren't doing the job and she had of cans of aerosol paint under the washroom sink.

Per Tip's suggestion, they spread the loot out on newspaper on the floor. Money. Stocks and bonds. Jewelry. Miscellanea such as lodge pins and class rings that were sentimental rather than intrinsically valuable.

Judith took photos. They looked over the array, shifted the loot around, and looked some more.

"Any ideas on how to go from here?" Judith said.

Tip said, "I believe the accurate term is laundering. How do we launder this for maximum value without risking arrest?"

"Very carefully," Judith said.

"I recommend a discreet and outside opinion," Tip said. "An advisor or panel of advisors."

"Buster and Carla," Judith said.

"They are splendid choices, but certainly not because they are to be part of or privy to a criminal hierarchy."

Judith ticked reasons off on her fingertips. "Because we can trust them. Because they have common sense. Because they are problem solvers. Because they've seen what's laid out on the floor."

"If Buster's not working this evening," she added.

The private eye flipped open his phone.

CHAPTER 30

Buster Hightower did have the night off at the Westside Bowling Lanes and Casino. Velma, the calypso accordionist, filled in when he did. She was a sweet lady with big graying hair. Velma favored pleated skirts, loose white blouses, and lipstick the color of his Caddy. The comic believed that Phil, the Westside manager, preferred Velma to him since he was sweet on her. Her rendition of "Lady of Spain" brought down the house, so he claimed. It happened that the tune was Phil's all-time favorite.

Buster feared not for his job. Velma cared for her ninety-something mom and couldn't be away from home that much anyhow.

Ace, Phil's third choice, wasn't available at all, nor would he be for a long time. Ace did card tricks and was currently in the hospital with multiple fractures. There'd been a skirmish during a high-stakes poker game—a fourth king had materialized out of thin air, so it was explained to the police—and Ace, the man with the phantom face card, had gotten the worst of the dispute.

Carla and Buster came promptly to Judith's, looked at the array, and looked some more.

"It's oodles and oodles more laid out like this," Carla said.

"We wished to spread it out, to better break it down and come up with ideas how to convert it into, shall we say, in its aggregate, a liquid asset," Tip said. "These assets positively belong to Judith. It does no one an iota of good sitting in a police property room for decades."

"Agreed," Carla said.

"Good old untraceable cash is the answer," Buster said, hinting. "It's as liquid an asset as an ice-cold beer."

"I have some in the refrigerator, Buster. But we're stumped how to make the conversion without attracting attention," Judith said, touching Tip's arm.

Startled, Carla looked at her. There was a glow in her eyes, a rosiness in her cheeks.

Oh dear! Matchmaker extraordinaire, she was seeing in Judith's body language and expression that they had moved beyond a chaste first date, skipping the preliminaries altogether. There was a fine line between playing Cupid and being a madam, and she had crossed it.

"We're talking money laundering here, not that I'm criticizing," Buster said. "Throwing dirty cash in the washing machine and having it coming out even dirtier. Ain't that one of them oxymoronics? I could do a set on that."

"Not now, Buster," Carla said.

The comic snapped his fingers. "Tip, you come from a rich family. Got any brothers or sisters who have big-time money connections?"

Carla said, "Is it wise to invite in others?"

Buster said, "No, really, I mean, are they collectors. You know, coins and artifactuals. Like this old money. They'd buy it at a discount and keep the deal private."

"Well, I do have an older sister. She married a remittance man and a drunk. Campbell travels extensively, often on her own. I should not say we are estranged, but we have not exchanged Christmas or birthday cards in years. I do not recall her collecting anything but lovers."

"Sounds like a fun gal, but not the answer to the dilemma," Buster said. "Your daddy's humongous law firm, it has to be crawling with lawyers, some of them inspirational to stale lawyer jokes. Can any of those boys help us out?"

"Buster," Carla said. "It's a firm with high-level corporate clients, not criminals."

"Carla," Tip said. "Trust me, Taylor and Taylor has attorneys who fit all stereotypes."

"You betcha. High-level corporation muckety-mucks. Criminals. Tell me the difference."

Judith and Tip laughed.

Carla rolled her eyes.

Buster said, "I rest my case."

Tip said that Buster had given him an idea. He cleared his throat, saying that residual spray-paint fumes made it difficult to speak. For that reason, he excused himself and went upstairs to make a telephone call that he said might lead to a solution. His difficulty was being overheard calling his mother "Mumsy."

At the head of the stairs, the door closed, he called her and said, "Mumsy, let me say how saddened I am for you hearing what you discovered regarding Father."

"I thank you for your Mr. Clounse. I had a right to know, to learn specifics regarding suspicions I held regarding him for ages. As our child, you have the right to know too, Tippy."

Her words were a bit slurred. Mumsy was no boozer, so a second mimosa would do that to her. "Are you all right, Mumsy?"

"Yes, I am, and since I have decided on a legal course of action, I am under control and centered."

"Oh?"

"Yes, Tippy. You would not be familiar with Attorney James Smith if you had met him yesterday. He appears as mundane-appearing as his name, a man who in actuality is a barracuda with razor-sharp teeth."

"The name is familiar."

"Coral snakes are innocuous-looking, Tippy. Another apt comparison to James."

"I am impressed," Tip said.

"There is an interesting story regarding Mr. James Smith. Five or six years ago, the firm promoted him to junior partner. James was not brilliant by any means, but an incredibly hard worker who let nothing stand in his way when he handled a case. He celebrated his promotion by inviting the senior partners and their families to a soiree at a lakefront estate he had rented for a weekend.

"Alcohol and good times flowed. James had an adolescent daughter, an attractive young lady replete with blue eyes, blonde hair, and freckles. She could be the farmer's daughter in those dreadful jokes.

"The fact pattern is unclear, but during the festivities she let out a blood-curling scream. Her mother ran from outside into her room and found her hysterical in her bathroom, a towel wrapped around her. Allegedly—that unlovely lawyer word—she was showering and had slid aside the shower curtain and there was your father, his pants unzipped, and he was, well, use your imagination."

"The tale was in a grapevine. I chose not to believe," Tip said.

"She claimed that she had been uncomfortable earlier because of the way he looked at her. Your father was long gone before the girl's mother came to her aid, so it was his word against hers. His red-faced outrage convinced me that she had prevaricated, that she was a sick little girl craving attention. That was the end of it, or so it seemed."

Tip filled her pause. "So it seemed? I did not hear that part."

"James Smith resigned from the firm the next working day and established his own practice shortly thereafter."

"Resigned as in forced to resign?"

"Akin to leaving a pistol with a single bullet in a capital prisoner's cell, I suspect. James is too much the gentleman to say so, to admit that he had been treated that shabbily, although in the professional sense he is not a gentleman. I say that in admiration and a degree of affection. Which brings me in my circumlocutory way of saying that I have retained him in the divorce action.

"His practice is eclectic and aggressive, Tippy. No grass grows beneath his wingtips. He has already sent workmen out to have our locks changed. When your father arrived at the house from Atlanta, I had thrown his clothes and toiletries out an upstairs window and told him to go back to his Trixi, preceding her name with a few choice adjectives. At a rare loss for words, he climbed back into his limo and departed for parts unknown."

"Trixi is her name?"

"According to your Atlanta detective, she dots the last 'i' with a bubble, one of the few words she can write."

Except for the suddenness of the events, Tip was not surprised either. Mumsy usually deliberated before acting. Her referring to their Lake Washington, eight-bedroom, seven-bath, complete-with-theater-and-swimming-pool mansion as a "house" always amused him.

"Does James Smith specialize in divorce?"

"No. Next time a bus passes by you, look at the side. It may be embellished with his one-eight-hundred-whiplash number. He advertises lavishly in the telephone directories, including those you see on a computer screen. James is versatile and talented and relentless. Real-estate law, criminal law, corporate law. His firm is large and staffed with specialists.

"And best of all, he loathes the air your father breathes. My settlement will be satisfactory, Tippy. Highly satisfactory."

"Another reason I called you, Mumsy, admittedly a priority,

is for an attorney recommendation for a situation I prefer not to be specific about. In general, the conversion of assets belonging to a client."

"Tippy, please tell me you are not mixed up in money shenanigans with those horrid South Americans! I feared for you so very much when you squandered the dregs of your trust in that Ferrari."

"Aston Martin. Have no fear, Mumsy. I may behave immaturely at times, but I am too prudent and law-abiding to be mixed up in an activity of that nature."

"That is the type of vehicle driven by the daredevil movie character, is it not?"

"Yes. Bond. James Bond."

"You are not living in a fantasy world, are you, Tippy, the private detection and a fascination with that outrageously sexist movie character?"

"Of course not, Mumsy!"

"Your Private Eye Yellow Pages advertisement."

"A business decision, Mumsy."

"You were and are a good boy, Tippy. I worried about you and girls too, how you attracted them. You and those you have dated, so many of the multitude were unsuitable."

"That was then, Mumsy. It is simply technical problems with the asset conversion that is stymieing us. Me."

"Please assure me that you and your confederates are not mixed up in shady business, Tippy?"

"If we are, Mumsy, we need an attorney who can assist in the conversion and make 'illegality' go away."

Claire Taylor sighed into the phone and said, "Just a moment. I will look up James's number. Trust your Mumsy, Tippy. James Smith is your man. I will contact him too and request that he handle your matter personally."

"Thank you, Mumsy."

"Before we say good night, your 'that was then' remark is intriguing. Is there something your mother should know?"

"I have met someone, Mumsy."

"Not among your customary debutantes, I trust?"

"Oh no."

"Those dreadful young ladies, all out for Taylor money. Lord help me, they have even taken to wearing tattoos and earrings in inappropriate places. Their parents must have been mortified at their debutante balls."

Thinking of the stunning ring that started this all, Tip said, "My friend, she is mature, Mumsy. She has no tattoos and her jewelry is conventional."

"Mature in years or in psychological maturity?"

"Yes."

"I shall sleep well tonight, Tippy, knowing that you are in good hands."

CHAPTER 31

Next morning, bright and early, at a quarter to ten, Dicky (Mad Dog) Coll unassed his bunk and dressed. Second (or third or fourth?) day in his skivvies, but no time for laundry, not with his agenda, "agenda" also being his word of the day.

At ten o'clock, doing as he was ordered, Vance Popkirk walked to the trailer and saw Dicky standing on the porch. He thought NOTED AUTHOR SWEPT INTO A HOOVERVILLE TIME WARP.

Last night, he'd okayed Poopkirk sleeping at a motel around the corner. The little pussy had been digging at his neck and armpits, saying he had an allergy to the interior of the trailer. Dicky, like Vinny, always thinking, had made Poopkirk leave everything he had in his pockets including ID and plastic, giving him cash to pay for the room, cash to the exact dollar.

Yesterday had been a bust, a big fucking zero. He'd checked in with Uncle Randall, leaving Poopkirk in the rental car as he was none of Uncle Randall's business.

All Dicky had to report is that the swell's sports car was parked at the old broad's haunted house for a long time, like it was gonna be permanent. What the hell were they doing in there, playing checkers? The guy was a twink. No way was he getting it on with Granny, who was a virgin anyways.

Uncle Randall wanted to know how come Taylor was there *for sure*, not a cockeyed theory, and Dicky said how the hell should he know. He didn't have X-ray vision. That pissed off

189

Uncle Randall like most everything he did, Uncle Randall who'd been giving him the stink eye the whole time. He asked where the pawned Datsun pickup was. Dicky said it was on the next block, parking being a bitch in that area of town.

Then Uncle Randall said to go back to the trailer park and sickle down the weeds, keep an eye on things, and get back to Judith Roswell's house by dark.

So that's what him and Poopkirk did. They headed back and Poopkirk knocked down the weeds while Dicky drank beer and listened to complaints from the trash that lived in the park. He asked them what the fuck they wanted, this ain't the Ritz. You got a leak in the roof of your trailer, that's what they make duct tape for. Rats? Hey, this here's a nature preserve and they're one of them protected species.

Something else he didn't get around telling Uncle Randall was that last night, the old red Caddy was parked there at Roswell's. If they were in the basement, they were fumbling around in the dark, as he didn't see any lights on.

Dicky hadn't the foggiest what to do next. He'd ask Poopkirk, who was walking back to him, drenched with sweat. He was a smart guy.

Harriet Hardin hadn't done a diddly except stew about Leamy Smith and Mutt Mullins, the two boneheads who made up Harry's Three Musketeers. She ate the meals that were brought to her room and walked to the liquor store for a bottle of cheap bourbon that she nursed while watching junk TV. She awakened from a boozy catnap, knowing her next step. She'd go on up to the big lady's insurance office if her Pinto could climb the hill. She'd give the insurance lady and her goofy boyfriend first shot at the straight scoop, see what they'd do with it. Like it or not, nobody was going to ace her out of what was hers.

★ ★ ★ ★ ★

As Claire Esther Jamison Taylor had implied, James Smith's features were so ordinary and bland that a person could not describe him five minutes after meeting him—late forties to early fifties, average height and weight, short sandy hair, pale roundish face. Completing the anonymity was his Nixon Administration blue suit, white shirt, and boring tie.

His name too, ironically, as common as the mysterious safe-cracking Smith buried somewhere in the *1954 Seattle City Directory*.

James Smith's law practice was not ordinary and bland. His office was so high in a downtown office tower that it had its own weather: fog at street level, blue skies outside his floor-to-ceiling windows.

Judith Roswell and Tip Taylor sat across a polished slab of a desk made from a single slice of ancient redwood.

Tip patted it and said, "James, this is the size of Rhode Island."

Smiling, Attorney James Smith scrolled through images of the loot on Judith's digital camera. They'd used hers because Tip had forgotten again to carry his.

Tip had said bluntly that they needed it laundered.

"We don't use the L-word, Tip," Smith had said. "We may be able to provide that service, but we term it 'asset transference.' "

"Then 'asset transference' it is," Tip said.

"Sweet," Smith said, looking up from the camera. "There was a news story four or five days ago. A charity received an anonymous gift of old cash, bonds and jewelry, which was strikingly similar to the same in these pics."

Judith and Tip replied with tight smiles.

"Mox nix and irrelevant," said James Smith. "Tip, I'm honored to have you and your mother as clients. That Claire is confident I have appropriate connections to perform this service is a compliment. Some attorneys might be insulted, but I'm long past making integrity judgments. It does take all kinds."

"We're pleased that you'll assist us," Judith said.

"Does it bother you, Tip, that I am representing her in what is certain to be a contentious divorce?"

"Not at all. Mum—my mother is entitled to whatever you can garner. To say my father and I are alienated is quite the understatement."

Smith rocked in his chair, his expression darkening. "Thankfully my daughter suffered no ill effects following her experience with him. There are rumors that she was not the first or the last inappropriately young lady he, well, never mind. It's irrelevant. My daughter is on the dean's list, bound for grad school. Majoring in physics, of all things. I have not lived with it as easily, nor has my wife. I'd be lying if I said there isn't personal satisfaction from my efforts in behalf of Claire."

Tip said, "Your anger is justified, James."

"The marriage dissolution is proving expensive to Mr. Taylor, and we are escalating," James Smith said.

"Thank you, James."

"You and Ms. Roswell do understand there will be surcharges and commissions, Tip? And that a time frame cannot be guaranteed?"

"We do," Judith said. "Can you give us an estimate?"

Smith continued rocking in his chair, contemplating the ceiling. "Off the top of my head, fifty percent."

"Ouch," Tip said.

"Very well. Forty percent. That's not unreasonable, guys. I'm not pro bono and there are layers of transactions and people, some of whom I will not permit in these offices."

Tip looked at Judith, who said, "Forty percent of something is preferable to a hundred percent of zero."

They sealed the deal with handshakes. At the door, James

Smith said, "Claire says you're driving a Lamborghini."

What hasn't Mumsy told him, Tip wondered?

"No. A DB9."

"I have an Aston Martin too. Just bought it, a 1965 DB5. Not the one in the Connery-Bond movie that was auctioned for millions, but virtually the same model, and not cheap either. It's my favorite ride, king of my seven-car garage. Tuning the three carburetors is a fun challenge."

"Have you mastered it?" Tip said, achingly envious.

"As soon as I think I have, not a hundred miles later, I read a wobble in the tach when doing above eighty-five. I find it relaxing, just me and my screwdrivers and the three twin-choke, side-draft carbs. For kicks, you can't beat the hum of the engine when you get it right," James Smith said. "Oh yes, and a glass of twenty-year-old port on the workbench."

In the elevator that they had to themselves, Tip Taylor bitterly wondered what he would be if he had not flunked out of Harvard Law School. In the elevator, Judith Roswell wondered if she had bought even more trouble.

Both wondered if and when they'd be caught kissing by the pinstripe set.

It happened at the thirty-first floor when they didn't break their clinch quickly enough.

CHAPTER 32

Harriet's Pinto cranked over a few times, wheezed, and *no mas.*

Cursing, too poor to own a cell phone, she went inside and called a cab from the senior apartments' office.

In the taxi, she shouted directions at the driver, not knowing how well he heard through that turban and all the grungy hair, telling him if he played dumb driving around in circles, he could shove what his meter read right up his ass.

Last Chance Insurance Agency was a funny name, she thought, like you insured yourself against the end of the world. When they arrived at the strip mall, Harriet saw Carla Chance had a funny mix of neighbors too. She figured the payday loan did the biggest business.

Harriet paid the cabbie to the penny, daring him to ask for a tip. If he wanted a tip, she'd give him one, some free advice. Take a shower.

He didn't, wiping his forehead in relief when she was out of his battered Crown Vic.

Harriet walked in and heard computer typing in a side office. There was a framed Yellow Pages ad on the wall: LAST CHANCE INSURANCE AGENCY. TICKETS? ACCIDENTS? DUI? NO PRIOR OR CANCELLED INSURANCE? SUSPENDED LICENSE? NO PROBLEM!

If I had a reliable car and money, this would be my kind of place to get covered, she thought. Harriet had fond memories of the Pinto in its younger days and its role in trying to running down a drunken ex. He'd slapped her hard enough to knock her over an easy chair when all she'd done was ask him for the fifth time that day when the hell he was gonna get off his dead ass drinking beer and watching TV all day, and find a job.

She smashed a dinner plate over the bum's head, grabbed the keys to the Pinto, ran to the driveway, and had it started when he charged out and pounded on the hood, calling her everything but a fairy princess.

Harriet hit the gas, goosing it, but he jumped out of the way. She smashed through the garage door. In reverse, she chased him across the yard, missing him again, and came within inches of T-boning a neighbor's car.

Okay, she'd had a few drinks, she told the cop the neighbor called. Harriet and her darling hubby were on private property (belonging to the landlords who evicted them the next day), so they couldn't haul her in for drunken driving. The insurance company paid to have the Pinto repaired. They did not take kindly to the facts of the incident and terminated her coverage. Luckily, uninsured Harriet hadn't had an accident since.

Carla Chance came out and said, "May I help—oh?"

"For real, you can insure anybody?"

What was this woman doing here? "Almost anyone."

"Didn't take me serious when I said we were gonna be partners, did you?"

Judith had phoned half an hour earlier, informing Carla of their agreement with Attorney James Smith. There was anxiety in her voice, as well as relief. This wild and aged woman was an unneeded complication.

"There is no partnership, dear. Don't delude yourself."

Harriet sat on an edge of the front desk. "Don't get all fancy-pants on me, hon. Maybe you got your paws on the burglary loot, but a lightbulb came on. Leamy Mullins?"

"Yes. The mysterious Mr. Mullins."

"There was a third player. Him and Harry and Leamy, I saw them together. When Harry wasn't in my britches, he'd actually talk to me now and again, or let me listen when he wasn't. He said they were the Three Musketeers. These boys, they weren't swinging swords, they were carrying acetylene torches and drills. You can count on it. After the Pioneer Safe Deposit Vaults safe-cracking job, I never saw two of the Musketeers again and or heard Harry speak of them."

"Interesting," Carla said, wondering if this was a ploy.

"More than interesting, honey. This second mystery man, no telling if he's dead or alive. If he ain't six feet under, he'll be liking to share the wealth. Now, you get boy stud on the horn and have him bring his hot body on over and we'll see what we'll see. You don't, I'm blowing the whistle. Partner."

"The gang's all here," Buster said as he walked into Last Chance.

" 'Gang' may be apropos, Buster," Judith said.

With her at his side, Tip plugged "Mutt Smith" and "Leamy Mullins" into every search engine at his disposal and came up dry.

"Are you absolutely sure of the names, Harriet?" Carla said.

Harriet's eyes were on her cutie pie and the old maid schoolteacher seated next to him. Her hand was on his thigh. Sure enough, they were playing hide the salami. She'd been aced out by an old prune of a schoolmarm who might've been a virgin. Not even in her mid-seventies yet and she was losing her touch.

Green with jealousy, she said, "It's been a year or three, but nightmares you don't forget."

Buster said, "Yeah, but could a letter or two or a name be switcherooed, like what goes on in the heads of folks who're perplexic?"

"Perplexic?" Tip said.

"Yeah. When you got perplexia."

"I'll translate," Carla said, squeezing her man's arm. "He means dyslexia. Harriet, no offense intended, so many years have gone by."

"Maybe I really do have the right names, maybe I don't. Maybe I'm playing games. I want partnership papers drawn up and I'll tell you," Harriet said, initiating her impromptu plan.

Carla said, "Tip, why don't you jumble the names and letters and see if anything happens. Buster has clairvoyant hunches that pay off. Don't ask me how."

The GOIPD graduate can often derive vital mystery clues from client hunches. Don't categorically dismiss them. Conversely, don't look a gift horse in the mouth.

Things did happen. In short order, Harriet's scheme collapsed, victim of a comedian who wasn't funny to her at the moment.

Tip Taylor read obituaries in local newspaper archives for Leamy Smith (1927–1954) and J.R. (Mutt) Mullins (1926–1954).

Mutt Mullins's body was found in a twenty-nine-cent-per-night flophouse room in Seattle's skid row, dead of a presumed overdose, a needle in his arm. His priors included drunk in public, home burglary, and possession of illegal drugs. No family was listed.

Leamy Smith was the loser in a jailhouse skirmish in Seattle's King County jail, victim of a shiv/shank slash to the carotid artery. None of the seven other prisoners in the holding tank saw a thing. A hothead, Smith had been arrested earlier that evening for instigating a fight in a tavern, doing considerable damage to persons and property. His rap sheet was longer than Mutt Mullins's: fighting, vandalism, attempted robbery of a grocer, car theft. From age sixteen on, he'd spent more time behind bars than not. A big, powerful man, when he held a job, he worked as a common laborer and hod carrier.

"Mullins was our singer, huh?" Buster said. "No cabaret gigs on his résumé."

Harriet pointed a witch's crooked finger and jabbed it back and forth. "That means my Harry Spicer kept the loot. Every penny of it. He died that year. That means it's in that house."

"You shouldn't make assumptions, dear," Carla said.

"You motherfuckers gave away my ruby necklace," Harriet screeched. "I want what's rightfully mine!"

"I am going in the bathroom for a bar of soap to use on that mouth of yours," Carla said, glaring at Harriet.

"I dare you. I double dare you!"

Carla stood up.

Harriet shut up.

Judith's cell phone rang.

"Yes. Yes. Yes. Yes! I'll be there right away."

Hands trembling, Judith closed the phone.

Her eyes glossy with tears, she said, "My uncle James. He's in the hospital. He's had a stroke. They don't think he's going to make it."

CHAPTER 33

At the freeway entrance, Tip accelerated hard onto Interstate Five, going through the gears fast, his right hand and clutch foot a blur. The speed limit was sixty, but there was no fine print restricting the length of time used to reach said limit.

"Zero to sixty in an eyeblink," he said, thinking *Bond . . . James Bond.*

"I'm not complaining, but I think you gave me whiplash."

"Speaking of which, your 'uncle' James was quick thinking, exceedingly clever."

The GOIPD graduate operates on his or her feet. This cannot be taught. The technique evolves in practical situations for yourself and your clients. Think outside of the box.

"The call was from James Smith, saying that his man would be by to pick up the loot in ninety minutes, and that ninety minutes meant ninety minutes," Judith said, nestled in the Aston Martin's buttery-soft leather. She had asked him to hurry to her house.

"Do we have plus or minus ninety seconds?" Tip said.

"I don't think so."

"I have always wondered how actors are taught to cry on demand," Tip said. "Is it by use of a cattle prod?"

"I minored in drama in college," Judith said. "You're taught to think of a horrible experience. When I was eight, a dog chased me while I was riding my bike and knocked me over. I had four stitches."

"I did not notice the scar."

"I didn't mention it."

"May I hunt for it tonight? Methodically."

"To your heart's content, sir. Please be thorough."

Dicky Coll had said they had to have what you call your window of opportunity to enter the Roswell house, "And do an inside and out and forward and backwards search."

Vance Popkirk said, "The house is old and large. It'd take so long, we could be arrested."

"Stop your goddamn whining before you give me a headache," Mad Dog said. "I can break into Fort Fucking Knox. All I need is fifteen minutes to tear the place apart. It ain't like we have a search warrant and gotta leave the place tidy."

Mad Dog had chased the rich boy's sports car to the big lady's insurance agency. Just before he was gonna boogie to the haunted house, it was hauling ass, going back the way it came. Driving Poopkirk's rental car, showing it no mercy, the renter a terrified passenger, his plan was in the toilet.

Could I, for once in my miserable life, catch a break? he asked himself.

A chaplain in Walla Walla preached a goddamn Sunday School God, a big bearded pissed-off dude in a robe, holding lightning bolts. Dicky tried praying to him for a while, like a week or two, but his bad luck didn't change, so fuck it.

Behind the wheel, doing eighty-five and ninety, he tried praying again for a minute or two. Nothing good happened, so the hell with it and Him.

A break. One measly break. Was that asking too much?

Eighty-nine-plus minutes after Judith's call from Attorney James Smith, there was a knock on her door.

She answered to a stocky man dressed in slacks and pullover, in the confectionary colors of a professional golfer, though she couldn't picture him on the links. He wore dark glasses and was as nondescript as James Smith, with the exception of a snake tattoo curling around a wrist and a knife scar on a cheek.

Without a word, he handed Judith Smith's business card. The card was proof who he was and their receipt.

She turned and nodded to Tip.

He passed her a heavy plastic trash bag. In it were manila envelopes filled with valuables, segregated as they had placed them on the basement floor.

Without a word, the man went to a large white SUV and drove off.

Idling at the corner, Mad Dog observed all.

Little did Mad Dog know that the loot had been in the basement laid out on the basement floor, his for the taking. He did guess that the bag contained the loot. Maybe contained it. Some or all.

What he knew for sure was that he'd recognized the guy who came to the door.

"He ain't no garbage collector, Poopkirk."

Vance Popkirk had no further thoughts of *Dead Man's Booty* and *Gone with the Wind: The Holy Bible*. Survival superseded art. "No, I think not."

"Know how I know for sure?"

Vance Popkirk only knew that he didn't want to know. "I do not."

"I recognize him from Walla Walla."

Inside Dicky's head, Vinny ordered him to *follow that car.*

"Hang on, Poopkirk. We're going for a ride."

Suspicious of the lack of GPS activity in the Datsun pickup, Randall Coll closed Coll's Jewelry and Loan: (A Family Business).

He couldn't afford to and he couldn't afford not to.

Coll drove to the trailer park. The truck was there.

The weeds too. Part had been chopped, a sloppy job. The others weren't as high as an elephant's eye, but they were getting there.

Coll pounded on the door and waited.

Then he fished out his key to the trailer, but he didn't need it. The moron had left the door unlocked.

Coll was in and out, slamming the door. It smelled to high heaven.

Where was the simpleminded bastard, how was he getting around, and what was he up to?

CHAPTER 34

Dicky Coll and Vance Popkirk kept the white SUV in sight all the way into downtown Seattle and into a parking garage. They'd played it cool, staying two or three cars back.

"Him in a fancy skyscraper, if it's the same guy, it don't fit, Poopkirk. We're talking serious white trash," he said, taking a ticket as the arm came up.

He gave it to Popkirk. "You keep it. You're paying the arm and a leg they'll charge."

"You have my cash," Popkirk said meekly.

Mad Dog looked at him. "All the plastic you're carrying, so don't give me no lip and don't be trying to confuse me. Your money's coming outta my pocket is what I mean."

No lip, indeed. His captor was living, breathing nitroglycerine.

Circling the ramp, one floor behind the SUV, Dicky Coll said, "Me saying I'd recognized the driver from Walla Walla? Know what's there at Walla Walla?"

"Yes, I believe so. Walla Walla is a southeastern Washington town known as a destination for wine connoisseurs. There are numerous appellations and vineyards and wineries in the region. Are you a wine lover?"

"You and your wine and your Walla Walla and your Appalachians." Coll's laughter released caustic breath and a condensed tale of *his* Walla Walla, how he'd done eleven years for a bum rap, on account of some geezer's bum ticker. How him and Vinny, they could never catch a break.

"He shouldn't of been out on the street, a footstep and heartbeat from dropping dead. Right, Poopkirk?"

Pressed against his door, Popkirk gulped. "Yes, right. How unjust."

"Okay, see, he's unassing his rig. Get on him, see where he's headed."

"Me?"

"I told you I seen him in the yard at the pen. Maybe he seen me too. Don't know him personal or why he was doing time. Don't wanna know. Scoot, boy. Haul ass!"

Vance Popkirk scooted. He hauled ass. He stepped onto an elevator immediately after their subject. Careful to stare blankly at the wall, he rode to an upper floor, where the man got off.

Popkirk rode to the next floor up, got off, and took the stairs down to the subject's floor, his timing perfect to see the man go from the reception area of a suite to an inner office of a law firm, carrying the trash bag. The law firm occupied the entire floor.

Popkirk rode down an elevator, pondering Judith Roswell and her connection to James Smith, Attorney-at-law LLC, a large and powerful law firm. He'd tell the awaiting beast that the man with the garbage bag had gotten off on a floor of law offices.

Which law office, he didn't know. There were three or four on that floor. A lie he hoped he could pull off.

On his redwood slab of a desk, James Smith emptied the manila envelopes. He examined each and said, "Impressive. Were you followed?"

"Yeah," said the man with the dark shades. "Two clowns, all the way from Roswell's. A nervous little guy who could use a shave and change of clothes, he got out their car downstairs in the garage and went with me into the elevator, his eyes on everyone and everything else. He was so obvious, a blind man coulda picked up the tail. He stayed on the elevator. I waited out front till he came down the stairs, making sure he saw where I went. Like you said to do if I was tailed. The other, I recognized from Walla Walla. A nutcase who thought he was related to a gangster from the old days."

"Good," said Attorney James Smith. "You earned your ten free billing hours while I work on your appeal."

"Eureka. I found it," said Tyler Polk (Tip) Taylor III, as he gently ran a finger back and forth on the small scar on the outside of her right thigh.

Unable to contain his curiosity until nighttime, they were taking an afternoon nap in the interest of dermatological research.

"Kiss it and make it well," Judith commanded.

Tip complied.

CHAPTER 35

"Folks ask me, hey, where do you get your material?" Buster Hightower said.

Having seen a screw on the floor in front of him, the comic was extra careful to keep his balance on the rickety platform between the dartboard and cigarette machine. He swept an arm. "It's all around us, here, there and everywhere. I read the paper every single day. The *Seattle Times* is a great newspaper. They print all the news that's fit to print and all the news that ain't.

"A while back, there was an article about this rancid putz who broke into a house and stole whatever he stole, but lost his sunglasses there. Later on, he rings the doorbell and demands his glasses back. The cops are on their way on account of the homeowner's nine-one-one call and haul him off to a place where you don't need shades."

Buster surveyed his audience in the cocktail lounge of the Westside Bowling Lanes and Casino. Seventeen plus Carla, Tip and Judith, who'd confessed her Uncle James lie, so nobody worried.

Not a bad crowd and most were smiling.

"See, what'd I tell you? If that ain't funny, I don't know what is. Here's another one that maybe ain't as funny, but as weird as they come.

"In Brazil, these guys greased railroad tracks out in the boonies. The train they were targeting lost traction on the grease and

206

spun its wheels, slowing way down. The crooks unhooked the containers they wanted, loaded them on tow trucks, and were taillights down the road. Know what they made off with? Fifty-five tons of corn. No lie. They did.

"So what the hell do you do with all that corn? Damned if I know. If I was the law, I'd be staking out Saturday farmers' markets. Brazilian crooks are smarter than the high percentage and majority of ours, like the master criminals who write 'this is a stickup' on the back of their own deposit slips. If they're gonna do that, shouldn't they be writing their notes on the back of their own withdrawal slips?

"I get material to bore you with from junk mail too. There's gold nuggets in that crud and no shortage of it to sort through. Like this catalog I got the other day. It's products for old people. How the hell they know I'm deep in the heart of geezerdom is beyond me. Big brother, maybe.

Buster took torn-out pages from his pants pockets. "This here is a dandy. A magic potion for your vertigo. Dab a little behind each ear like perfume and you won't fall on your keester like I do all the time and am about to do again. Guaranteed or your money back if you survive.

"On this page, shoe shims if one leg's taller than the other. How does that happen? And soaps and creams to restore your skin's youthful moisture, which I never had to begin with.

"On this page, all manner of sunglasses that'll protect your delicate eyes even in the dark. Could be one of these pairs is what our dummy of a crook lost during his burglarization of that house. You'd have to go to his trial to find out as the law's holding them as evidence.

"Umpteen weight loss pills and umpteen diet books that show you how to lose weight without having to take them pills. You buy out the catalogs, you'll live to be a hundred, which you gotta do to have time to pay it off."

Buster swigged his beer as his audience laughed and applauded.

"Okay, any of you who's had the unpleasure of seeing me before has probably heard me rave and rant about retirement planning seminars. How many out there have got dinner invites from them?"

Over half raised their hands.

"We're talking the mother of all junk mail. You call the number on the invitation and reserve a spot. They feed you your choice of chicken and fish, then bolt the doors shut. Your money or your life. Let them make you rich while they're making themselves rich or you don't escape with your hide intact and in one piece."

Laughter and knowing groans.

"Hey, I'm gonna tip you how to get rich. You're hearing it here first."

"How many out there been to a mall in the last thirty days?"

Every hand went up.

"How many of you folks got tattoos done on your bods?"

Ten arms went up.

"There're franchises and chain stores for damn near everything, right? Everything from soup to nuts. And the malls are clogged with these brand-name places to spend your hard-earned money. So why not a chain of tattoo parlors? Could be they got 'em elsewheres, but I haven't seen any in this area. It's virginal territory."

Laughter, plus two couples looking at each other with "hmmm" on their faces.

"Call it Needles Are Us or Tattoo Barn.

"That's it for silliness, boys and girls. Pumpkin time for yours truly, so that means one or three stale lawyer jokes."

Bottoms up for Buster until the booing subsided.

"What's black and brown, and looks good on a lawyer?"

Silence.

"A Doberman pinscher."

Whistles and chuckles.

"Two-part question. Do you know how to save a drowning lawyer? Answer, take your foot off his head. The other part of the question, you gotta guess. How do you save a drowning lawyer?

"No? Stumped? Take your other foot off his head."

"Last one. I promise. What's the difference between a lawyer and a bucket of pond scum?"

A drunk in a corner yelled, "The bucket."

"Give that man the door prize," Buster said.

"What's the prize?" the drunk asked.

"You think I'm gonna say a door, right? C'mon, that's the stalest gag in the whole entire world."

Everybody waited.

"The door," Buster said. "See you next time. I hope."

Simultaneously, as Buster Hightower ended his set by poking fun at lawyers, Dicky Coll was not poking fun at lawyers. He raged about them to Vance Popkirk at a tavern two blocks from the trailer park.

It was easy walking distance, but Mad Dog had ordered Poopkirk to drive them in the Datsun pickup, his philosophy being that there was no use wearing out your shoe leather when you can ride on someone else's tire rubber.

He raged about Randall Coll, Uncle Randall who didn't visit him a single, solitary time in the eleven years he was in the joint, how he was treating him like shit on the outside, bossing him around like he was a retard, a Mongolian idiot, and making him drive beater cars while Dicky was working his ass off for him at the trailer park for peanuts.

Dicky raged about shyster lawyers, how he couldn't afford to hire one and the loser of a court-appointed lawyer wouldn't defend him eleven years ago. Plead guilty, he said. Bull-shit.

"I shoulda known that the swag from that safecracking job in the olden days wound up in the hands of greedy shysters in that swank office building, Poopkirk. The motherfuckers got more money than God and they got their hands on mine," Mad Dog said, not for the first time after taking a long pull on a beer that was not his first.

On the barstool beside him, Vance Popkirk sat rigidly, nursing the schooner of draft beer his captor had ordered for him. He initially asked for a glass of Perrier with a twist of lemon and received a blank look from the bartender and an elbow from Coll that may have cracked a rib.

"You trying to get us both killed with your faggot drink, them in here thinking we're queers?" Coll had asked him.

If I had an ounce of common sense, Popkirk thought, I'd go to the restroom, call the police, and be free of this cretin. But he'd blow career possibilities out of the water. If he stayed patient and overcame obstacles, he'd obtain access to Roswell for *Dead Man's Booty*. These misadventures could be secondary story lines for *Gone with the Wind: The Holy Bible*. He'd stick it out.

"If they'd give me a decent shyster or if I'd had the dough to hire me one, I wouldn't of got eleven years for an accident. My girlfriend, the cooz, not only didn't she pitch in and help pay for my defense, she dumped me. I got twenty-three dollars and fourteen cents off that old boy, so I shoulda took the fall for petty larceny. Toss in assault as I had my hands on him, fine. I'd of been sent up for two years max.

"Just goes to show that lawyers got their hands on my loot, Poopkirk. I wish you'd saw what lawyer office that ex-con went into with the goodies. If I knew which shyster he was handing it to, I'd be all over him like a bad smell," Coll said, thumping his chest. "Nobody fucks with Vinny Coll. Just ask Gerald Roswell."

A bad smell, Popkirk thought; how appropriate.

And *Vinny*. God help me, Vance Popkirk silently beseeched the flyspecked ceiling. The lout thinks he *is* the 1930s homicidal gangster. And, Lord, please advise me what I am going to do with my knowledge of Attorney James Smith?

And who is (or was) Gerald Roswell? Presumably a relative of Judith Roswell.

Roswell, New Mexico, such a promising commonality, seemed now a sick joke.

The warpage of his predicament: PARALLEL UNIVERSES COLLIDE. CUBS WIN WORLD SERIES.

Randall Coll had seen infinitesimal movement in the GPS in the Datsun pickup's toolbox. He'd driven out to Kent to find it in the lot of a neighborhood tavern within sight of the trailer park.

He parked in a strip mall lot across the street and watched his numbskull nephew perched on a barstool, talking the ear off a guy who looked like he had no business in a beer parlor, a fern bar being right up his alley. The guy who maybe drove the new rental car parked at the trailer.

Randall pulled away. First thing in the morning, he'd call his DMV acquaintance and have him run the license number.

By some miracle, Harriet Hardin's Ford Pinto started. She put it in gear, but the miracle ended with a mechanical shudder and moan. She caught a bus into downtown Seattle, a taxi to Capitol Hill and the treasure house, where nobody was home except the goddamn cats. They'd dumped her at home again when the party at the weirdo insurance agency broke up, brushing her off. She was getting damn sick of that and thought she'd finally gotten lucky by making her own luck.

She let herself in with the last door that would work with her skeleton key and saw that she had no luck. In the basement of Judith Roswell's house, Harriet Hardin sat cross-legged in the basement where her room was sixty-odd years ago. To the best of her recollection, she sat at the same spot her butt was when—so long ago—she was laying in bed. The same spot where Harry would yank her panties off if she didn't get them off quick enough herself to suit him.

She stared and stared at the fake brick front on the floor and the metal box built in the wall.

Empty metal box.

Empty metal box that had her loot.

Empty metal box that had her ruby necklace.

No luck with money; the cupboard was bare.

No luck with love; the schoolteacher virgin had hot pants after all, acing her out for Cutie Pie.

Numbly, Harriet curled up in the fetal position like she had when Harry was done with her and tippy-toed upstairs to Ella. She thought of the kids she didn't have, thanks to a coat-hanger abortion arranged by Harry. She wouldn't've been mom of the year, but the bastard shouldn't've robbed her of the chance to try.

Harriet was facing the stack of milk crates. When she was a kid, like she told the dildo who tried to kill her, milk was delivered in glass bottles, unhomogenized. If you didn't get it inside fast enough, cats would dig out the cardboard caps and lick the cream. Cats ran loose in the neighborhood, so Ella ran out as soon as she heard the milkman coming.

Poor clueless Ella. Like herself, a nice, sweet lady who didn't deserve a Harry Spicer.

CHAPTER 36

"Are you going to show me your etchings?" Judith asked Tip.

"I am. Every last etching I do not have, for as long as it takes."

"Art appreciation and culture. It sounds very educational."

He kissed her in the car and said, "We shall make up the academic rules as we go."

In the basement garage of his Tacoma apartment, Tip opened the Aston Martin's passenger door for Judith. She had topped off Orange and Vanilla's food and water bowls, and packed a small bag. They'd come directly from Buster's show at the Westside.

Tip entered first and tensed. He smelled expensive cologne. He flicked on the lights.

Seated in a leather easy chair, a patrician man with excellent posture held a small glass of eighteen-year-old single-malt Scotch, neat. Though dressed in frightfully expensive clothing that defied wrinkles, the man's garb was nonetheless wrinkled. Although clearly lean and fit, a continuation of his days rowing on the Harvard crew, he appeared slouched and beaten, with a two-or-three-day growth of beard. Tip had never seen him like this.

"Father."

"Tyler. My apologies for the intrusion. Your friend and neighbor on this floor was taking out his garbage when I happened by. He has a key and was kind enough to let me in."

Judith looked around Tip and gasped. The visitor was Tip's identical twin, separated by twenty-five years.

"You are always welcome, Father," Tip said evenly.

"Forgive me for sitting in the dark. I wanted to avoid any opportunity to see my reflection." Tyler Polk Taylor II stood unsteadily and said, "And you are who, Miss . . . ?"

Tip introduced Judith to his father, who said, "My pleasure, Miss Roswell. Tyler, you are wondering why I uncouthly barged in on you, in light of our differences."

Standing rigidly, Tip said, "I am listening."

Tyler II did not speak. He looked at a wall and Tyler III's framed Gumshoe Online Institute of Private Detection diploma. A gold seal designated Tyler Polk Taylor III as an honor graduate. It was a perusal intended to be insulting.

Without comment on the pitiful achievement, he said, "You are aware that your mother and I are experiencing marital difficulties?"

A GOIPD graduate answers when opportunity knocks, when he is able to reverse roles, particularly when he has home-turf advantage in a given situation. He turns the tables. He seizes the moment.

"She keeps me apprised," Tip said. "As a matter of fact, she consulted me for a recommendation of a private investigator in the Atlanta region. Think what you may of my new profession, my fledgling career, the best of us deliver our client's money's worth. Her Atlanta detective surely did. Case in point, Trixi, a young lady, a very young lady, who dots the second 'i' with a bubble."

Shocked that his wastrel son and namesake's jutting jaw was displaying fangs, Tyler II said with the unflappable calm of a highest-level corporate attorney who discussed millions as if gratuity change left at a coffee shop. "Do tell? So you say. An alleged Trixi."

"Father, please do not insult me by scattering 'allegeds' on

214

the floor between us, denying the facts."

"Did this so-called investigator participate in your mother's choice of a divorce attorney?"

Tyler III shook his head. "She decided that completely on her own. I presume that you do not approve of her choice of James Smith."

Tyler II sipped his Scotch and looked out at the view, seeing but not seeing the downtown lights. This is not what he dreamed of for the boy. He had envisioned Harvard Law with honors, then III joining the firm, which ultimately would become Taylor, Taylor and Taylor. Upon which his son would sire an appropriate male heir from suitable stock, to subsequently become a partner in Taylor, Taylor, Taylor and Taylor.

This woman with his son, this older woman, struck him as pleasant enough and certainly devoted, but not breeding material even if menopause were not looming. Tip would never develop circumspection, he feared. Romantically or vocationally.

While Tyler II collected his thoughts, lost in said thoughts, as Tip remembered him being so frequently at home, to the chagrin of Mumsy, Tip took Judith's hand and led her into kitchen, set two wine glasses on the island, and poured Malbec into them.

His father entered the kitchen and said, "This James Smith, this ambulance chaser of hers, was formerly with the firm, you know."

"Mumsy told me the entire story, Father. There had been jungle drums."

Mumsy? Judith almost choked on her wine.

"Doubtlessly her slanderous version. The alleged bathroom encounter with the young lady and Smith's dismissal."

Tip raised his free hand. "What is done is done."

His father raised his voice. "Not in every context is it done.

That shyster, that pettifogger, that jackleg, he managed to have my assets frozen at blitzkrieg speed! Your mother threw my belongings out a window as if they were rubbish. That is why I stand before you in the visage of a street tramp."

"We all have our ups and downs, Father."

"Spare me the banalities, Tyler. Frankly, I came here because I have limited funds at my disposal and nowhere else to go. You are thinking Atlanta? Yes, I could scrape up the cost of a coach ticket, but once Trixi's family discovered I was destitute, they would treat me like roadkill. Besides, have you an inkling how miniscule legroom is in coach?

"And the firm . . . *my* firm? I have taken a leave of absence. My subordinates would willingly pass the hat, but I could not endure the pity, the ridicule behind my back.

"Again, Tyler, our differences. You are within your rights to throw me out. I can hail a cab to transport me to a fleabag."

"Father, please, you can stay in the guest room for as long as you like."

Father thanked son with a friendly nod. And so it was. Face saved, Tyler II reclaimed his chair, his single malt, and stared into a region of the universe known only to him.

Later, as Judith and Tip frustratingly snuggled in bed, he said, "Your place or mine is perhaps no longer an operative question."

She replied by kissing his cheek. "At a swanky place like this, wall insulation should be good."

Vance Popkirk thanked his lucky stars that Dicky Coll—or Vinny? (Popkirk was confused now too)—had a limit. Fifteen beers, eighteen? In spite of paying for them, he'd lost count. With help from the bartender, who said "good riddance," they loaded a newly unconscious Mad Dog into the Datsun pickup.

At Coll's trailer, Popkirk liberated from his comatose form

and the trailer the personal property Coll had removed from him, most critically his wallet. He then let the air out of all four of the creature's tires. The hissing of air and settling of the vehicle did not awaken Coll.

Popkirk drove the rental car to his motel, at which he hadn't even unpacked. He hurriedly collected his belongings and drove into Seattle. He selected the first hotel he saw with an underground garage, parked and took a room.

Exhausted, he crashed on the bed, not even bothering to get out of his clothes. In the morning, he thought before falling asleep, he'd pay a visit on Attorney James Smith, a man who may be persuaded to invest in an innovative reality TV show. And for a percentage of royalties stake him to living expenses while he wrote The Great American Novel.

In bed, unable to sleep, Carla asked, "Do you think it'll be over for Judith, Buster? The stress and the unsavory people that her discovery brought on?"

Also unable to sleep, he said, "I hope it ain't the beginning of anything else, toots. You know, the cash that lawyer's gonna get for her from the take-out laundry."

"What do we do?"

"Whatever we gotta do that they ask us to do . . . that we're able to do, even if we ain't able to do it."

"I'm sorry I asked, Buster," Carla said. "You're making the ceiling spin."

CHAPTER 37

Next day, cup of morning coffee in hand, Randall Coll phoned his DMV acquaintance and occasional drinking companion.

"Aren't we even yet?" the man whined.

"I'll tell you when we are."

The DMV man informed him that the car at the trailer was registered to an airport-area rental agency. Coll hung up on him without a word, phoned the agency, saying that he was worried about his cousin, who had called him after picking up the car but hadn't showed up at his house yet. "My cousin's old and can't face the reality that he's beginning to have bouts of early dementia."

The clerk told Coll how sorry he was and gave him Vance Popkirk's name and an East Coast address, and the name of an airport-area motel.

"If you find the car and your cousin, we'll send someone to pick up the car. Just say the word."

Coll hung up on him without a word, phoned the hotel, and was informed that Mr. Popkirk checked out late last night, forwarding address given, but permission denied to divulge it. Coll gave the clerk his dementia pitch, to no avail. Coll hung up, his hemorrhoids throbbing and his headache in full bloom.

Who was Mr. Vance Popkirk, where was he now, and who was he to Randall's shit-for-brains nephew?

His phone rang.

"Uncle Randall?"

"Who else? What's up?"

"In the middle of the night, it must of been, some vandals, kids you gotta figure, you know, kids who were brung up wrong, juvenile delinquents, you know, they let the air out of the tires of this cheap Jap pickup truck of yours, or they flattened them while they was stealing it."

"Where is it, at the trailer? Please tell me that it is."

"Sort of."

Sort of. "Stay on the phone. I'll be right back."

Randall Coll went to the medicine cabinet, shook two aspirin out of the bottle, and returned, chewing them. "Talk to me."

"Well, they must of drove off down the road when they let the air out of the tires, and the tires came plumb off the wheels, and they abandoned it there in the street."

"Why would your juvenile delinquents let the air out of the tires and steal it?"

"There's no accounting for kids these days, Uncle Randall. They're dumb shits."

"They left the truck where?"

Dicky was speaking from a rear corner of the trailer, out of sight of anyone on the street or sidewalk, knowing he couldn't tell the truth, even half the truth, how he'd woke up half an hour ago in the truck and saw Poopkirk's rental car was gone. Brutally pissed, he lost his cool, and headed north, bound for the haunted house, goosing the old pickup, figuring to find the little bastard there, going for the loot his own self. Until he was on the street, hearing and feeling the *thumpety-thump-thump*.

"They're hitching it up to a tow truck. Could you come on down and get me?"

"Don't go away," Randall Coll said, slamming down the receiver.

★ ★ ★ ★ ★

"Just push the number 'four' on the face of the microwave, Father. No, there, on the keypad. That signifies four minutes cooking time at maximum wattage," Tip said. "Your meal should be done. No, remove it from the carton first and pierce the plastic. Otherwise, steam buildup may cause an explosion."

"I know, in theory, how these ovens work," Tyler Polk Taylor II said in his own defense. "An individual understandably lacks basic experience in simple tasks when others assume the drudgeries in one's life. It is not a mental deficiency."

"I understand, Father."

Tyler II did as instructed, placed the frozen french-toast-and-bacon breakfast in the microwave and said, "Household servants and, on the rare occasion, your mother, did the cooking. As a youth, you enjoyed working with her in the kitchen."

"You did not approve, Father. I saw it in your face. The kitchen was for ladies."

"Water under the bridge, Tyler. I literally cannot boil water for coffee. You have no domestic help whatsoever?"

"I do not and no further justification on your part is required. If you want coffee, you must boil water, Father. All I have is instant. Two minutes in the microwave should be adequate," Tip said. "You are welcome to go out to breakfast with us, my treat."

"No, if it is all the same to you, I shall stay in. Somebody might recognize me. This is all too, too mortifying."

"You shall be fine in time, Father."

"In your absence, am I welcome to watch your television, Tyler?"

"That goes without saying, Father. The remote control is on the table by my easy chair."

"Well, to a degree, I do know how to operate those household devices. Your mother programmed shows somehow and kept command of the remote control. Do either of you know if soap operas are currently telecast."

Judith and Tip said they did not.

"I shall research that question. They are oddities of American culture I have never had the time or inclination to explore. The insipid daytime talk shows, Tyler. I can rationalize this squandering of free time as research into contemporary American mores, yes?

"Yes, Father. If you wish."

In the garage, inside the Aston Martin, Judith said, "He's into soap operas?"

"Soap operas," Tip repeated. "This lion of the Pacific Northwest legal fraternity. Incredibly, yes."

"Do you think he's becoming agoraphobic?"

Tip closed his eyes and started the engine. "Of all places, here? Please, please, no."

Attorney James Smith sat stock-still across his immense slab of a desk from the small, natty man who wore far too much cologne.

"My, that is quite a story, Mr. Popkirk. Money and gems and securities from a long-ago unsolved burglary are allegedly in my possession. That you merely request exclusive rights for your concept and minimal seed money, to finance the first episodes. Tell me the name of your proposed show again."

"*Dead Man's Booty*," Vance Popkirk said. "The Pioneer Safe Deposit Vaults caper and its denouement will be the first episode."

"Frankly, that you aren't asking for a share of the alleged valuables strains credulity. Valuables I *allegedly* possess, you understand?"

"My reward, artistically and monetarily, will come when I sell the concept. Creativity is its own reward."

"As a future best-selling novelist and an independent producer of reality television, yes, you are indeed, as you describe yourself, a Renaissance man and a polymath," James Smith said. "However, my associate your Mr. Coll supposedly recognized is a long-time penitentiary inmate on probation."

"I discerned as much."

"Working pro bono, I'm mainstreaming him back into society as a responsible and law-abiding citizen."

"That is highly laudable of you, Mr. Smith."

"You have to understand that for me to utilize him in an illegal activity would be irresponsible and unethical."

"I do."

"To jeopardize his freedom, well, he is reputed to be a crude and unstable character. Have we suppressed those proclivities? I cannot say. Character behavior does not change overnight. Who can say how he'd react to an individual who might cause his probation to be revoked?"

A threat? "Not to worry. I'll blur the faces and use no names. I am aware that the process remains underway, so we'll have to re-create it. You'll have veto power on the script."

The ineptitude of the pair behind Smith's man's SUV had paid off. Attorney James Smith knew with whom he was dealing, a deluded pseudo intellectual on a fishing exhibition, hinting blackmail. His commission on the Roswell money wash-and-wear transactions and his piece of the Taylor divorce settlement comprised considerable moneys. The last thing he wanted was a publicity splash.

"Ever tune multiple carburetors on an older engine, Mr. Popkirk? A classic English sports car like a nineteen-sixty-five Aston Martin DB5?"

Popkirk hesitated, searching for an analogy that applied to the here and now. "No, I don't believe I have."

"Synchronization under the hood, synchronization in life's

endeavors, both vitally important. A minor aspect out of tune spells failure for all."

A veiled threat heaped upon the previous veiled threat? Pop-kirk nodded.

James Smith stood and extended a hand.

"You win. You have a bargain, Mr. Popkirk," he lied.

"I knew you were a reasonable man, Mr. Smith."

"Please let my secretary know where you're staying. We'll be in touch just as soon as we're through," said James Smith.

"Learn how to read a bus schedule. I can't take in cars fast enough to keep up with you destroying and walking off from them."

"Bus schedules? Nobody can read bus schedules, Uncle Randall. You gotta be one of them linguists."

"Hire an interpreter."

Unable to come up with a snappy reply, Dicky pouted.

"Talk to me about Vance Popkirk, what you and him have been up to."

"How did you know?"

Randall Coll tapped a temple.

"Yeah, shit. The Clairol gift you got. Poopkirk's a TV guy. He says he wants to make a movie out of the loot thing."

Dicky Coll told his uncle the rest of the story.

"Everything is gone from that old house?"

"One of the lawyer crooks on that downtown office floor the Walla Walla ex-con took it to, they got it, Uncle Randall. Every last dime."

Randall Coll leaned against his car, hands on the doors. His moronic nephew sat on the stoop of the trailer, severely hungover. The moronic nephew who was of no further use.

The loot was being laundered into untraceable money, cold hard cash by a slippery lawyer and his underworld connections.

Randall's hemorrhoids throbbed and his flat feet burned as he thought of the Roswell woman and that stunning ring. All his work and expense—to no avail. He had accomplished nothing but bring his nephew out of the woodwork. If the pawnbroker had eaten breakfast, he'd lose it.

Randall Coll carefully got into his car.

"Hey, where're you going, Uncle Randall?"

"Elsewhere."

"Hey, what about me?"

"The weeds. You and the weeds."

Dicky Coll got up and went for the sickle. When his mean and nasty uncle was out of sight, he dropped the sickle and went inside for a nap.

Word of the day: abandoned.

Buster Hightower, a man with time on his hands, was asked by Carla Chance, a woman with scant time on her hands, to do something useful.

"I ain't the right person for the job, toots. You're talking excessively stressful pressure and I got no formal training in the profession."

"I didn't mean it the way it came out, Buster. I know you're on at the Westside tonight and that's very useful. You make people laugh. I mean during the day. Please be a dear and run into town and check on Judith again."

"Tip's keeping a close watch on her. Wouldn't I, ahem, be in the way, Ms. Matchmaker?"

"Don't be snotty, Buster. She's turned over those valuables to a shady character and a lawyer."

"Lawyers and shady characters, they're synonymical. They're Siamese twins," Buster said. "I gotta have reinforcements and you need a day off."

"Well."

"C'mon, kiddo. Give Pearl a jingle. Ask her to run the office today."

Pearl was a retired insurance broker who liked to keep her hand in.

"Well, I don't know."

"C'mon," Buster said. "Besides, half your companies' honchos and policyholders are in the slammer. They're not gonna call you with their one phone call."

"Don't be snide. Not half. Not that many are incarcerated on any given day."

After breakfast, Judith and Tip arrived at her place to see a disheveled Harriet Hardin having her breakfast on the front stoop, the door wide open. She was eating cereal out of a box and drinking a glass of red wine, the bottle conveniently beside it for refills.

"Did you know you've been robbed? They cleaned out the safe you got in the basement you and Harry forgot to tell me about. The cupboard's bare."

"How did you get in, Harriet?"

"I got my secrets."

Judith poured the wine out into shrubbery, stepped around her, and said, "Please come inside and eat at the table. I'll get you a glass of milk."

"Yuck. That comes from the underside of a cow. You know what else they do down there."

"Coffee, then. I'll brew a pot."

"Did you hear me? The loot's gone."

"The neighborhood heard you," newly arrived Carla said.

Harriet looked at Tip. "Cutie Pie, you look like you had a rough night. Why don't you and me go upstairs for a siesta?"

"Regular or decaf?" Judith said.

Judith had left the false front on the basement floor and the box door open. If someone broke into the house—a frequent occurrence lately—she felt they wouldn't tear her home apart if they knew the loot was gone.

Tip had agreed with her reasoning. *The GOIPD graduate must be pessimistic and anticipate criminal and/or unethical activity and advise his or her clients to plan for it, to mitigate potential losses. Prepare for the worst, hope for the best, remembering that it's always darkest before the dawn.*

He offered Harriet a hand. "Permit me to help you up."

She refused, knocking over the cereal box as she unsteadily regained her feet. "Only if you're gonna carry me off to bed and screw my brains out, which isn't likely with her here."

Judith stared at her blankly. She was beyond blushing in the company of this woman, or even being angered.

On the way into the house, Carla stared at her, thinking there wasn't enough soap in town to thoroughly wash out Harriet's mouth.

Tip's cell phone beckoned Harvard Yard. Saved by the bell, he thought, excusing himself and going back outside.

"How long have you been here, Harriet?" Judith said, bringing a glass of milk to the dining-room table.

"Overnight. I slept where I used to sleep in the bad old days when Harry was teepee creeping, except I curled up on the floor since there was no bed. You oughta do something about your locks."

Judith said nothing.

"So where is it?"

"Where's what?"

"You know goddamn well what."

"It's gone, Harriet, not to be seen again," Judith said.

Inside, at the dining-room table, as coffee was served, Tip brought in the cereal box and said, "Who would like to caravan to Lake Washington for lunch? Everyone present is invited."

CHAPTER 38

At the wheel of his Aston Martin DB9, Judith as his passenger, Tip led Buster's 1959 Cadillac Eldorado to the east side of Lake Washington. He stopped at a stretch of lakefront residences obscured by fences and tall hedges, and punched in a code on the call box. A formidable steel gate slowly swung open.

At walking speed, the cars negotiated a curving and sloping flagstone driveway that cost as much, Buster guessed, as all the asphalt and concrete at their condo complex combined. Pruned shrubbery crowded each side. They came to a clearing where gardeners were busy at flowerbeds. Sprinklers arced over a golf course of a lawn, making rainbows.

They parked in front of an umpteen-car garage and got out. Lake Washington was flat and glossy, dotted with boats. On the other side of the lake, the Seattle side, the tallest downtown skyscrapers spiked upward at the rear of residential hills.

"Holy bleeping cow!" Buster said. "This view. If there was a tarpaper shack on the lot, it'd be worth a zillion bucks irregardless."

He ogled the house too, a dwelling that was not a tarpaper shack. It struck him as a frat house with its brick facing and gables and dormers and the shake roof.

"Be it ever so humble," he said to Tip.

"Mumsy—my mother finds it comfortable."

"Regardless of her well-deserved hard feelings regarding your father, she must be lonely," Carla said.

Oh no, Buster thought, looking at her. No subtleness this time. We're talking romantic blitz. Forgive and forget.

Reading Buster's body language, Carla took his arm and said, "Buster, the man has weaknesses. All men do. Male menopause? Who knows? If he's learned his lesson and comes back, begging on his hands and knees, he's eligible to be forgiven, isn't he?"

"Yeah? What if it was me with a cradle-robbing hang-up?"

"That's different," she said, kissing his cheek. "I'd geld you with whatever was handy in the silverware drawer. Didn't you get your midlife crisis out of your system before we met?"

"I sure as hell hope so."

Claire Esther Jamison Taylor met them at a lacquered, oblong wooden table on a parking-lot-sized brick patio with a built-in brick-and-stainless-steel barbecue, the type used on television cooking shows. She was a slim, gray-haired woman in her late fifties. Once very pretty, Carla thought. Unresolved grievances in Claire's eyes were dated; her estranged husband must have been a trial. Her slimness seemed a result of tension rather than diet and exercise, and her skin was prematurely wrinkled from parlor tanning, the poor thing.

She'd had some expensive maintenance too, the sort done by aging TV anchorwomen. Repair of sagging eyelids, skin tightening, and a chin tuck. Sad and costly, Carla thought, and impossibly ineffective. She couldn't turn the clock back far enough to please a man who regarded as erotic the cheerleader pages of a high-school yearbook.

Buster watched a uniformed Hispanic maid in a light blue uniform and white lace collar setting the table with snacks and pitchers of what Claire had in a champagne piccolo. A strapping young Honduran cook with an EDUARDO name tag was applying marinade to a rib roast.

His eyes were on the barbecue activity too. The kid looked

like he could be Ricardo Montalban's grandson.

"You could rotisserate a steer on it," Buster told him.

Eduardo smiled and said, "Yes sir."

"Are you related to Ricardo Montalban? You know, the guy on that old TV show with the midget?"

"No sir."

"Buster, back away before you have smoke inhalation," Carla said.

"Welcome to my home and to mimosas," Claire Taylor said. "Please, help yourself to the snacks and beverages. Isabella will fill your glasses. Lunch will be served shortly."

"You're speaking my language, hon," Harriet said, taking the first glass.

Mumsy was starting early and this wasn't her first, Tip observed. But under the circumstances, it was forgivable.

His cell phone rang.

Facing away from the others, Tip said, "Yes, Father."

"Is this an awkward time?"

He took a few steps and said, "I shall manage."

"Tyler, there is no television schedule in your daily newspaper that was delivered this morning."

"Newspapers have been doing away with them, requiring you to purchase TV schedules separately, Father."

Tyler Polk Taylor II sighed. "I suppose I can channel-surf to zero in on a station of interest, an aforementioned soap opera, if the timing is right."

"I watch television infrequently, Father, but I know there is a channel devoted to local scheduling."

"Programming?"

"It scrolls. Times, channels, program names."

"I shall try. Thank you for your advice, Tyler. Good day."

"Good day, Father."

"My house guest," he told Judith. "First the microwave as a

learning experience, now the television."

They sat down to eat and Claire Taylor raised her glass. "To everybody's health and happiness, with an exception, and to the outset of my new life."

Glasses clinked and Harriet said, "Yeah? What's going on? Is that exception here at the table? You're not talking about me, are you?"

"Harriet, it's not you. We can discuss this later," Carla said.

"Carla is right," Claire said. "I am over the initial shock, Ms. Hardin. My husband has a new romantic interest."

"He must be loaded to afford this layout," Harriet said. "If it doesn't work out with that gal, I'll take him off your hands."

Claire Taylor's smile exhibited one hundred thousand dollars' worth of dental work. "Thanks to my attorney, before long he will not be loaded. No offense, Ms. Hardin, but either one of us is far too old for his tastes."

"How old is this little cookie of his?"

Everyone but Claire studied their meals.

Emboldened by several glasses of champagne and orange juice, their hostess said, "I am informed that she shall reach legal age before the end of the decade. Her name is Trixi. She dots the last 'i' with a bubble and I am told that her freckles are adorable."

Harriet said, "I was her a long time ago, hon. I had a filthy old man of my own, whether I liked it or not. What's with guys his age who're hot for jailbait?"

Even fueled by mimosas, Claire was no match for Harriet. She studied her meal and asked if everyone's meat was cooked properly. Everyone said it was. And wasn't the weather positively glorious?

After lunch and thank-yous, everybody gathered at the cars but Tip, who said he would be along momentarily.

Carla told Buster, "Her husband is a disgrace, but poor Claire is lonely. She misses him."

Buster Hightower groaned. "You ain't gonna let this go, are you?"

"We'd be killing two birds, Buster," Carla said. "Reuniting two unhappy people and getting Mr. Taylor the Second out of Tip's hair. Judith confided his problem to me."

"Jeez, don't let our hostess hear you," Buster said.

Claire Taylor did not hear her. She was with her son adjacent the patio, just outside a screened porch the size of Carla and Buster's condo.

"I thought you had the right to know, Mumsy."

"That is impudent of him, Tippy, to arbitrarily make your home his home, given his treatment of you in past years."

"Father is vulnerable on his own, sans you and his high-priced support system. To Father the operation of a microwave oven is as bewildering as a supercomputer."

"On a happier topic, Tippy, I approve of your choice of female companion."

With that, Claire gave her son a teary-cheeked hug.

It wasn't fair, Dicky Coll groused as he walked through neighboring apartment parking lots, scouting for a car to steal. All the newfangled stuff they installed in them in the last eleven years, the alarms and computerized shit, no way in hell could he poach a newer ride.

Out of the blue, he had hisself a brainstorm.

That old hag he'd snuffed out. He walked to the old-folks apartment home she'd lived in, and there it was in the parking lot, that beat-to-shit Pinto of hers that wasn't doing nobody no good sitting there taking up space. God rest her skuzzy soul, ghosts don't drive.

Thanks to screwdriver magic popping the ignition lock, and even with the battery on its last legs, it cranked over once and fired up, and he was taillights down the road. He'd sorted through the papers in the glove box of Poopkirk's car. He'd remembered the name of the rental outfit and that it was close by the airport. He'd go on over there and give them a sob story, how he had to get ahold of Poopkirk on account of a death in the man's family and how he lost his address.

Nobody messed with either Mad Dog Coll and lived to tell about it!

Completely forgetting that Vinny died at the tender age of twenty-three.

CHAPTER 39

"That fast?" an astonished Judith Roswell said to James Smith, attorney-at-law. "I don't believe it."

Smith smiled. "Believe, Judith, believe. We didn't even have to put it on eBay. Tip, my best to your mother. I'm doing what I can for Claire and her unfortunate situation."

"She is delighted with the service you are providing, James," Tip Taylor said.

Smith had called Judith when they were on the way back to her house after lunch.

"Without further adieu, Judith, your share is one-ninety-six-five, Judith."

"Oh my goodness, just shy of two hundred thousand dollars?"

"I had hoped for more, but I didn't want to push our luck."

"I'm not complaining, James. That's wonderful."

"I can cut a cashier's check in your name, Judith, but I strongly recommend cash, so you can spread it out with different banks and investment instruments. That big a lump sum sends up red flags, you know, suspicions that it's drug money."

"This isn't really legal, is it?"

James Smith laughed. "Asset transference is a gray area. What isn't legally flexible in this day and age? Perchance, investing in Girl Scout cookies is pristine. Please ask me no specific questions."

Judith thought of Buster Hightower and his stale lawyer jokes.

She said, "I know exactly what I'll do with it."

Smith looked condescendingly at Tip, who said, "Trust me, James. Her idea will be creative, it will be perfection. Please do as she asks."

Dicky Coll didn't like what he was hearing from the loser behind the counter at the car rental place, a scrawny, balding young guy in a dipshit uniform.

"You're saying you got some company policy irregardless that I go and ask you a harmless question?"

"Sir, corporate headquarters makes that decision."

Dicky tugged on his foul, too-tight T-shirt to show the outline of his .25 Browning automatic he'd stuck in his belt in case he met this sort of resistance to reason.

"See, what the deal is, my uncle Vance Poopkirk, he got a brain tumor." Dicky tapped a temple. "What happens is if he's out on his own too much, he does funny things. Poopkirk walking in front of a bus, you don't want that on your conscience, do you?"

The clerk had taken a call earlier from Vance Popkirk's cousin, who said he suffered from dementia. Now he was informed that this man's uncle Vance "Poopkirk" had a brain tumor. The rental clerk wanted this foul-smelling whack job out of the office before he wet his pants. Let him, the doomed Popkirk/Poopkirk, and the cousin sort it out, to hell with corporate policy.

"In that case, sir, for compassionate reasons we can make an exception," he said, writing down the name of the renter's hotel. The clerk gave Dicky detailed verbal directions to the hotel, answering repetitious questions and writing them out on a pad.

Impatiently, Dicky whipped the old Ford Pinto. After going around in circles, he blundered onto a freeway entrance and eventually made it to a downtown Seattle exit. The Pinto promptly ran out of gas and died at the end of the ramp.

Dicky coasted to a NO PARKING zone and walked off into a breeze and light rainfall. Thinking, that stingy old dead bitch, running her junk car on fumes.

Luckily for him, Poopkirk's hotel was less than three blocks, a tall ritzy skyscraper. The lobby was decked out in brass and marble. There was a uniformed twink at a concierge desk, whatever the hell that was about.

Dicky went to the front desk and asked for Vance Poopkirk.

The clerk looked at his computer screen and said, "Do you mean Mr. Popkirk?"

"What'd I just say? Me and him, we're business partners, so it's important we connect as soon as we can. Something important came up."

The clerk tried hard not to make a rash judgment regarding the individual at his desk. This had been taught in his hotel management courses. In a high-tech city such as Seattle, billionaire software magnates often dressed like street people.

"Mr. Popkirk is in room eleven-forty-seven, but I show he's out."

"Yeah? How do you know he's in or he's out?"

"By his key card usage."

"Okay, whatever." Dicky looked at the cocktail lounge to his right. "He comes in, tell him I'll be there waiting."

Dicky went into the lounge, ordered a beer and a steak sandwich, charging it to room 1147. If the hotel and the parole board and Poopkirk and anybody else didn't like it, they could lump it.

Upon his triumph in Attorney James Smith's office, making it perfectly clear to the lawyer who had the upper hand, Vance Popkirk took advantage of the downtown venue. He called on a firm that rented professional camera gear. He reserved what he required, had a quick lunch, and returned to his hotel. Upbeat in spite of a vague uneasiness that he was being followed, he planned to go to his room and take another stab at launching *Gone with the Wind: The Holy Bible.*

"Sir, Mr. Popkirk," the desk clerk called out as he passed by. "Your business partner asked you to join him in the lounge."

Smiling broadly, Popkirk strode triumphantly into the cocktail lounge to join James Smith, attorney-at-law.

Crooking his finger, French fries stuffed in his mouth, his worst nightmare said, "Have a seat, Poopkirk. Me and you, we got us some catching up to do."

CHAPTER 40

"It's a dark and stormy night, boys and girls, as you can see out the window, hearing the lightning and seeing the thunder, thanks to us being close to the summer soluble and having long days and twilight. Once again, we appreciate all nine of you coming out tonight. Phil does too. Phil's the manager of the Westside Bowling Lanes and Casino," Buster said from his rickety stage (the screw was still on the floor). "That's Phil peeking in from the doorway, checking that I don't say anything politically indecently invalidly incorrect. Too late, Phil. I'm far along in the set, so the dirty subversive stuff is done and gone.

"Whoops, now you see him, now you don't. Bye, Phil. He must of overheard a bowler tossing a strike into the next lane. It's weird what you hear with one ear while the other's eaves-dropsying.

"Speaking of ears. You never know when someone walking down the street's deranged or not. Is he talking to himself or does he have a baby cell phone attached to an ear like an ear-ring. That's why I carry pepper spray. You're covered both ways. Let him have it and he goes down screaming or with an electric pop when you short out his baby phone."

As Buster raved on, Carla Chance and Claire Taylor sat together, drinking mimosas. Carla was acquiring Claire's taste for them, but not in the patrician woman's quantity. She had persuaded the separated Mrs. Taylor to meet her here and take in Buster's show.

When the comic paused to chugalug his beer, Claire said, "He is quite amusing. Your man is unafraid to take on any subject or offend any person, is he not?"

Carla said, "As Buster is fond of saying, he's an equal opportunity offender. May I ask you a question, dear?"

"A question to you first, if I may."

"Why yes, of course."

"My intuition advises me that you enjoy the role of liaison, of intercessor in matters of romance."

"Well, I hate to see people unhappy if that's what you mean," Carla said.

As Buster drained his beer, Claire said, "We must have a chat later."

"Let's make that sooner, Claire. I have an idea."

"Look," said the comic, "I get razzed for being computerphobic, like it's an old-age disease, like bedsore fungus, or varicoasted veins. Sticks and stones, as far as I'm concerned. Maybe we oughta catch that illness, an epidemic of it.

"I read in the paper about a guy who got arrested for trying to buy drugs with fake money he printed on his computer on one side only. Damn lucky for him he's alive and well in the pokey. If that boy didn't have a computer, he'd of found an honester line of work, like armed robbery. Notwithstanding, he needs himself a lawyer.

"There's a lawyer I know of who might work for him since he's jurisprudentializingly doomed as it is. He's the lawyer who said his last good case was of Miller High Life. Phil has him on retainer here.

"Speaking of beer. How come wine has to breathe and beer doesn't. You uncap the wine to let it breathe and catch its breath, right? Will it suffocate if you don't, like a chipmunk or lawyer or other critter who doesn't have air to breathe? Beer goes flat if you leave it open to breathe on account of the bubbles go away.

Is that the same as suffocating? I'm confused.

"What confuses me too is junk mail. On the same day last week we got a flier from this nut-job preacher predicting that the end of the world's right around the corner and a catalog peddling pills and food supplements that'll make you live longer and healthier. What if the preacher is right and the world's ending next week, why should you buy the pills and supplements?"

Throughout his set, Buster kept an eye on Carla and Claire. They were a pair of intense girls, acting like best buddies now, Carla doing the majority of the talking. He was eager to wrap up and find out what the hell was going on. If he knew his Carla, she had Tip's daddy locked up outside in the trunk of her car, ready to lead him in here with a string attached to a ring through his nose.

"So I shoehorned a lawyer joke in there without warning you. Sue me."

He waited out the good-natured booing.

"No joking. Here's a good lawyer candidate to represent the rancid putz with the counterfeit money, a lawyer who walks in the courtroom and high-fives the prosecutor.

"I'm gonna end with a homework assignment. You go through the checkout line and there's tabloids on one side and candy bars on the other. How come no broccoli and poison-ivy ointment? Explain it on paper in less than five thousand words."

CHAPTER 41

It was a dark and stormy night at Judith Roswell's. Windows rattled. Lightning flashed through curtains. Shutters rattled and banged. Wind whistled through chimneys.

Judith whispered, "Tip, were you always a satyr?"

Satyr inflated Tip's chest, broadened his shoulders. He thought of Sean Connery in the early Bonds and his routine conquests.

"It is entirely your fault," he said, a hand inside her pajama bottoms.

"Harriet may hear us and come up," Judith said.

"And hop in bed with us? I think not. Orange and Vanilla are at the top of the steps on sentry duty, and Harriet has made her sentiments concerning cats clear."

"Tip, I heard her."

Tip did not hear her, but took Judith seriously. *A GOIPD operative receives all data with an open mind and makes no snap judgments. To take everything with a grain of salt could be costly to the investigation.*

"I did. She's prowling around, searching. I know every creak in every floorboard in this house."

Harriet had been relegated to a downstairs bedroom. She was snooping around and heard them, too. Him putting the blocks to the schoolmarm, giving the mattress a workout! She was tempted to charge up there, throw aside the covers, and pile on. Show Cutie Pie what a real piece of tail was.

But those goddamn cats at the top of the steps, staring at her with their creepy eyes, like she was a catnip mouse, they'd claw her and trip her up, sending her tumbling down the stairs. Those old ladies where she lived who'd had busted hips, they could barely move around, let alone have any fun with the opposite sex.

She'd confine her search to the main floor, ransacking the place, drawer by drawer, and find *something* of value. She was entitled.

Then she heard Cutie Pie's phone ring upstairs, those stupid schoolhouse bells. Good. She could work faster, use her flashlight, and make noise.

"Father?"

"Tyler, I have visitors."

"At my apartment?"

"Yes. Your mother, accompanied by an older couple. As I perceive it, the lady is an insurance vendor and the gentleman is a local entertainer. Are you acquainted with them?"

"Indeed I am. They are the salt of the earth."

"Events are occurring very, very fast. The insurance lady had to demonstrate how to silence my television program with a 'mute' button. There are a plethora of buttons on that device and I have misplaced my reading glasses. I was in the midst of a reality program where the contestants live in the jungle and eat a variety of hideous flora and fauna. This came on the heels of a talent contest. The singing was for the most part atrocious. Past winners have inexplicably become celebrities, earning millions of—"

"Father, excuse me. You are rambling."

"Yes, yes, admittedly I am. All this is disorienting to the extreme."

"Is that Mumsy I hear in the background?"

"I fear it is, Tyler. She is strongly suggesting that I agree to

241

counseling. Perhaps at the behest of the insurance lady who is shaking her head at me, as if I am addled. Regardless, the quasi-suggestion is in the form of an ultimatum."

"Counseling?"

"Your mother is of the perception that I have a problem in the area of sexual fixation with adolescent girls and that this alleged aberration is curable. Why, Tyler, do women believe they can repair men when no repair is required?"

"Realistically, Father, you do have that problem."

"I am not going to debate this alleged psychological shortcoming with your mother and her newfound friends. Nor am I with you. If I cooperate, your mother will suspend her divorce action. I telephoned you to ask your opinion."

"I wholeheartedly agree with Mumsy, Father. She is not being unreasonable."

"I regret that I was so busy with the practice to participate to a greater extent in your upbringing, delegating those responsibilities to your mother. Your sister, God knows where she is, was untamed. I accept Campbell as a joint parenting failure, but you, the male sibling—"

"Father, if you are intimating that I am a mama's boy, I am terminating our conversation."

"No, no, please do not. As I age, I increasingly say and do things I subsequently regret. Your mother insists that the counseling be at a residential facility. Does this color your opinion?"

"No, Father. In that environment, your treatment will be proportionally more intensive and, hopefully, effective in a shorter period of time."

"But I will be living in rudimentary conditions with the mentally ill and outright criminals. With perverts and sex fiends!"

"Three words, Father."

"Yes?"

"Attorney. James. Smith."

"I shall take your recommendation under advisement. Good evening, Tyler."

"Good evening, Father."

Judith said, "I overheard. What will happen?"

Tip smiled. "Thanks to Carla, I will regain my apartment."

CHAPTER 42

Dicky Coll had polished off two steak sandwiches and drank five beers at Vance Popkirk's hotel. Filled up, with the budding best-selling author in tow, they rode in his rental car and parked a block from Judith Roswell's home.

Looking out through windblown torrents of rain, Dicky sized up the haunted house, saying, "Poopkirk, the rich swell who's been dicking the old gal if she ain't still a virgin, his fancy sports car's there in front and all lights are out. If we're quiet like mice, we're gonna get away with tiptoeing around in there till we find us some goodies. The loot may of flown off, but there's antiques and shit for us."

"We?"

"I didn't bring you here to sit in the car with your thumb up your ass," Dicky said. "Those two flashlights we stopped to buy along with them clothes, I'm gonna wear both sets and hold a flashlight in each hand?"

"Well, no, but what if we're discovered and they notify the police?"

"There ain't gonna be no cops and we ain't leaving till we find something of value I can sell or till we find nothing. If it's nothing, I'm gonna be in a bad mood."

"That's different from your perpetually bad mood?" Popkirk didn't say. He did say, "How can we avoid being seen or overheard?"

"You ain't seeing that it's a stormy and dark night? We got

this rain and wind working for us." Dicky lifted the black sweat-shirt they'd also bought with Popkirk's credit card. "And my itty-bitty buddy tucked in my belt, I hear noise, nobody's call-ing nobody. Let's boogie."

As ordered. Popkirk followed his captor out of the car and onto the property, his handmade Italian wingtips soaked, absolutely ruined. Any thoughts of a Roswell, Judith, and a Roswell, New Mexico, linkage were gone. Likewise, *Dead Man's Booty* was a dead issue.

Survival was Popkirk's first and only priority.

MASSIVE COVER-UP. AREA 51 ALIEN BODIES BURNED BY SECRET AGENTS, BURIED IN DESERT WITH 1950'S CURRENCY.

A block from Judith Roswell's home, Randall Coll sat in a seven-year-old Kia he'd taken in that afternoon. It had 151,800 miles on the odometer and a disturbing shimmy. Coll swapped a set of luggage and cash to get the customer to the bus station and out of town. As the title to the Kia looked legit, Coll asked no questions.

He had driven here at sundown to see what he could see. Thanks to his laundry list of aches and pains, he couldn't sleep anyway.

He was about ready to leave for home and give shut-eye another shot when a car parked not fifty feet ahead of him. It was the automobile rented to Vance Popkirk. Coll could make out the license plate in the wet bluster, a number that was imprinted on his memory.

Out of the car came his nitwitted nephew and presumably Mr. Vance Popkirk, his tavern companion. Like cartoon burglars, they wore black sweatshirts and stocking caps, and carried flashlights. Coll watched them walk around the side of the old house, giving them time to break in while he unzipped a bag that contained a pair of top-of-the-line night-vision goggles a soldier had brought in several months ago.

The kid had said they were a souvenir from Iraq, where he'd been fighting for his country. At the end of his long spiel, Iraq became Afghanistan. It was the pawnbroker's judgment that "souvenir" had a wide definition. He didn't give a damn if they came from the War of 1812. Coll gave the kid a fifty-dollar bill, no questions asked.

Randall Coll moved the car ahead to better see what there was to see.

A stocky man in a Windbreaker stood behind a tree, seeing what there was to see. The man had a snake tattoo curling around a wrist, a knife scar on a cheek, and a cell phone in his pocket.

He got into his car, punched in a number and received a response on the first ring.

"Sorry to be bugging you at all hours, boss."

"No worries. I asked you to call and I wasn't asleep. In fact, I just finished a conversation with a wealthy client who asked me to put her divorce action on hold. It'll cost me mucho bucks, but the client is always right even when she's dead wrong."

"They got in through a side door. Didn't take long, so they must of had a key or a pick. This is the same two ding-dongs from the hotel bar. The guy with the bullshit reality TV pitch. Him and a fat pile of shit I'm pretty sure I saw where I, you know, last resided. Fatso's obviously in charge."

"No names, please. No specifics. The airwaves have ears."

"Yeah. Sorry."

"Stick around to see what transpires, but don't become aggressively involved. If anything hairy occurs, bail out. The chance Mr. Reality TV is going to shoot off his mouth and bring unwanted attention to us is negligible."

CHAPTER 43

Orange and Vanilla hopped onto the bed. They heard what the humans hadn't.

"Your bodyguards," Tip whispered, stepping into his pants, thinking *Bond James Bond.*

"Where are you going? Shouldn't we be calling the police?"

"Not yet."

Harriet reached the dining room. She aimed her flashlight at silverware in the drawers of a hutch. It was sterling, a whole lot of good that'd do her. She didn't have a gunnysack to haul it off and even if she did, it'd bring her two grand, tops, chicken feed. Antique china, too. And the way her luck was going, she'd land in the clink.

She heard and felt a breeze.

Into a hallway, sopping wet, were two guys dressed in black. Jesus H. Christ, one of them was her one-night stand from hell.

Harriet knew that the game was over, that she had no chance at a bonanza. So why not have a little fun?

"Psst."

Vance Popkirk and Dicky Coll squinted in her direction.

"I am the ghost of smothering past," she rasped.

Neither man replied.

Harriet pointed her flashlight upward at her face. "Boo!"

Dicky Coll screamed.

Vance Popkirk screamed.

Harriet advanced. "Boo, Needle Dick! Boo boo boo!"

Arms flailing like a dog paddler, Dicky backed into Popkirk, caroming him against the dining table. Off-balance, Dicky bounced into a coatrack and grabbed it, falling on one knee. He lifted the rack and aimed it at Harriet, as if a battering ram.

"You old scuz, you ain't spose to be alive," Dicky said, eyes wide. First, Uncle Randall developed a case of mind reading, then this old witch comes back from the dead. What next?

"You didn't think I was so scuzzy the other night, you loser. You screw as good as you smother."

He threw the coatrack aside, pulled the Browning .25 out of his waistband, and came at her, gun extended. "Where is it?"

"Where's what?"

"You know fuckin-A well what."

"Good luck. You and me both, sugar, we're drilling a dry hole. Get used to it."

"Why don't I just blow your head off and be done with it and find what's left my own self. That's what Vinny would do. No muss, no fuss."

"This Vinny of yours. You were babbling in the bar about Vinny. You say he was a big-shot gangster, but dollars to doughnuts he was your boyfriend when you were in Walla Walla, your lover boy."

"The police are on their way," Tip lied from the foot of the steps.

Standing behind him, Judith said, "Wait and give yourself up or run for it and hope for the best, Mr. Coll. Those are your sensible options."

Dicky Coll laughed. Displaying a rare insight, he said, "Ain't gonna be no police busting in on us. The cops get mixed up in it, the lid's off and you got more explaining to do than me. Where's what's left? And don't nobody say they don't know what I'm saying. Somebody speak up."

Harriet lunged for him, fingernails first.

Mad Dog slapped her.

Harriet fell against the china cabinet and held onto an edge before she fell. "Three of my ex-husbands hit harder than that, Needle Dick."

Mad Dog pointed his gun at Judith and advanced. "Lady of the house, come here. Come to papa. Me and you, we're gonna go for a ride in your save-the-planet car."

He turned to the others. "I'm gonna get a safe distance, then I dump her. You three, you call anybody or try to leave before I call, she's toast."

Fight Dirty and Live, Tip thought. The GOIPD postgrad course and the promo depicting a small guy defeating a big guy with various tricks. In retrospect, he should have shelled out the additional $139.95.

He sidestepped in front of Judith and said, "You will have to get by me first."

"It's your funeral, rich boy."

Tip vividly remembered the intro trick: *A swift kick to a shin and a swifter kick to an area above the shins. A thumb poke to an eyeball. Most creatively, grabbing a finger with a hand cupped over the other, then jerking it backward, vertically, until a bone or joint snapped or dislocated. Never underestimate the element of surprise.*

Tip wagged a finger in reproach, making Dicky grin.

"You rich-boy puss—"

That element of surprise gave Tip a split second to plunge forward and snag Dicky's gun hand and raise it. Dicky got off two shots, grazing Tip's shoulder and shattering a ceiling lamp. With his other hand, the private eye grabbed Dicky's middle finger and bent it upward.

Crazed on adrenaline, Dicky clasped Tip's wrist with his other four fingers. It was a standoff not favoring Tip, whose shoulder felt as if it had been seared with a branding iron.

Harriet had by then crawled to Dicky. She held onto an ankle and sunk her teeth into a calf.

Mad Dog yelped and fell backward, her dentures impaled in his leg. Tip took advantage and put all his weight forward, bending Dicky's middle finger ninety degrees, snapping it loose at the joint. He released Tip and went down to a knee, shrieking.

A heavy ceramic tray shattered on the top of his head, putting him down for the count. Judith had taken from the china cabinet a 1939–1940 New York's World Fair souvenir that had been lovingly displayed by Grandmother Ella Spicer.

Dicky Coll lost consciousness, his last thought a word of the day: incarceration.

Judith sacrificed it for the best of reasons.

Grandmother Ella would approve.

In the heat of the moment, a small envelope hidden between the plate and the glued-on pedestal dropped to the floor.

CHAPTER 44

Arriving at Judith's after their trip to Tip's Tacoma apartment, Carla, Claire, and Buster hurried inside. Bringing up the rear, Buster was damn near knocked off the porch by the tabloid reporter who ran out full steam ahead. He didn't even have time to razz him about Elvis.

No sooner had Buster regained his balance than a large flabby man brushed by on his hands and knees, the contact with the comic loosening a set of dentures from a bloody pant leg. The sight and sound of the guy made Buster think of a hog escaping a slaughterhouse chute.

"We heard yelling and what might have been gunshots," Claire said. "Oh my God, Tippy!"

She rushed to her son, who sat, cross-legged. Judith had cut away his shirt and was dabbing disinfectant on an ugly gash in a shoulder.

"Tippy!"

Had Ian Fleming given James Bond a mother, he wondered? He should research that. "I am fine, Mumsy. Splendid."

"Are the police coming and an ambulance on the way?"

"They aren't and won't be, Carla," Judith said. "It's a long long story."

Unsteadily, Harriet Hardin walked by him to retrieve the dentures, cussing up a storm, words Buster couldn't understand though knowing what they were.

"It's Grand Central Station here," Buster said.

★　★　★　★　★

"It's Grand Central Station there, boss, and a Chinese fire drill too. It stopped raining, so I'm out of the car, behind a tree."

"How so?" said Attorney James Smith. "My apologies for being redundant, but the airwaves have ears."

"Well, our boy lit out like a scalded ape in a rental car. Fatso too, wobbling and stumbling. He's groggy. Wait, a car parked up the street blinked its headlights. Blinked them again and honked. Fatso's going to it."

"This is becoming too exciting. We know what we have to know. As far as we're concerned, the well is dry. The pot is empty. You're done for the night."

"You don't have to tell me twice, boss."

"My hand hurts like a motherfucker, Uncle Randall. My head too. They clobbered me with a frying pan or something. It had to be made out of cast iron."

At the wheel of the Kia, Randall Coll said, "What do you want me to do?"

"Take me to the hospital, the emergency room. Hey, how'd you know I'd be here?"

The pawnbroker tapped his temple. "Have you forgotten? I have ESP. I read minds."

"Oh yeah. The hospital, okay?"

"Think about this," Randall Coll told his nephew. "You're out late, you've been drinking, you have no money, you're on parole."

"But my finger, Uncle Randall."

Randall glanced at his swollen hand and gave a diagnosis. "You have swelling. It looks dislocated, not broken. Take two aspirin and go to bed. You'll have to flip people the bird with your right hand until it heals."

"Let me out and I'll walk to the nearest hospital."

Randall slowed.

"Unless it's still raining."

"Are you wet or dry?"

"Dry."

"Therefore it's stopped raining. Sit back and shut up. I'll take you to the trailer park."

"I guess that's okay."

"I'll expect those weeds sickled down by the end of the week. You have one good arm and hand."

They sat around the dining-room table. Judith had poured glasses of wine for everybody except Buster, who said he'd developed an allergy to grapes.

"They make me break out in hives."

"Buster," Carla said.

"May I find you a cold beer?" Judith said.

"If it's not any trouble," Buster said.

Judith went for a beer. Tip was shirtless, arm in a sling, gauze taped to the wounded shoulder. Harriet couldn't take her eyes off the exposed flesh.

Claire couldn't look at her Tippy, for fear she'd cry.

"One last time on this subject. Why do you think Grandfather Harry folded those pages in the city directory? Any ideas?" Judith said as Buster drank.

"Vital mystery clues," Tip said. "He must have known a descendant would someday find the loot and want the full story out."

Carla said, "A muddled form of immortality."

"That's my guess too," Judith said.

"Harry," Harriet said. "Harry didn't think with his brain."

"Harriet," Carla said.

"Save yourself a trip to the sink for a bar of soap, honey. Harry's full story was Harry. Period."

Buster said, "The loot's bye-bye. Cash in your bank. End of story."

Tip said, "I am in accordance, Buster."

Claire gestured to her empty wine glass. As Judith refilled it, she said, "There is always another story, Tippy. Just ask your father."

Judith opened the envelope that was hidden between the ceremonial plate and its glued-on pedestal. "Let's see if we do have another story at this table."

She read aloud, "To whom it may concern, who will eventually discover this note, family members or new residents of this home. I, Ella Hitchcock Spicer, am addressing this to Harry Spicer. Forgive my rudeness for ignoring you and speaking to Harry beyond the grave. First, Harry, let me say that I don't hate you for being a criminal or cheating on me. I do hate you for being a pedophile. What you did to that waif was low even for you. I hope you're burning in hell for what you did to poor little Harriet.

"On the other two counts, it'd be hypocritical of me to damn you. Despite what you believed, I was not deaf, dumb, blind or stupid. I know what you and your two pals (The Three Musketeers—how revolting!!!) did over Washington's Birthday nineteen-fifty-four. I know where you hid it and I helped myself to what I needed for living expenses, not the least being booze.

"As far as sex goes, do you remember Brad, our milkman? When you were at work and Harriet was asleep or gone—thanks to me, Brad was late for the next stop on his route. Guess why? Brad and I in *our* marital bed!!!!

"Those were the best days of my life and my worst day was when Brad announced that he was reconciling with his wife.

"I have spoken my piece,

"Ella Hitchcock Spicer

"March eleventh, nineteen-seventy

"PS: If the reader of this guesses my reference to Washington's Birthday nineteen-fifty-four, have a happy Easter egg hunt."

Tears streaming, Judith said, "That was a week before she died. Her drinking worsened because of Brad, not because of Harry's death."

There was not a dry eye in the room.

Carla cradled a sobbing Harriet on her lap.

"There there," she said. "There there."

EPILOGUE

VANCE POPKIRK caught the first available flight home. His experience attempting to sell *Dead Man's Booty* had made him borderline agoraphobic. Dicky (Mad Dog) Coll stars in his nightmares, sometimes twice in one night.

Popkirk is devoting his waking hours to *Gone with the Wind: The Holy Bible*. He's mightily pleased with his progress, having gotten to "Once upon a time, it was a dark and stormy night in the holy land of Oz."

TYLER POLK TAYLOR II fulfilled his promise to enter treatment for what others regard as a problem. Taylor is a patient at the Northwest Institute for Aberrant Sexual Behavior (NIFASB).

Outwardly, he is making exceptional progress. Taylor, a veteran attorney, says all the right things.

He keeps a nude and suggestive photo of Trixi under his pillow, his masturbatory inspiration.

CLAIRE ESTHER JAMISON TAYLOR kept her word to her estranged husband and discharged Attorney James Smith. Reuniting with him, however, is not in the fine print.

She had follow-up maintenance done by her plastic surgeon and began a torrid affair with Eduardo, the ruggedly handsome young Honduran cook at her estate. When she asks Eduardo if he is aware that he resembles a young Ricardo Montalban, it's his signal to perform. Unfailingly, he replies with a smile and does so.

HARRIET HARDIN CALLAHAN MILLER KLINE PARKER JACOBS SMITH met a pimply, awkward, pear-shaped, twenty-nine-year-old software whiz at a bar within walking distance of her seniors' apartment complex. His name is Richie R. Ralf. Richie owns rrrWare. Although most PC owners don't know they have rrrWare installed in their computers, the machines run faster because it is.

Harriet and Richie got to talking, him saying that he did his drinking in ordinary places where nobody knew him. He said he was "socially inadequate," a laughingstock in swinging singles bars. Harriet put her hand on his thigh and told him not to sell himself short. They had more drinks and Harriet took him home and took his virginity.

Richie R. Ralf and Harriet Hardin Callahan Miller Kline Parker Jacobs Smith Ralf are building a new home on Lake Washington. The Ralfs and Claire Taylor will soon be neighbors.

RANDALL COLL read an article in the paper, a request for the public's help by the Seattle Police Department and King County Medical Examiner's Office in identifying a male murder victim whose fingerprints aren't on file.

There was a sketch of the victim, and his height, weight, and approximate age. What made the article jump off the page was "GGR" tattooed on his fingers, and the fact that the man had succumbed to a single gunshot to the head from a Browning .25 automatic pistol.

Randall Coll double-checked the inscription on the back of the cheesy Rolex knockoff he'd taken in from Dicky. There it was: *to GGR from MAJ.*

Coll closed Coll's Jewelry and Loan: (A Family Business)

and hung his GONE TO LUNCH. He wasn't going to lunch and he wasn't coming back after the lunch he wasn't going to eat.

He drove to the same suburban mall where he had opened Pandora's box and released from it his sub-mental nephew. He walked slowly past the same cell-phone kiosks, ignoring the same pitches from the same or different twerps, in due time reaching the same stand-up pay phones that wanted the same fifty cents, highway robbery.

Randall Coll dropped two quarters in the slot, dialed a police station. He passed on an anonymous tip that he guaranteed would lead them to the killer of the unidentified GGR.

Randall Coll hung up and smiled. Rarely did he smile, but he had accomplished two goals. He had performed an important civic duty and he had gotten rid of a royal pain in the ass.

He is not a happy man, but he is less unhappy.

DICKY COLL was served a search warrant at the trailer. The tiny pistol was found on him, jammed into his waistband, plain as day, a parole violation that in itself assured him a trip downtown.

Ballistics on Dicky's Browning matched the slug found in GGR's gray matter.

The suspect was picked out of a lineup by the bartender at the tavern around the corner from the alley, the murder scene.

Presented with an overwhelming fact pattern, the suspect did not yield. He denied knowing any GGR, let alone following him from the haunted house. He told the interviewing detectives to "Figure it out your ownself, coppers. Vinny wouldn't sing like no canary neither."

The suspect's court-appointed attorney had advised him to plead guilty in the hope of a lesser sentence. According to a newspaper article, the suspect advised him "to go take a flying f*** at a rolling doughnut."

The suspect got daily media coverage, lots of it.

He was the hottest story in town.

He was red hot.

Dicky (Mad Dog) Coll was a center of attention. He even had groupies in attendance at courtroom appearances, lonely women who thought he was complex and dashing.

He was having the time of his life.

Word of the day on the day he was sentenced to life in prison: gunsel.

JUDITH ROSWELL'S plan for the $196,500 was this. She paid $180,000 to her creditors, using the $16,500 for short-term living expenses. She kept track of Dicky Coll's trial in the papers and on the TV news. It was hard to avoid.

Judith suspected that GGR, the mysterious murder victim, was Gerald G. Roswell. She felt a twinge of guilt for not coming forward to identify GGR and claim his remains.

TYLER POLK (TIP) TAYLOR III sold his gold Rolex and the Aston Martin DB9. To tell time, Tip purchased a digital watch at a department store. He got around in a used white Toyota Prius, a twin of his lover's.

He moved in permanently with Judith. They invested the proceeds of the sales in tuition to a culinary arts school for him and a business management class for her. Upon their graduations, they converted the main floor of her home into an organic tapas bar. Creative remodeling and interior design allowed seating for fifty.

They named the restaurant BOTÍN, Spanish for "loot."

Asked why by diners two or three times a night, they said the name came to each of them in a dream, on the same night.

A harmless white lie.

Tip's latest fantasy, replacing 007: Stardom in a TV cooking show of his own.

CARLA CHANCE and BUSTER HIGHTOWER resumed life as usual . . . until their next adventure strikes.

LEARN MORE ABOUT THE NEXT BUSTER HIGHTOWER ADVENTURE!

In *Gold,* the fifth Buster Hightower mystery, Carla and Buster visit Panama City, Panama. She's attending a convention of international insurance agents and arranged a stand-up gig for him. He began his stand-up-comedy career with a partner named Blinko Potts. The last he heard, Blinko owned a bar in a historic district of Panama City. Buster looks him up. Blinko, nicknamed for his blinking, blinks even faster. He shows Buster a diary he swapped for a customer's bar tab. If you can believe the diarist, he was mixed up in the disappearance of forty tons of Nazi gold in 1940 Lisbon. Blinko believes him. The man was murdered two days after turning the diary over to Blinko.

Is the gold within their grasp? The volume of forty tons of gold, a heavy element, is less than two household refrigerators, not all that difficult to hide. At today's prices, its value is well over $1 billion.

ABOUT THE AUTHOR

Gary Alexander has written thirteen novels, including *Loot,* fourth in the Five Star mystery series featuring as protagonist a stand-up comic named Buster Hightower.

Disappeared, the first Buster Hightower novel, has been optioned to Universal Pictures.

Alexander has written more than 150 short stories, most to mystery magazines, and sold travel articles to six major dailies, including the *Chicago Tribune* and the *Dallas Morning News.*

He's served as Regional Vice President of the Mystery Writers of America.

Dragon Lady, his Vietnam novel, is being published as an e-book by Istoria Books.

He lives in Kent, Washington, with his wife Shari.

Please visit him at www.garyralexander.com.